LUCID

LUCID

MICHAEL S. MILANO

PRAXIS
BOOKS

ISBN: 979-8-9914581-0-8 (Paperback)
ISBN: 979-8-9914581-1-5 (Hardcover)
ISBN: 979-8-9914581-2-2 (eBook)

Library of Congress Control Number: 2024947795

Edited by Michael J. Totten
Cover design by Matt Roeser
Layout by The Book Designers

Published by Praxis Books
25 SE 2nd Ave Ste 550
468
Miami, FL 33131

PraxisBooks@protonmail.com

To my parents,
Priscilla and Robert Milano

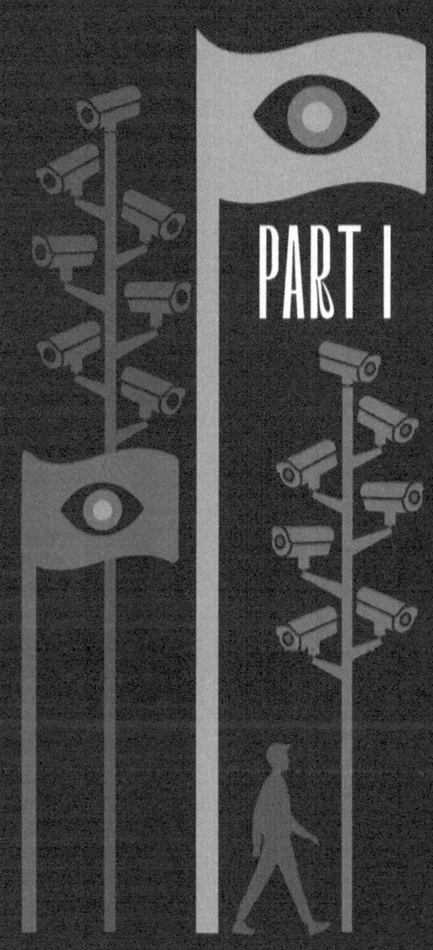

WEDNESDAY FEBRUARY 2, 2084

CHAPTER ONE

Several hours remained before curfew. Rain plummeted to the earth's surface as men and women were released from their daily drudgeries. Multicolored umbrellas proliferated through the streets of a city where downpours were a common occurrence. The local citizens were eager to maximize their free time. One man, however, was unfazed by these bleak surroundings, for today victory was assured. Radiating an aura of confidence, he strutted like a world champion pugilist entering the ring against a broken-down rival. Visions of financial windfalls clouded his mind. Glancing up through the dreary skies, he laid his eyes upon the sign of his destination: The Emerald.

Among the bright lights and towering office buildings of the downtown metropolis, the small Irish pub served as a portal into the past. Fenestration of the pine-green and carmine-red storefront was achieved through a trio of arched windows. Ivy climbed the white window grilles and crawled along a faded awning. Vintage lanterns flanked the entrance, inviting pedestrians to forget their troubles by entering a world of intoxication.

A mechanical voice greeted the man: "Welcome, Antony Sartori."

As entry was granted, green arrows flashed in sequence along the glass tops of the optical turnstiles. For those who traveled on unsure footing, a slippery floor was an obstacle not to be overlooked. Antony wiped his feet on the doormat. He cautiously crossed the watering hole, counting the swiveled wooden stools along the way. The sixth, his lucky number, was occupied by an unfamiliar face. Peeved, Antony slanted his eyebrows inward as he considered his alternatives. At the eleventh stool, his favorite prime number, he sat down and beckoned Clara with a wave.

"Be right with you, hon," the middle-aged bartender said. She pointed at the local historical photographs that lined the walls as she resumed her discourse with the couple seated at the bar. "Completed in December 1961, months before the World's Fair, the iconic Space Needle stands 605 feet tall. It amazingly took only 400 days to com—"

"Can I get a beer when you get a chance?" Antony said.

Clara glowered in his direction. He'd apparently broken her concentration mid-recital. After glancing back at the black-and-white photos, she excused herself from her other customers.

"I love you, Ant." Clara feigned a smile. "But the interruptions are rude. Not everyone has heard my history lessons on loop."

The clock was ticking, and Antony's superstitious rituals required a beer in hand before game time. He impatiently tapped his fingers on the mahogany bar top. The impenetrable confidence he possessed upon entering the establishment was fading as tip-off approached. His venturesome hobby had produced a string of profitable nights, but each and every one of those had begun with a drink. Uncertainty derailed his positive mental manifestations. While searching his pockets for his betting ticket, he came across losing wagers from the prior month, and apprehension entered his thoughts.

Winning wasn't everything; it was truly the only thing. Prosperity Dividends, a form of universal basic income, offered little in terms of financial maneuverability. When Antony's life had fallen apart, he choose to literally bet on himself. By combining his passion for sports with a proficiency in probability, he created a new income stream.

"Seattle minus eight and a half." He held up a wrinkled betting slip. "It's a lock."

"Is that so?" Clara said with a grin, always skeptical of the contradictory nature of the guaranteed gamble.

"Most definitely, I caught a huge break."

"Oh really?"

"Thanks to a stroke of good fortune, I placed my bet well before the Peppers suspension was announced. Then I doubled down before the line was adjusted. It was only a matter of time before someone noticed that man was on steroids."

"Ain't that the truth?" Clara giggled as she slid over a

frigid pint of the pub's celebrated microbrew. "So, when are you going to pass some good luck my way?"

"The formula has been nearly flawless over the last three weeks. But let's not jinx it."

"I'm just glad your money is on our boys. I'd hate to kick you out again."

Antony shamefully shook his head to absorb the low blow. "How many times do I have to tell you that I learned my lesson?"

He broke eye contact while raising his mug. The muddy liquid's aroma of toasted oak and fruity undertones seduced his olfactory receptors. After a few gulps, he slammed the half-empty glass back onto the bar. He could not allow the embodiment of the pessimistic perspective to persist. He finished off the frosty beverage in haste.

Whenever money was at stake, Antony's emotional reactions intensified. Clara refrained from further teasing one of her regulars. She poured a second pint as a sudsy peace offering.

"If there's anything else you need, Ant, let me know."

Under a kelly-green beanie, Clara's cherubic features were offset by a pair of enchanting heterochromatic eyes. Dressed in tight black jeans and a T-shirt with "The Emerald" embroidered across her busty chest, she navigated her tasks with the gracefulness of a ballerina. After placing an order in the kitchen, she emerged wearing her customary rainbow-colored rubber gloves. In a single elegant swoop, she collected bancor shares as payment from customers, then pirouetted away to execute her mysophobic rituals. The handful of smart bills were collectively submerged into a large jar of disinfectants. One hour later, the money would be hung-dried across the mischief of mousetraps nailed to the shelves behind the bar.

Antony casually followed Clara's movements before shifting his focus overhead. The ceiling-mounted plasma televisions offered bar-goers an experience conceived decades earlier. Developments in holography had pioneered a new wave of technologies in the media industry. Despite the cost, holographic platforms were commonplace in living rooms throughout middle-class households. In a lonely, world-weary society, one couldn't put a price on the value of entertainment. Antony personally had succumbed to the allure of the technology years earlier, but he preferred the convivial ambience of The Emerald on game days.

On the pregame telecast, the talking heads spoke of the competition as a foregone conclusion. In the background, the visiting Hippogriffs from Berlin jogged horizontally around the perimeter of the microgravity court. Meanwhile, the Seattle Supersonics' star player sprinted down the baseline. Using a teammate as a springboard, he vaulted himself high above his opponents, then reversed course in midair by kicking off the walled playing surface. Soaring over the hardwood, from beyond the three-point line, he threw down a monstrous slam dunk. This athletic demonstration, along with the panel's prognostications, reassured Antony. Visualizing the victory, a triumphant smile graced his face.

Moments later, the robotic greeting of new arrivals silenced the pregame analysis: "Welcome." Several men scampered inside, proceeding in height order, each appearing more anxious than the last, the coinciding announcement of their names loud enough for everyone in the bar to hear. Decked out in green-and-yellow Sonics attire, the group fidgeted as they searched for a booth. For a weekday, the pub's occupancy was exceeding expectations.

Antony acknowledged his fellow regulars with a slow nod. The timing of their entrance was another good omen.

"Shots all around," he shouted while twirling his index finger overhead.

Compelled by karma, Antony's altruistic actions were payment for future happiness. He repeated this generous act multiple times throughout the first three quarters. An insurmountable lead served as a catalyst for copious amounts of ingested alcohol by all onlookers. Midway through the fourth quarter, momentum switched allegiances. With a collection of reserve players roaming the floor, the visitors narrowed the gap on the scoreboard.

"A shooting foul by Seattle gives Berlin a chance to cut this lead to eight." The announcer's lethargic tone underlined the fact that with only seconds on the game clock, the result was already in the record books. Beyond the pure competition, it was these moments the gambling community agonized over;

what were meaningless points to one, could build an empire for another.

Antony gnawed on the collar of his brown wool overcoat. "Miss it!"

The notoriously poor shooter made his first of two attempts from the charity strip. Then and there, Antony felt the true pressure of the moment. His gut churned. A time-out exacerbated his stress. The teams nonchalantly strolled toward their respective coaches for instruction. As a sign of respect, The Emerald's patrons returned their attention to the game. In the midst of the lull, Antony leapt up from his seat. Unable to watch his fate unfold at the hands of another man, he hurried toward the restroom.

His erratic pacing began when his shoes touched the beige ceramic tiles. One, two, three steps forward, pivot, three steps back. He clumsily bounced off the grimy walls of the diminutive lavatory. Like drawing a line with a distorted ruler, his feet performed this drunken dance. Several minutes passed. Given the absence of an uproar, Antony concluded that the free throw had fallen.

The realization of the defeat stopped his frantic pacing mid-step. Slowly, he approached the crestfallen image that stared across from him in the mirror. Leaning in toward the reflection, he put his hands on the countertop. Gray-and-black hair wildly protruded from his scalp like the quills of a porcupine. Dark stubble concealed his dimpled chin. Anchored by a snub nose, his facial features, while handsome, appeared a touch too small for the olive-toned oval canvas. A pair of listless hazel eyes told the story of a man molded by tragedy.

"Am I destined to become a failure?" He directed the slurred utterance at his likeness. Win or lose, gambling was by no means constructive for society. For the individual, productivity was an indispensable element for a moral life. Antony reluctantly nodded his head up and down. Below the surface, he harbored a set of deviant self-serving motives. These shameful, selfish inclinations would be responsible for his approaching financial hardships. Overconfidence in his statistical analysis of the Zero-G Basketball Association compelled him to constantly increase the amount of his wagers. Regrettably, tonight's mishap not only included February's Prosperity Dividend but a sizable portion of his recent winnings. When taking into account his drunken generosity, a net loss for the month was all but certain.

Once upon a time, Antony was a highly respected robotics engineer. Over thirty-two years, he'd built a reputation as a prominent figure with a specialization in mobility systems. During the late stages of his career, he spent his days directing teams of up-and-comers within the propulsion industry.

Everything changed seventeen months ago. On an ill-fated afternoon, his team sought to unleash the immense energy embedded within magnetic fields. Inspired by astronomical observations, the experiment delved into the acceleration of particles by manipulating the phenomenon of magnetic reconnection. Discoveries in this field had the potential to enhance plasma engine capabilities, thereupon transforming space exploration.

In the center of a metal, honeycombed workstation, the team placed their latest experimental device, a toroidal vacuum vessel wrapped in field coils with a plasma ejection chamber. They attached a cryogenic power generator to the circumferential magnets, then pumped heated ionized gas into the torus.

Antony always took a hands-on approach during preliminary design testing. Behind a galvanized steel protective barrier, while observing through a thick polycarbonate viewing window, he controlled amperage and current direction.

The experiment swiftly revealed itself to be an abysmal failure. Nonlinear distortions, caused by tangled magnetic field lines, introduced instability into the system. A breakdown of the frozen flux condition resulted in the topological rearrangement of the plasma's magnetic field. Within the toroidal chamber, thermal energy was converted into kinetic energy. Streams of charged particles smashed into the walls of the torus at thousands of kilometers per second. Sensing that something was amiss, Antony stepped out from behind the barrier to deactivate the device. At that very moment, shards of shrapnel were expelled haphazardly throughout the laboratory. Lodged deep within his unshielded right leg, the fragmentations of the explosion left a mangled appendage. The on-site medical staff administered the grim diagnosis, an above-the-knee amputation.

In the aftermath, a robotic prosthesis restored Antony's mobility. Ridding himself of uncanny feelings of disconnectedness was a different story. The advanced anatomical substitute imperfectly replicated the appearance and natural movements of his lost limb. Fortunately, an infusion of wealth turned the kaleidoscope, transforming the blue into the rosy; his prosthesis was only temporary.

A biological scaffolding was constructed from digital photos taken of Antony the previous summer. Its three-dimensional cultures were filled with his skin cells, which were subsequently reprogrammed to induce pluripotency. Freshly formed muscle tissue was exercised regularly to prevent atrophy. Newly engineered bone was stress tested to ensure durability. Seven months later, the biofabrication process reached its conclusion. Antony would endure months of grueling rehabilitation. While he would eventually regain full functionality, the path toward reacclimation remained rocky.

In the bar's restroom, with clinched teeth, Antony ferociously shook his head back and forth, attempting to erase the deeply ingrained traumatic memories from his hippocampus. The experience was another instance where he'd failed to control a situation. Throughout his life, he'd fervidly attacked futile challenges, unwilling to accept reality. A solitary man was never in control. Hoping to regain his composure, he cupped his sweaty hands and splashed cold water onto his face. Shrouded in disappointment, he sluggishly exited.

Clara smiled at her grief-filled companion. "Let's get you another drink."

Antony's response was one of the many guttural noises in his despondent repertoire. The low growl was more appropriate for a dying wild animal than a civilized human being. An incomprehensible request for a bourbon on the rocks followed. His muttered words were superfluous from the get-go as his anticipated request was already in the process of being poured.

"You know I can read your mind, baby," Clara said. She batted her eyes while sliding over the small stemmed glass. Out of habit, she twirled her golden strands of hair. These simple acts had captured the hearts of countless suitors over the years.

"Thanks." He raised the glass to his lips. The pungent bite of American whiskey invaded his languid palate. Before swallowing, he swished around the liquid, saturating his taste buds.

"Can you do me a favor?" Clara asked.

Antony fixed his vapid gaze upon her. He folded the coasters within reach to and fro. The cardboard circles crumbled and changed shapes between his fingers. "That depends," he said at last.

"Stop thinking about that free throw."

"Please," he replied dourly, "not now."

She ignored his taciturnity and continued with her consolatory pep talk. "Ant. It's only one game. This wasn't your first bad beat. And it won't be your last. You'll bounce back. Tonight was nothing but a setback. There's still half a season for that formula of yours to figure th—"

The breaking-news jingle from the televisions interrupted her condolence speech. On each of their screens appeared the esteemed chair of the Pansophical Corporation.

Leonard Fields stood motionless center stage, seemingly undaunted by his task at hand. In his early forties, the man was a bulldog, thick in the chest with a powerful square-shaped head. His slick espresso hair was sideswept. Below his flattened nose sat a lampshade mustache. As a member of the board of directors, Fields wore the company's prestigious white double-breasted blazer over a black-and-white striped dress shirt complemented by a solid black tie. Overhead behind him, "Pansophical" was printed across a black circle in white bold letters. As Fields stoically approached the podium, the camera panned to reveal the full extent of the backdrop. A white elongated ellipse enclosed the black circle to form a prodigious eyeball. The alternating color scheme was mesmerizing. As if under hypnotic incantation, The Emerald's patrons converged on the main television. Staring intently into the camera, Fields began his address.

"Citizens of the world. Your unwavering loyalty has been a guiding light during these tumultuous times. Our society stands on the shoulders of each and every one of you. Thanks to your hard work, thanks to your fidelity, we at the Pansophical Corporation have facilitated tremendous improvements in living standards. Together we have raised the tides, and across the seas, all boats have been lifted.

"In spite of the diabolical crusades carried out by Praxis, the glaring problems plaguing previous civilizations have ceased to exist. With each passing day, we move closer to restoring our communication infrastructure. Developments in medicine have extended lifespans. Technological break-throughs have helped us avert climate catastrophe and have freed humanity from many menial tasks. The prosperous gains that pervade our economy have led to a fair and just society, free of poverty."

Fields paused and aggressively cleared his throat. The gesture served as the precursor for a topical shift in the oratory. The chairman's serious expression persisted, but as he continued, solemnity infused his words.

"Regretfully, I do not stand before you this evening to sim-ply recount the innumerable enhancements in life quality that have occurred under the Pansophical Corporation's guidance.

"Make no mistake about it, mankind remains at war against a microscopic foe. Three hours ago, on the border of the Floridian peninsula quarantine camp, the Tembakoo virus claimed the lives of another hundred innocent victims in the town of Waldo. Initial tests by the World Health Organization estimate the fatality rate upon infection for this mutated strain to be of upward of 87 percent. Do. Not. Panic. An aggressive response by the best and brightest minds within the medical community have mitigated the risk of exposure. All evidence indicates that this recent outbreak has been contained.

"If you are experiencing any of the typical Tembakoo symptoms, contact the Department of Health Services immediately. Vaccines are being manufactured as we speak and will be available shortly at designated locations.

"The Atlantic Territories of North America have been elevated to threat level red. Citizens in this region are required to stay indoors until further notice. The rest of the Americas have been elevated to threat level orange. Unvaccinated citizens within these regions are now permitted to mask up in public. Curfews worldwide will be instated one hour early.

"My fellow citizens, your well-being is of the upmost concern. Our efforts will be tireless in combating this deadly challenge. We are united as one. We will never surrender. Long live Pansophical!"

Fields issued the directive by vehemently pointing into the camera lens. The television then faded to black. As the screen completed its transformation to the absence of color, the corporate slogan emerged.

The Emerald's patrons repeated the phrase with an impassioned fist pump accompanying each word. The thundering chant reverberated through the establishment.

Immediately following the unifying ritual, the woman closest to the television refashioned her jacket into a mask. Panicking, she wrapped its sleeves around her face. "Vámonos." She directed the muffled command at her boyfriend. He hesitated. "Vámonos!" She yanked on his arm. The young couple bolted for the exit. On the way out, he tossed a handful of bancor shares behind the bar.

The apocalyptic threat of Tembakoo always lingered in the shadows, yet under the newest normal, life felt placidly secure. Now to the contrary, the chairman's words formed a grim conception within Antony. Trepidation crept up his spine. Perhaps Homo sapiens were not equipped to ward off the relentless vultures circling overhead; perhaps evolution was prepared to crown its next king. Tembakoo's first wave had left billions dead, reminding mankind of the prospect of extinction. The burning question was whether the species' reprieve was permanent or only a temporary injunction.

Over the next half hour, The Emerald emptied out. Antony and his affable bartender stayed behind.

"How about one more?" He glumly looked at Clara. With a gulp, the remaining bourbon occupying his glass disappeared.

"Not tonight," she answered.

"Come on." The crispness of his speech was jaded by the

distilled spirits. "Don't make me endure the wrath of Mother Nature just yet."

Clara paused from cleaning the rubber bar runners and pointed up to the shamrock-shaped neon wall clock. "You know I love your company, but you need to get going."

A pair of black miniature flags, each featuring a minimalist eyeball, bookended the tubed timepiece. Antony's sightline followed Clara's directional command. The optical emblems of the Pansophical Corporation bored into their organic counterparts. His head wobbled unsteadily. From right to left, from front-to-back, he attempted to counterbalance the spinning room to determine the time.

Clara giggled while watching him struggle. "Forty-five minutes until curfew, hon."

"Oh, well, I have plenty of time."

"You may only live twenty minutes away, but that's twenty sober minutes."

Her playful jab was nevertheless a serious warning. Curfew violation penalties ranged from large fines to jail time. In the midst of a crisis, sentences levied were exponentially more severe. Still, Antony's angst-ridded intoxicated state reduced his sense of urgency. He leisurely rose to his feet and reached both arms with elbows bent behind his back. At the height of the stretch, gaseous-filled cavities formed around his facet joints, releasing a string of gratifying pops.

"Fine. Guess hitting the road is my only option." He broke a slight smile while strolling toward the exit. "I'll pass by later in the week to square away that bar tab. Take it easy, sweetheart."

"Goodbye, Antony Sartori," the monotonic gatekeeper said, drowning out Clara's valediction. The system always had the final word.

CHAPTER TWO

ear the corner of Harrison Street and Pontius Avenue, Antony's procumbent body laid still. Minutes earlier, he had tumbled into the intersection. During daylight hours, this false step off the curb would have had ruinous ramifications, but at the present, the streets were rightfully deserted. As his concussed state waned, his sprawled-out limbs regained their strength. He struggled to his battered knees in the caliginous crossroad.

Crimson plasma oozed down his hairline. Gravity slowly forced the hematic discharge into his unsuspecting mouth. The sweet metallic taste served as a sensory perception beacon. Methodically with both hands, he scoured his skullcap for the source.

"What hap-pened here?" he murmured. His inquiring mind spun, rampaging through recollections like funnel clouds touching down in tornado alley. A debilitating headache hampered his cognitive processing. Gathering information was an arduous task. Persevering through the discomfort, he began to replay the night's proceedings. He remembered

Leonard Fields's global address, but the subsequent sequence of events was a mystery. All the more perplexing was a vivid childhood flashback that continually rebuffed his attempts to access the blacked-out segments.

The out-of-the-blue visual hallucination transported him back to his first day of elementary school. Anxious to tell his parents about everything he had learned, he tried to run off the bus. His would-be sprint was short-lived. One of his classmates had tied his shoelaces together. Throughout his formative years, he was on the receiving end of this juvenile prank. Ridiculed as "Antony Accidents," the laugher of his peers had haunted him as a youngster.

Reminiscing over personal episodes beyond a few months prior was a forced exercise in fabrication. Antony apperceived the events that shaped his life rather than remembering them as if he had experienced them firsthand. In a sense, it was like he had constructed an autobiography after memorizing a collection of short stories. This latest juvenile recollection was an eerie abnormality. It was unique; it was real.

Releasing a bewildered sigh, Antony sluggishly stood. He surveyed the desolate junction for the answers he sought, but no clues were revealed. Aside from himself, the only movement belonged to the blinking bulbs of the judiciously arranged security cameras. The reddish luminescence reflected off the street signs, glass windows, and pools of rain water, setting the intersection ablaze. Now was not the time, nor the place, to ruminate over past embarrassments.

The pulsating illumination signaled a tripped motion sensor. Attempting to escape was futile, but that never stopped one's basic survival instincts from kicking in. Five hundred feet from the site of his fall, Antony's wobbly gallop was thrown into a trepid halt.

"Public Safety, don't move!"

Perpetrators were rarely afforded the opportunity to comply with this command on their own terms. Three blocks away, mounted on the roof of a black Humvee, Medusa's Stare swirled into place. The multipurpose energy weapon thermographically scanned the scene to pinpoint the trespasser. The weapon's operator calibrated its amplitude and frequency settings. A high-pitched murmur was released. Before discharging, the cannon's tapered nozzle glowed a vibrant blue. Slicing through the foggy night air, the paralysis ray struck Antony precisely in the center of his chest. The frigid benumbing sensation quickly traveled outward, immobilizing his extremities.

"Citizen," the Humvee's PA system blared, "you're in direct violation of Pansophical Corporation bylaw 17-3. As per the curfew directive, you're trespassing on lands designated as non-civilian. All your rights and freedoms have been temporarily rescinded. A failure to fully cooperate with the upcoming judicial proceedings will result in immediate incarceration."

The notification alerted law-abiding residents in the vicinity of the street-side happenings. An inrush of lumens shaped the darkness. Ocular ensigns of the Pansophical

Corporation dangled from flagpoles, peppering the steel structures with pride. Awoken from their peaceful slumber, onlookers peered out their freshly lit windows to witness a man staring into an unblinking authority.

The Humvee's driver side door flung open. The infamous Sergeant Leroy Bannister exited the vehicle. He stalked the pavement like a bloodthirsty jackhammer entering a granite quarry. Nano LEDs, interwoven into the fibers of his formfitting uniform, could produce a near limitless palette of colors on demand. His monstrous frame adopted a blackish-red hue, mimicking the environment. Behind him, his seven chameleonic soldiers spread out along the street. They raised their assault rail-rifles to eye level. Their laser-sighted scopes locked on to Antony's incapacitated body.

Antony's eyes darted back and forth between the dancing malignant circles on his torso and the advancing Bannister. The sergeant's sheer size could intimidate a man into submission. Internally, Antony's heart pounded on his chest wall. Maintaining a rational mindset was desirable, but autonomic signals betrayed his apprehensive state. Fear was birthed in a petri dish of unfamiliarity, and he was reliving the days before microbiology.

Inches in front of the frozen transgressor, Bannister stopped and lifted his head in observance of the burgeoning audience. Like an actor preparing for an impending curtain call, he seemed to revel in this moment. When his sightline returned to the street level, his darkened face shield receded to unveil a protruding scarred brow, a broad nose, a rigid jaw line, and a scowl for the ages.

"Do you know what time it is?" Bannister asked Antony. "Or are you unable to tell time?"

Antony was taken aback by the condescending tone of the colossus before him. Instinctively, he made an effort to turn away, but Medusa had not yet relinquished her grasp.

"Citizen, are you aware of the curfew that forbids you from being out at this hour?"

Shallow breaths originated from Antony's upper chest as he formulated a timid response. "Yes ... I-I-I'm aware."

"Aware?" Bannister's eyes narrowed. "Yet you disobey the laws of the Pansophical Corporation?"

"No. Never. Never willingly, that is."

"Is that a fact? Or maybe you just believe that you're special?"

If only I were, Antony thought heretically. The prospect rarely if ever occurred to him. The concept was foreign for a man molded in a crucible of chaos in a world ravaged by a ruthless pathogen. Above all else, distinctiveness was antithetical to the precept of being united as one.

"No," Antony said with a sigh. "I'm far from special."

"Damn right." Bannister's nostrils flared. "You're nothing but a drunkard about to feel the hand of justice."

Bannister tapped twice on his wrist, prompting a gray control panel to appear on his forearm. He initiated an RFID scan via this graphical interface. A red progress bar replaced the array of buttons. It steadily became green as information was gathered.

A tinny voice emanated from a speaker on the outside of the sergeant's helmet: "Scan complete."

"Let's hear it, Benton," said Bannister.

"Citizen name: Antony Sartori. Home address: 1186 Sanctuary Lane Apartment 7F, Seattle, Washington. Age: Fifty-four. Physical description: Caucasian male. Six foot, one inch. 172 pounds. Vaccinations: Up to date. Profession: Unemployed, psychologically unstable. Previous offenses: None."

In the matter of a minute, the artificial intelligence system had scanned Antony like a bag of groceries, then publicized his personal information to all within earshot. He shivered at Benton's hasty dehumanization.

Bannister glanced over his shoulder at his men and chuckled. "It appears that we have another member of the parasitic class."

"Laugh, all of you, if you must," said Antony.

"Jobless and mentally unsound," Bannister carried on. "Antony Sartori, you are human greatness defined."

"I wasn't always this way. Prior to my accident, I was an engineer for Pansophical. Imagine for a moment losing your leg. And subsequently your wife. Sanity drifts when the fetters of reality are removed."

"You'll speak when spoken to!" Bannister punctuated his bellowed instruction by chopping down Antony with a swift kick.

Just as Antony crumbled to the unforgiving asphalt, the effects of Medusa's Stare ceased to impair. His muscular system regained its vitality. Writhing in pain, he grabbed his left knee while sheepishly looking up at his assailant.

"Pathetic," Bannister said. "Keep the sob story to yourself. Consider this your one and only warning. We serve the Pansophical Corporation and protect its citizens. But Public Safety doesn't cater to deadbeats. Step out of line again and watch what happens."

Verbally defending oneself when facing Bannister's vitriolic barbs was a dangerous game. Antony came to recognize that the stage belonged to Bannister, and Bannister alone. For the briefest of moments, Antony's mind wandered into the future. Fatalities caused by a Public Safety beating or bullet occurred frequently. He imagined his name appearing as an afterthought during a late-night news telecast. The visualization left him petrified. A swollen knee became the least of his worries.

Accompanied by a sneer, Bannister dragged his rugged boot toe backward, then thrust it through a puddle of rainwater. Water molecules haphazardly splattered Antony's unsuspecting frame. He closed his eyes as the droplets trickled down his face. In a stare-down with an unwavering foe, sometimes the only option was to blink.

With the hierarchy of dominance reestablished, the sergeant's gaze dipped to his forearm controls. He scrolled past an assortment of advanced uniform configurations before pressing the video surveillance button. A second query menu popped up featuring the names and corresponding timestamps from recent scans. His visor dropped down into place. "Time to take a walk in the shoes of a parasite."

"Additional parameters required," stated Benton. "Please provide start and end points for surveillance footage."

"Yesterday, February 2, nine o'clock. That's our start point. End point is the present. And set replay to twenty speed."

Bannister issued the commands as if he were Chronos himself. Control of the present required knowledge of the past. He seemed to relish the act of fast-forwarding through a life he deemed to be insignificant.

Minutes passed. With a mistrustful grumble, Bannister broke the prolonged silence. Returning to his control pad, he scrolled through Benton's analytical arsenal. At his fingertips awaited dozens of tools, each bolstering Public Safety's crime prevention capabilities.

"Did you know that seemingly innocent movements can reveal one's thoughts?" Bannister activated the Jungian Lens. "What do you have to hide, Antony Sartori?"

"Analysis underway," Benton said, its robotic tone juxtaposing the subtle aspects of communications that evolved to facilitate human interactions.

How would Antony look when the veil he adorned was removed? Like a nude model posing for a virtuoso sculptor, his minute imperfections would imminently be revealed. He feared how his involuntary gestures and facial expressions would be deciphered by this emotionless algorithm.

Criteria for suspicious activity was broadened during curfew. The bar was lowered even more so following outbreaks of Tembakoo. Antony was keenly aware of Bannister's relentless reputation as an investigator with no tolerance for dubious behavior. His peerless zeal toward law enforcement and his unquenchable thirst for righteousness were legendary. The countless names declared as "dangers to humanity" by his gavel dwarfed those of other officers. Three weeks earlier, Antony had witnessed his handiwork in the flesh.

Jasper Turner lived a happy fulfilling life. Without exception, the residents of Sanctuary Village viewed him as delightful. Upon retirement, he moved his antique rocking chair to the apartment lobby. Every day at the break of dawn, he lumbered down a single flight of stairs to his beloved rocker. Throughout the day, he regaled all who would listen with tales of his childhood, astute societal observations, and a never-ending repertoire of jokes. News of Jasper's charming personality extended beyond the complex. People across the neighborhood paid visits to the lobby solely to bask in the worldly, kindhearted disposition of the senior with the trademark beard.

Antony had grown incredibly fond of the elderly gentleman. The two regularly spent hours upon hours engrossed in conversation.

Born and raised inside the apartment complex, Jasper was content with spending his final days within its familiar walls. He had amassed an abundance of financial resources as a result of a frugal lifestyle. Thanks to the local children, who performed his weekly errands, along with a personal nurse, Jasper had no need to venture outdoors.

During the wee hours of a traumatic morning weeks earlier, roles had been reversed. Awoken by Sergeant Bannister's boisterous insolence, it was Antony who gaped down from his window at his close friend. Antony incredulously watched the scene unfold. Mired in ethical conflict, he found himself simultaneously commending and condemning the protectors of peace.

Jasper exhibited no trepidation in the face of the unfeeling muscle of the Pansophical Corporation. Surely Jasper understood the gravity of the situation, yet he responded to Bannister's barrage of questions candidly. He cited a desire for fresh air as the reason of his curfew violation. He repeatedly took deep breaths, filling his lungs with unprocessed oxygen molecules. Accompanied by a smile, he asked the Public Safety officers whether this simple pleasure was not his right. The outward display of Jasper's unwillingness to submit enraged the temperamental sergeant.

"Take a seat, grandpa!"

Bannister violently jabbed Jasper in the chest with his index finger. The force knocked the feeble old man flat on his back. Like a turtle waving at the celestial crescent overhead,

Jasper frantically attempted to use his extremities to restore his body to an upright position. Bannister's maniacal chuckle echoed through the deserted streets. The Jungian Lens would serve as the star witness for the prosecution. Ten minutes of ostensibly harmless footage, analyzed through a magnifying glass, would unearth suspicious intentions. Bannister lifted Jasper and threw him on his shoulder in the manner one would carry a large bag of concrete.

Hours later on the morning news, mixed among other "dangers to humanity," the name Jasper Turner scrolled across the bottom of Antony's holographic television. No one ever saw Jasper again. The residents of Sanctuary Village no longer had the privilege of listening to his life lessons. The world was forever deprived of one of its last remaining sources of benevolence.

In the aftermath, the absurdity of it all overwhelmed Antony. From his perspective, Jasper was hardly a threat to anyone, let alone humanity. Bewailing, he spent the following days replaying the calamity. Although he struggled to pinpoint the motivations guiding Jasper's uncharacteristic behavior, the incident engendered doubts within him about the infallibility of the Pansophical Corporation. Never before had he questioned the justness of a Public Safety hearing, but now he inescapably harbored smidgens of skepticism.

Bannister received a status update from Benton about the scofflaw in the street, one Antony Sartori. "Nonverbal behavior analysis complete."

Playback resumed on the inside of his tinted visor. Location data on the sidebar was replaced by a series of twenty-one rotating emoticons. Each pictorial representation included a likelihood percentage bar. For those lacking an interest in unconscious communication, the recording epitomized the mundane. The footage featured Antony seated on a blue cushioned bucket seat, alone, within a Hyperloop pod. While staring out the window, he readjusted his pants, then scratched his forehead. His pupils followed the natural beauty that sped by outside. 78 percent sadly fearful, 55 percent awed, 53 percent sad, 31 percent fearful, 17 percent sadly angry. The percentage bars were updated with each facial expression or change in body language.

Scanning the scene, Bannister squinted in search of incriminating details. He grew increasingly disturbed as he speculated about the reasons Antony ignored the surrounding amenities. Travelers had the luxury of watching television, listening to music, playing immersive games, or altering the interior design of their transportation vessel. What would cause an individual to pay no heed to the entertainment options at their disposal? Why would someone not take advantage of the possibility to escape reality? An hour later, over 250 miles inland, Antony disembarked in Spokane.

Bannister growled. "Open those damn eyes, Benton. For a super AI, you're clueless. This drunk is a danger to society!"

The Jungian Lens failed to corroborate the suspicions that permeated his bones. With an outstretched hand in the form of a claw, he took a small step toward Antony's trembling frame. Flight response was activated, and Antony scurried away from the looming threat.

"Sergeant." The timorous words arose from one of the men. "None of his risk identifiers topped our minimum thresholds."

Bannister turned away from the wounded prey that quailed at his feet.

Obscured by a face shield, the other Public Safety officer continued. "Didn't the board caution you about rejecting Benton's findings?"

For several seconds Bannister glowered at his subordinates. He waited for the source of the punctilious warning to claim ownership. Even with a rifle in hand, the fainthearted officer refused to oblige.

"Before any of you question my judgment, remember who is in charge. A lengthy look at any citizen will show probability spikes of anger, disgust, or hatred. I refuse to be bound by the ignorance of a machine." Bannister returned his focus to the subject of the interrogation. "Play time is over. Tell me what you're hiding."

Antony's response was nearly inaudible. "One year ago, my wife was diagnosed with Tembakoo."

"And?"

"And today has been difficult. We first met outside Central Station in Spokane. I had never seen anyone so passionate about their work. Dominique ..."

Antony whispered her name as if each syllable were sacred. Tears welled up in his eyes. A wave of melancholy swept over his countenance as the salty liquid steamed down his cheeks.

"Sergeant, he speaks the truth," one of Bannister's men, Nikola Fedorovich, said, unable to hide his Russian accent. "This man pulls at my heartstrings. Guilty of violating curfew, yes. But he's no threat."

Without delay, Nikola holstered his weapon in the scabbard strapped onto his back and began typing commands on his control pad.

Benton's high-pitched update broke the uneasy silence. "Personal history retrieved." On Bannister's heads-up display, the surveillance footage of Antony was replaced by an extensive multimedia dossier.

Bannister was accustomed to being challenged during judicial proceedings but not by his men in the field, let alone the young, shy Nikola. In a rare moment of emotional restraint, Bannister pressed his lips together. He skimmed through the tragic story of a bright man with untold potential. He passed over intricate details of Antony's life without a second glance. Bannister sped by photos, snippets of conversations, and employee reviews. His pace slowed when he arrived at the accomplishment section. Numerous items were listed. A master's degree in engineering was followed by inventions conceived within Pansophical laboratories. The file concluded with a description of Antony's amputation, an infected patient transfer form for Dominique Sartori, and a psychological assessment that diagnosed Antony with borderline personality disorder.

The advanced background query provided credence to Antony's words, but it failed to evoke even an iota of compassion within Bannister. With calm deliberation, he looked over his shoulder and stared down Nikola.

"Benton, resume playback at normal speed."

Until proven otherwise, Antony was a guilty man. Nikola drew his weapon and aimed it back at the despondent shell before him. Order was reestablished, and the investigation proceeded.

On the video, Antony exited the pod with his head down. He carefully stepped over the gap onto the gray concrete platform. After multiple steps, he raised his field of vision, then turned to marvel at the passing vehicles. Seconds turned into minutes. Locked in a visceral trance, he was oblivious to the arriving and departing passengers.

Eventually, Antony strolled down the station's staircase toward the administrative department. Along the way, he caressed the handrail as if attempting to extract the molecular history from its metal surface. At the bottom of the descent was the office of the chief transportation officer for the Pacific Territories of North America. He lifted the door's nameplate to reveal a crudely drawn woman with a globe in her outstretched hand. There was a Hyperloop pod perched on the North Pole and action lines circling the planet. The corners of his mouth raised into the shape of an effervescent smile. The simple sketch marked the end of his pilgrimage. After replacing the nameplate, he hustled up the flight of stairs back to the platform.

"Pathetic." Bannister's lips curled in disdain. "The human race marches on, yet here you are wasting your days reliving the past."

Antony said nothing. While it had been the sergeant who earlier announced his refusal to participate in a mental joust, it was Antony who stepped away from the field of competition. Just as a state of blankness washed over his visage, an all-points bulletin offered him refuge.

"Attention," Benton announced. "Attention, all squads. Report to Heritage Park. We have officers in hot pursuit of four armed non-citizens transporting contraband by robo-mule. They are disguised in hyper-realistic masks of Pansophical board members and are wearing thermal-resistant black jumpsuits. The materials in their possession are a global threat. It's to be destroyed immediately upon seizure. Proceed with caution and prepare to use deadly force. This is priority number one."

The investigation was terminated prematurely. One of the officers approached Bannister and handed him a citation, but it slipped through his burly fingers. It fluttered in freefall before landing on the wet ground. Briefly, Bannister considered throwing Antony into the prisoner containment unit, but his wariness had waned. More importantly, time was of the essence.

Bannister begrudgingly recited the sentences that had been drilled into his memory at the academy. "Citizen, you have been found guilty of Pansophical bylaw 17-3. This judgment is final and not subject to appeal. The evidence gathered during these judicial proceedings has been added to your permanent record. All your rescinded rights and freedoms have been restored effective immediately. As a penalty for today's offense, you've been fined 15,000Ƀ. Payment will be due in three months' time."

Antony stared vacantly at the citation as the officers jogged away to attend to the global imperative.

Bannister lingered for a moment. "I suggest that you make sure our paths don't cross again. If there's a next time, you won't be gimping away with a measly fine."

CHAPTER THREE

ntony peered through the frosted glass doors of Sanctuary Village Apartments. It took him a moment to confirm his location. Upon doing so, his haggard eyes descended onto the building's biometric security panel. He placed his hand on the optical scanner, only to be denied access. Authentication was impossible due to the dried blood and pavement that encrusted his fingers.

Psychological trauma had dimmed the luminance of his inner light bulb. The gatekeeper's refusal to grant passage left him confounded. He released a few short breaths while running his fingers through his hair, then mindlessly plopped down his other hand.

The security system buzzed. The crossed-out friction ridge patterns belonging to his soiled phalanges appeared on the entry panel. Underneath, a message blinked in red: "Access Denied."

Irritated, Antony jiggled the door handle. The rattling echoed through the empty lobby. Three failed attempts later, he remembered his contingency plan. This was not the first time that he had been locked out. Years earlier, on a night when the system went haywire, his wife had stashed a backup key inside an unmarked sealed envelope. Antony slid over to the apartment's cluster of mailboxes. He slowly typed Dominique's birthday into the keypad of his box: 062133. After tearing open the envelope, he aligned the key's pointed teeth with the pins of its locked counterpart. With a turn, the barrier of entry was removed, and he stepped inside.

Antony emitted a prolonged sigh as the door closed behind him. Now firmly away from the roving militants, a sense of relief washed over his physical mass. The journey following his precarious exchange with Public Safety had been a blur. Neurons corresponding to advanced thought had ceased to fire. His legs had instinctively followed the path laid out during previous drunken treks from The Emerald. As a biological locomotive, he had moved resolutely along his guide rails toward home.

Within the safety of the foyer, the mental anguish that dominated his thoughts became secondary to physical suffering. Pain receptors forced this cognitive transition. The assault he had endured at the hands of Sergeant Bannister manifested in the form of a hematoma. He gingerly dragged his feet along the gold letters of the monogrammed navy entrance mat. Blinking repeatedly, he became acclimated to his surroundings. The room came into focus.

Two beige leather armchairs, lined with brass nails, diagonally faced a faux fireplace. Stacked sandstones flanked the fiery ghosts that danced across the bundle of imitation logs. An oval walnut coffee table was positioned between the chairs. Atop the table, a dark-bronze desk lamp provided light in addition to the scattered sconces.

Feeling the effects of the crushed muscle fibers, Antony heedfully bent his left knee, elevating his heel rearward. He simultaneously reached down for his ankle to extend the stretch. Balancing on a single leg proved to be a challenge. The bourbon still tenuously held the reins controlling his center of movement. He wobbled on his fragile support beam like a malfunctioning gyroscope. In an act of desperation, he grabbed the back of the wooden rocking chair next to the doorway. The angle of its curved rails increased rapidly, disrupting his equilibrium. On the verge of another self-inflicted fall, he released his battered limb just in time. Laboriously, he climbed onto the chair that had once served as a watchtower for his worldly companion.

Dust accrued on the chair's armrests and intricately crafted spindles. The once-spotless windows that looked out into the world were now opaque. These tangible signs of neglect further fueled the grief that permeated his day. He squinted through the filth into the darkness and began to reminisce about his daily conversations with Jasper.

On a half-day Friday, over two decades ago, Antony galloped down the sidewalk with childlike enthusiasm. A propulsion project and an unexpected promotion consumed his thoughts. Swinging his leather briefcase, he was undismayed by Seattle's record high temperatures on that July afternoon. Dress shoes were hardly ideal for this level of activity, but his excitement would not be contained by restrictive attire nor slowed by the heat. Large white oak trees supplied cover from the sun's relentless barrage. The intermittent shade, however, did not prevent Antony from sweating through his collared dress shirt.

Both of the apartment complex's doors were ajar. A pair of fans served as substitutes for the building's malfunctioning air conditioner. Greeted by a gust of hot air, Antony's eyelids reflexively clamped shut.

Across the lobby, Jasper was attempting to drag a rocking chair out from inside the elevator. The older gentleman struggled to impose his will on his wooden foe. Back and forth the chair rocked, creaking while it swayed, as if laughing in triumph over its opposition. Panting in temporary defeat, he leaned his shoulder into the elevator's door track to reactivate the motion sensor. Whereas a white bushy beard blanked his face, not a single hair sprouted atop his smooth skull. Woolly eyebrows perfectly complemented his facial hair while directly contrasting his mocha complexion. He wore a plaid short-sleeved shirt embroidered with an anchor and slim ivory khakis.

On the way over, Antony raised his hand to acknowledge his fellow apartment dweller.

"Antony ... how are you on this hellacious afternoon?"

"You know, Jasper," Antony said, dabbing his brow with his sleeve, "I'm not one to complain, but something needs to be done about the heat in here."

"Tell me about it." The oval wire-framed glasses that rested on Jasper's bulbous nose had fogged over. He removed a whale-printed cloth from his pocket and wiped away the moisture. "I'll be out of your way in just a minute."

Jasper gathered himself and took a backward stride in the direction of the exit. With his seasoned fingers wrapped around the chair arms, he strenuously yanked at the furniture, grunting all the while. The combination of blistering temperatures and dreadful humidity transformed the relatively easy task into an arduous endeavor.

Upon hearing the sounds of physical strain, Antony set down his briefcase and hopped inside the elevator. "Allow me to lend a hand." He latched onto the chair's outermost back spindles.

"It wasn't long ago that no object was immovable." Jasper released a low-pitch chuckle in between labored breaths. "Through determination alone, my body was an unstoppable force."

Although Jasper's response was conceived in jest, Antony recognized the underlying truth of his words. The sands of time unrelentingly buried beings of the flesh without discrimination. He waited patiently, permitting Jasper an opportunity to gather his thoughts.

"We all have our limitations," Jasper said after recuperating. "I appreciate the help."

"Don't mention it. So, where are we moving this?"

"Over by the door." Jasper's light-brown irises deliberately guided Antony along their projected path. He released the arm supports, placed his hands flat under the seat, then lifted the front of the rocker off the ground. Antony followed suit. Without further delay, they awkwardly carried the chair to its desired location. Once lowered, Jasper spun it around to face the sidewalk.

"Why are you casting away your possessions anyway?" Antony asked.

"Guess you haven't heard. Our building just hired the best damn security guard in the land. And at no cost!"

"Quite a bargain, but I suspect Luis will be awfully displeased to find something new cluttering his lobby."

"Luis won't dare say a word. A fierce bark, but that dog has no fangs. That whole stickler-for-cleanliness routine is a ruse. Have you seen the inside of his apartment?"

Antony smirked. "Maybe he'll grant you amnesty as a seniority perk."

With the indomitable confidence of a grotesque gargoyle accepting its post on a medieval skyline, Jasper settled onto his wooden perch. "Outside of my time at sea, I've lived here for seventy-six years."

"Seventy-six years," Antony repeated in astonishment. "Really?"

"Unbelievable, right? And thoughts of relocating never crossed my mind. Lil Mama raised me all by herself in that apartment upstairs. My days were spent as a cashier at our family bakery. Nights were spent over a hot furnace, baking goods for the following morning. I helped as much as I could. A life of luxury it was not, but we had all that we needed. And most importantly, we had each other."

"That's all that matters at the end of the day."

"So true."

"Well, if anyone makes a fuss about this right here"—Antony patted the rocker—"retell that story, and they'll shut their trap."

"Great, another chance for me to play my old man card."

"Why hold back? Today the lobby adds a piece of furniture. Tomorrow we'll all be forced to navigate piles of your discarded trash."

"Our family heirloom is not, as you so elegantly insinuate, a piece of"—Jasper used his fingers to make air quotes—"discarded trash."

Antony uncomfortably shifted his weight. "Believe me, I didn't intend to off—"

"Relax." Jasper laughed. "Possessions don't define the man. It takes more than bad-mouthing my rocking chair to offend me regardless of the number of Turner bottoms it has supported over the years. The stories it would tell if we could unlock the information deep within its grains.

"Look at me rambling on. In the months you've lived here,

we've exchanged words. But this is the first time we've truly spoken. Here I am, sucking the oxygen out of the room. Tell me, what has you so excited today?"

"Today has been a good one," said Antony. "I work for Pansophical, as an engineer in their propulsion division. My development team over this past year has been designing nanobot prototypes with little success to speak of. This morning was my quarterly review."

"And I assume it went well?"

"Shockingly, it couldn't have gone better. Now, my boss, Cassandra, is difficult to deal with, to say the least. Don't get me wrong, she's brilliant, but her pessimism and tendency to belittle is unbearable. Her patronizing responses to incompetence have brought employees to tears. Those that have shown weakness have been lucky to escape her office with a tissue, let alone their job."

"Sounds like a joy to work for."

"You don't know the half of it. There's an urban legend that Cassandra concluded her introductory meeting as project manager by screaming, 'Off with their heads.' That evening she supposedly cleaned house with a group email. I initially thought that this was a rumor conceived to terrify new hires. But now I have little doubt that it occurred."

Jasper set his chair in motion with a soft chuckle. "When did guillotines replace pink slips as the firing method of choice? Back in my day, we forced crewmen to walk the plank for shoddy work."

"The higher-ups at Pansophical have learned that nothing increases productivity like threats of decapitation."

Mimicking a beheading, Antony drew the fingertips of his flattened hand crosswise his throat. While making croaking sounds, he tilted his head. In a deformed expression, his tongue drooped from the corner of his mouth.

Together the men chortled.

When the laugher subsided, Jasper raised his eyebrows in curiosity. "So, how were you able to stave off execution and enter the good graces of Cassandra the Terrible?"

"Plain and simple, she was blown away by my design. I can't remember a single time when she even praised a proposal before today. Not only did she green-light my blueprints for production, she promoted me to staff engineer!"

"Impressive. What was so special about these blueprints?"

"Ummm. Where to start? Have you ever seen how a single-celled organism moves? Using its flagellum?"

Jasper nodded.

"Nanobots move in a similar manner, with an artificial muscle that operates as a propeller. There's problems, though. This tends to be energy inefficient. And deployment speed is an issue."

Antony paused. When he continued, his words increased velocity like the head of a landslide with his enthusiasm serving as gravity.

"My design is also based on biomimicry. It uses a pair of flagella, constructed from carbon nanotubes, affixed to opposite ends of a helical-shaped nanobot. These two flagella obviously can't operate simultaneously. The solution I devised was for the nanobot to wrap its leading flagellum around itself to create a unified thrust. Whenever my nanobots need to change direction, they simply reverse the orientation of their flagellum. Logistically, the mechanisms are straightforward. A voltage change rotates a motor that is connected to a ho—"

"Whoa, whoa, whoa," Jasper said with a smirk. "I don't want you to overheat. Remember that I'm a simple sailor, not a biologist, not a mechanical engineer."

"I have a tendency to do that," said Antony, embarrassed. "It's rare that I discuss this stuff outside the office."

"Actually, I first came across those tiny machines while working as a boatswain. It must have been fifteen years ago. I was stationed on a polar research vessel. We sent out an entire swarm of them to clean the Weddell Sea, near Antarctica. Our environmental engineer, Dr. Honjo, placed a clump of them in the palm of my hand. I swear, as a whole, they were no larger than a grain of salt."

"Difficult as it is to imagine, they've been further miniaturized. Ten thousand nanobots then amount to over a million nowadays."

"Amazing. I still remember how Dr. Honjo would ramble on and on about how his miracle workers could swim around and break down pollutants. Knowledge never falls by the wayside, but it was too cold to pay attention to his lessons on those Antarctic mornings. I've had plenty of ice cream headaches, but those were real brain freezes.

"Anyway, congratulations on the promotion, Antony. Technology transforms the world. I've always admired the people who actively serve as the shapers."

Antony grinned graciously, reminded of the inherent commonalities between men. "I appreciate the kind words. Throughout my life, I've aspired to be one of those people."

"Keep on this path. And it will happen."

"I hope so. I dream of the day when my contributions change humanity for the better."

"Maybe it's already happening."

"Anything's possible. If my most recent design can lift energy restraints, the applications are endless."

Jasper glanced up, his eyes emanating genuine inquisitiveness. "When did you become interested in all this nano stuff?"

"Middle school. It's a bit of a long story."

"Unless you have somewhere better to be, I'm all ears."

"It was back in fifth grade. My teacher, Mrs. Bennett, fell ill and was diagnosed with pancreatic cancer. In a failing education system, she was a difference maker, an inspiration. Never did she play the victim, never did she allow the tumor to affect her cheerful disposition. The other faculty members only discovered that she was ill after noticing the yellowing of her eyes. Unfortunately, the doctors likewise had been late to identify the disease."

Jasper's voice grew heavy. "Lost my Uncle Denzel to pancreatic cancer."

Antony placed his hand on Jasper's shoulder. "Sorry to hear. It's a terrible disease."

"It was long ago. Go on."

"Well, it was a week before Mrs. Bennett's procedure. She taught as if it were any other school day. During our last period, she announced that she was being forced to take a leave of absence. It was in those final minutes that emotional restraint was lost. We cried as one with the specter of the unknown in plain sight. Before dismissing us, Mrs. Bennett passed around a vial of nanobots. She told us that she would soon be receiving an injection of these mini-machines. And that they would hunt down and destroy her cancer.

"The dignity she maintained in the face of death left a lasting impression. Her final act in that classroom paved the path for my life's work. Immediately after school I started researching. From those inauspicious beginnings, I was forever captivated by the field of robotics."

In concurrence, Jasper chimed in. "Even a small spark has the potential to set our inner fire ablaze."

Jasper's words transcended Antony's daydream and ricocheted around his skull. The lifelike characteristics of the flashbacks mirrored his earlier childhood recollection, but now, as then, the peculiarities of the medium took a backseat.

A blank curtain lowered over his visage.

What is a hamster to do when its wheel is removed?

Antony contemplated the extinguishment of his life's driving passion. To fill the waking hours, he devoted himself to his sport handicapping endeavor. Without question, the hobby-turned-occupation provided a challenge. However, the vexatious hiccups had decreased enjoyment for the experiencing-self, and the lack of a societal contribution had left his remembering-self perpetually unfulfilled. The merging of these dissatisfied selves was embodied by the seamless wet mass within his pocket. Tonight's losing betting ticket and the curfew citation combined into a crumbled lump of failure.

Wrapping his fingers around the coalesced form, Antony released his stress with a prolonged violent squeeze. The cathartic response brought about a more balanced emotional state. After calmly straightening his posture, he placed his hands squarely on the rocker's armrests and returned his body to a standing position.

The temporary inactivity caused the muscles and tendons to tighten within his damaged knee. The effects of the alcohol had diminished, yet locomotion remained difficult. He gingerly crossed the lobby in the direction of the elevator. He focused on the inherent intricacies of his movements as he made each meticulous step. In front of the elevator's sliding doors, he lifted his head toward the floor display and pressed the call button. The elevator dial steadily rotated from right to left. It lit up when the transport arrived at the ground floor. Less than a minute later, he disembarked seven stories up.

Burned-out bulbs rendered every other light fixture through the corridor useless. Still-life photographs decorated the walls. Down the glimmering hallway, Antony tentatively advanced. From his periphery, he caught a glimpse of his reflection off the metallic frames. On account of his mangled gait, his mirrored image bobbed up and down. The menacing scowl of Sergeant Bannister fleetingly flashed in his mind's eye. These reminders of the harrowing evening sent a shiver down his spine.

Nearing the end of the hall, Antony spotted the craggy profile of Fritz McGregor, a man eroded by time. Before he fully turned the corner, he was accosted by Fritz's adenoidal voice. "Who goes there?"

Fritz paced back and forth with the precision of a metronome. This routine trek had taken a toll on the cobalt-colored carpet underfoot. The indelible trace fossils left by his bare feet resembled a prehistoric trackway.

Antony's lips curved upward. Reflexively, he extended his hand in an affable greeting but caught himself mid-movement. He retracted the gesture. Over many interactions, he had learned that adhering to societal norms was not a priority for his eccentric next-door neighbor.

"Hello, Fritz. Why are you awake at this hour?"

"Sixty minutes in an hour." Fritz made the statement

matter-of-factly without altering his calculated course.

"There's sixty seconds in a minute too. But neither of these facts are relevant to our current hour, which happens to be late."

Earlier in the week, Fritz had drawn the ire of Mrs. Rothstein, the self-appointed hall monitor. Searching for suspicious behavior, she patrolled their nearly empty building. Fritz's pacing had set off a squabble. From the land of the dreaming, Antony was abruptly aroused by Mrs. Rothstein's shrill chastisement. It was an unpleasant incident that lasted almost a half hour. Unfortunately, neighborly bickerings of this sort occurred with some frequency.

Antony hunched his shoulders, rotated the vertebrae in his neck, then stuck his head directly in Fritz's path. "Thankfully, we don't have to worry about our safety here inside." He spoke his final words softly in an effort to encourage consideration. "But please, please remember, Fritz, there's people trying to sleep."

Behind a pair of oversized, thick, black-rimmed spectacles, Fritz's magnified green eyes locked onto the figure thwarting his movement. A bubble level was mounted above his glasses via toothpicks and duct tape. At least for the time being, horizontal perfection had been achieved.

"On the perilous Serengeti, no animal is safe." Fritz's eyes darted upward as he spoke. "Only the fit survive. Drought plagues the endless plains. Tensions run high in the battle for limited resources. Migrating herds of wildebeest search in futility for rain-ripened grass. Internal strife erupts among the zebras. Gazelle numbers enter endangered territory as starvation and dehydration prove to be unconquerable foes. The face of the ecosystem transforms, but life perseveres. The mass deaths of African grazers serve as an all-you-can-eat buffet for predators far and wi—"

Fritz's apartment door opened. Startled, both men shifted their attention to the adjacent auditory stimuli. In the open entranceway, with arms folded and a tapping foot, stood Fritz's sister, Norah McGregor. A ribbon-and-lace-trimmed white nightgown was draped over her portly physique. A green satin scarf was fashioned into a sleep turban, concealing her hair.

"Fritzy," she said, "get your butt inside this very instant!"

Fritz lowered his head and scurried inside like a mischievous child hearing a parent's disapproving tone. Norah's hollow eyes followed her younger brother's acquiescent action before landing upon her neighbor.

"Oh my gosh! Antony, you're covered in blood."

"I've certainly seen better days. But I'm fine."

"You don't look fine." She frowned. "Are you sure you're okay?"

"I'll survive. Really, it's nothing to worry about."

"Worrying is what I do. Now you stay put, I'll be right back."

Norah disappeared into her apartment. Shortly after, she emerged wearing a floral robe, a pair of vinyl exam gloves, and a contoured translucent filtration mask. Without saying another word, she hurried to Antony's side and wrapped her fingers around his upper arm. While she attempted to lead him inside, he laughed at her melodramatic response. At first he resisted, but he quickly caved to her compassionate tugs.

As he crossed the property line, the fresh ozone-laden air of the McGregor's apartment stormed his olfactory system. The residence existed as a mishmash infused by the temptations of modern technology with decor befitting a century prior. He followed Norah through the foyer past the slender wall-mounted waterless washing machine and the live-grass purification panels. They entered the living room, where a mustard-colored loveseat was the only sitting option for guests.

Antony plopped down and scooted side-to-side in search of a comfortable position. High-pitched squeaks emanated from the plastic-covered cushions.

Norah cringed. "Hold still."

To begin the physical examination, she combed through his hair to ascribe the location of the vascular trauma. With the scrupulous attention of an avarice prospector sifting through a creek bed, she examined every square inch of his scalp. Both individuals remained mute. The silence was randomly broken by the animalistic growls emerging from Fritz's bedroom.

"Phew," said Norah. "It's nothing serious, just a medium-sized gash and a nasty friction burn. I'll have you patched up in no time."

"Excellent."

She stepped back and tenderly peered down at him. "So, what happened to you tonight?"

"It started with a drunken stumble on my way home from The Emerald." Antony swallowed hard. "Followed by a regrettable encounter with Public Safety. All in all, a night I'd prefer to forget."

Norah wrapped her arms around her dispirited friend. The hug instantly boosted Antony's oxytocin levels. He relished the physical contact. On days when the populace was reminded of infectious agents, personal space became a priority beyond common courtesy. Small acts of kindness were too often lost in the shuffle when traversing an inimical landscape.

Norah rubbed Antony's arm. "Wait here while I grab my first aid kit."

Feeling relaxed, Antony scanned his surroundings. There was a biofuel recycling tank alongside the kitchen archway. For a few seconds, he watched the mechanical fish pluck organic material off the McGregors' dirty dishes. Next, his eyes were drawn to the ornate double-doored oak bookcase on the opposite wall. Behind the protective glass, a collection of porcelain plates lined the shelves. Each one depicted a city and its most famous respective landmarks.

Antony read the names aloud. "Paris, Rome, New York, London, Cairo, Bangkok." He stressed each syllable, striving to trigger hippocampal neurons, aiming to unlock personal anecdotes from his own travels. With eyes closed, he sluggishly lifted his battered frame and hobbled toward the decorative dinnerware for further inspection.

Dong. Dong.

Antony paused mid-step, startled by the grandfather clock's temporal announcement. Coinciding with the second chime, Fritz bustled into the room, flannel shirt misbuttoned, oversized jar of pickled eggs in hand. In his hurried state, he clipped Antony's shoulder yet continued in stride. A mahogany cherry console piano sat nestled in the far corner of the living room. An unlatched empty mason jar rested on the lid of the musical instrument. Fritz placed his egg-filled container on the piano's fallboard. With his veiny fingers wrapped around its threaded metal lid, he torqued his upper body and opened the jar. He plunged his hand into the vinegar, removed one of the prolate spheroids, then dropped it into the other jar. Satisfied with the transfer, he deliberately closed both containers. Antony had witnessed this obsessive ritual on a multitude of occasions, but he was still surprised by the abstruseness of the act.

"For the Woolly bear caterpillar, patience is a virtue. Calling winter home has its drawbacks. In its pre-metamorphic form, this caterpillar must feed over several summers to store enough energy for its transformation into the Isabella Ti—"

"Fritzy," Norah said, "what have I told you about dripping that egg juice all over my piano? Grab a towel and clean that up before it stains."

Fritz unquestionably complied with his younger sister's request. Holding the full jar of pickled eggs, he dashed out of the room. Although the siblings shared half their DNA, the differences between them were blatant. Fritz's thin frame stood hunchbacked, which further accentuated his diminutive stature. Norah's rotund physique possessed a posture that a steel girder would envy. Six decades had left Fritz hoary with withered features. Norah's quest to delay Father Time had resulted in a glowing hue and the appearance of a forty-year-old. Fritz's echolalia was the source of verbose zoological soliloquies; his autism overrode customary behavior. Norah's empathetic bedside manner permeated all her interactions.

Antony turned away from the kitty-cornered keys of ebony and ivory. With wide eyes and lips parted, he faced Norah. "Whenever I'm here, I can't help but marvel at all your souvenirs from abroad. I'd love to have an opportunity to visit some of these foreign lands. What were the highlights from your trip to England?"

"Unfortunately, I've never been," Norah replied. "All my life it's been near the top of my places-to-go list."

Antony's nose wrinkled. "Norah ... what about that?" He tapped on the bookcase's glass door to draw her gaze to a photograph. In front of Westminster Abbey, a vibrant beauty in her late twenties posed wearing a bearskin hat.

Norah stared at the photo for several seconds without moving.

"Of course!" Her confused countenance changed into one of

elation. "That vacation exceeded my wildest hopes and dreams! Come to think of it, those were the best days of my life!"

Dumbfounded, Antony blinked repeatedly as he returned to the couch. "How could that slip your mind?"

"If you want, I'll tell you all about my trips the next time I see you. For now, let's get you bandaged up so I can get back to bed."

Seemingly unconcerned by the lapse, Norah shielded Antony's puzzled eyes and sprayed an antiseptic onto the gash. Next she sprinkled a tiny vile of nanobots around the site of the tissue damage. After fashioning a head bandage using a roll of gauze, she unleashed a beaming smile and sent Antony on his way.

CHAPTER FOUR

eariness washed over Antony's physiognomy upon closing the door to his cluttered castle. Leaning against the sealed entryway, first his knees buckled, then his entire frame crumbled. Reflected photons converged on his retina, bringing the apartment into focus.

At the sight of his fallen robot, Antony's eyebrows furrowed. "Unis, you are utterly useless."

In his absence, the second law of thermodynamics proclaimed its existence. Toppled on the floor, his ballbot invention lay like a skyscraper designed by a geometrically obtuse architect. Its single wheel remained fruitlessly in motion. Scattered along the floor were partially folded clothes. Underneath the littered attire, several tablespoons of detergent had soaked into the plush vanilla carpet.

From Antony's crouched position, he painstakingly removed his ragged gray suede sneakers. The faint grinding hum of Unis's motors and spinning inverse rollers served another blow to his fragile confidence. After casting away his footwear into the open closet, he straightened his legs and moved toward the mechanical sounds of distress.

Antony allowed his arms to hang freely, bending over at the waist to rescue his automated assistant. He wrapped his fingers around the helpless bot's elbow joints and vigorously yanked at its fulcrums. Once its locus of movement made contact with the ground, it was off. Unis raced away like an education-loathing child hearing an afternoon school bell.

In pursuit of the single-minded mechanical contrivance, Antony headed in the direction of the broom cupboard. On first footfall, his heel entered the puddle of cleaning solution left behind from the bot's bungle. His jaw clenched as he continued the chase. Inside the cramped hallway offshoot, his indefatigable assistant was giving laundry another go. It turned the detergent dispenser knob using one its three-fingered grippers, and with the other it caught the free-falling liquid within a cup.

"Enough messes from you today," Antony grumbled. He stomped down on Unis's power switch, then removed the detergent-filled container from its grasp.

As he lifted his head in contemplation, the cause of the washing mishap became apparent. Balancing algorithms were executed within Antony's prefrontal cortex. In an effort to accommodate multitasking capabilities, he had earlier altered the internal values of a set of Unis's potentiometers. By overcompensating for the weight of a second laundry load, he had disrupted the robot's hemispherical balance. Upon tracing this chain of causation, he meekly smiled.

Antony braced himself for the impending hoist. Employing a widened stance, he lowered down into a sumo squat and clenched the handles on the ballbot's base. Although the robot was half as tall as its creator, it was nearly twice as heavy.

In the act of lifting Unis, Antony exhaled against his partially closed vocal folds to release an emphatic grunt. As a result of countless trials, he had grown accustomed to lugging his hefty invention around the apartment. Today however, the task was exceedingly difficult due to his damaged knee. He took a deep breath before waddling backward out of the cupboard. With his forearms extended perpendicular to the floor, he clumsily advanced down the hallway.

Pitter-patter, pitter-patter, pitter-patter. Antony's short steps moved the duo past the lavatory on their right then the padlocked master bedroom on their left. No one had stepped foot in the latter for almost ten months.

With the exception of two off-centered medium-sized frames, the seafoam-green hallway was bare. These walls once bustled with life, radiating elation in the form of a collage of photographs. The assemblage of still shots from around the globe had told the love story of Dominique and Antony, a couple cosmically entangled. All mementos from those joyous years had been sealed away. Antony could not endure the persistent reminders of her absence; he could not withstand the inadvertent taunts by his former self who had obtained true happiness.

Only a pair of mechanical drawings had survived the

emotional purge. Encased within a walnut frame sat a topographical map of the rapid transportation system. Resembling a cardiovascular diagram, the color-coded rail lines diffused as veins across the Pacific Territories of North America. The tracks transported vitals over the landscape, converging at their heart, Spokane, Washington. Within an identical askew frame, bordered by a thin white mat, was a Hyperloop patient diagram. These entities had combined to shrink the world in the same manner as their transit predecessors. Communities separated by hundreds of miles were henceforth considered local. Under the supervision of Dominique, an inspired life force had been infused within the vascular network. At present, the system remained in listless operation.

"Here we are." Antony nudged open the door at the end of the hall.

The darkness morphed into light as the motion sensors were triggered. Breadboards, jumper wires, and electronic components were strewn about the tinker's workshop. Overhead, a ceiling-mounted wireless access point glowed red. In one corner sat a small soldering station, and in another was a plastic organizer full of parts. Affixed to the back wall was a workbench with a built-in oscilloscope and power supply.

"Last stop on the Sartori express," he said while lowering Unis onto the static dissipative vinyl tile.

Freed of the burden, Antony stared into the deadened eyes of the being he had conceived. A protruding horizontal clear band protected Unis's high-resolution cameras.

Its main visual capturing apparatuses faced forward and backward, whereas smaller cameras pointed sideways. These sensory devices combined with lidar to provide Unis with an omnidirectional range of vision and outstanding depth perception.

"How I wonder what you are capable of." His breath slowed. "Unis, can you think?"

He pondered the question Alan Turing had posed over a century ago. His invention did not merely replicate a series of predetermined directions. Unis operated in a dynamic environment, where inputs were acquired and analyzed. Through semi-supervised learning, its prior experiences shaped future decisions. Analogous to a human, Unis gained new knowledge and skills by employing systematic processes.

Antony reflected on a scene he had watched unfold the prior afternoon. On the Hyperloop platform, there was a pigtailed girl, no older than four, who was eager to understand the ticket ordering procedure. She tugged at her older sister's purple fleece sleeve. Her sister responded to question after question with a simple instruction: "Just watch." The precocious child's eyes became glued to the kiosk screen as her sibling entered the destinations for their upcoming journey. Upon completion, the elder sibling canceled the order. She lifted up her younger sister with a reverse bear hug and encouraged her to try it all by herself. Without complication, the child entered the necessary information. In the process, she even corrected a minor oversight.

Were these little girl's actions not identical to those enacted by Unis?

Antony cupped his fingers around his chin. Both human organism and the inorganic bot successfully reacted to a range of stimuli and subsequently altered their worldviews and behaviors. He stroked his cheek with his thumb in contemplation.

Introspection, flashes of creativity, intuition—the vast differences in cognitive capabilities became readily apparent. The fact that this internal investigation preoccupied his own gray matter was evidence of Unis's limitations. His diagnosis of the dissimilarities between them quickly branched off into thoughts of hardware reliability. The solid state hard drive that logged Unis's experiences was essentially infallible. While Unis was restricted in the realm of cognition, Antony recognized the irrecusable advantages it possessed in other areas.

"You know"—he patted Unis's titanium rectangular head—"there was a time when our memories weren't so different. Growing up I never forgot the smallest of details. Now I barely remember even my fondest of days." The affectionate gesture for his lifeless companion caused the spring hinge in its neck to open and close. Up and down its head moved as though it were nodding in agreement.

Exhaustion overrode Antony's urges to fiddle. Sluggishly, he exited his workshop, then trudged down the hall. In an effort to suppress an approaching yawning spell, he entered the spatial confines of the living room with his lips forcibly sealed. Deep breaths bizarrely kindled phantom limb pains in the months following his above-the-knee amputation. While the distressing sensations no longer occurred, he continued this antiquated practice of repressing serial yawns. Overcome by fatigue, he could not forestall the autogenetic actions from thermoregulating his central processing unit.

Inside the living room's slate-colored walls, disorder reigned supreme. Leaning stacks of notes and calculations established permanent residences in every corner. The motor housing of a ceiling fan vibrated. The spinning maple blades caused the mountains of documents to perpetually tremble. Antony sidestepped the jumbled heap of clothing on his way to the whiteboard that hung on the back side of the front door.

Regardless of his energy levels, maintaining an accurate record of his handicapping enterprise was a priority. He scrunched up his face while snatching the dry eraser markers from the board's magnetic cup holder. As if in a bid to erase the events themselves from the chronicles of history, he vigorously wiped his gambling ledger clean. Wins were akin to a parental obligatory pat on the back, losses crushed the soul like a persuasive, loquacious atheist. His grip tightened around the writing instruments. Lost in the moment, his fingers tingled and turned blue due to the dearth of oxygen. When his fist opened, tension was replaced by the acceptance of defeat. The ruinous events that transpired earlier that evening were carefully recorded.

Turning away from the ledger, he evaluated his belongings

through a lens of bancor shares. Within his internally created world, the superimposed values mirrored a department store catalog. A particleboard coffee table covered with water stains, 195₿. Two wilting weeping fig trees in ceramic striped pots, 90₿ each. A ten-speed mountain bike with a punctured tire, 840₿. A panoramic canvas of an exoplanet captured by the Habitable Worlds Observatory, 375₿. He hesitated before appraising his smartphone. The dead pixels that populated its flexible OLED could be repaired cheaply, but thanks to a host of unreliable mobile networks and the indefinite World Wide Web outage, this columnar device was little more than a paperweight. Outside his holographic television, the room was devoid of anything worth reselling.

Unemployment had taken a financial toll, but it was the rehabilitation sessions that pauperized the former senior engineer. He solemnly shook his head back and forth. The decibels of his mind chatter ratcheted up with each passing thought. Flashbacks of tormenting trips to the pawnshop ran recursively over his visual pathways. Improvements in the fluidity of his gait were positively correlated with a reduction of material goods. By the time of his final visit to Capital Jewelry & Loan, the shop contained more of the Sartoris' possessions than his seventh-floor apartment. Emotionally traumatic events of the past prompted unknowable questions about the future. Worries of mounting debt flooded his cerebral landscape like a blocked tributary. Lost in the unrelenting barrage of inner musings, he stood frozen.

A low-pitched beep originating from the holographic platform snapped him out his trance. His pupils were reflexively drawn to the source. Scanning the surroundings, a biometric beam emanated from the device. Upon registering Antony's ocular features, its lasers began to warm up.

Five slumberous strides later, Antony collapsed onto his sliding sofa bed. The black corduroy cushions accepted him like an old catcher's mitt longing for its stitched companion. The negative space of the bed was uniquely molded to the contours of its owner. His fatigued body instinctively found its cozy indentations. Before his eyes, a hologram materialized.

Revolving overhead, an intricately detailed relief globe rotated on its axis. The earth began to desaturate midway through its orbit. As the blues, greens, yellows, and oranges abated, "Breaking News" was imprinted upon the monochromatic sphere. Into the proverbial nothingness, these images soon faded, and a news studio came into view.

Behind a frosted glass desk emblazoned with the Pansophical logo sat Camille Rodin. She wore a light-gray pencil skirt, a two-button jacket over a white blouse, and a pair of black heels. In the background of the futuristic set were walls of surveillance footage featuring smiling citizens. The news ticker displayed weekly changes in the global happiness index along with other technocratic measures of prosperity.

Antony's droopy eyes rolled over the projection like high tide over a sandy coastline. Starting at her stockings, his pupils moved up to the silver vixen's dome then back down again. In an identical manner to the day prior, the diurnal wave passed over with little thought. While he only faintly consciously recognized it, he counted on her presence; he depended on her as a paragon of truth.

Through the eyes of the citizenry, Camille Rodin, Pansophical's chief information officer, was a collection of amorphous features. Universally, viewers perceived similarities between themselves and her, sparking attachment. Whenever news broke, neurons corresponding to trustworthiness fired across the globe.

"Good day, my fellow citizens," Rodin said. "We have a major story developing in the Pacific Territories of North America. Earlier today, Public Safety officers in Sacramento apprehended and convicted a twenty-nine-year-old man, a Praxis terrorist, for plotting against humanity. The whereabouts of his anarchist cell were revealed during the interrogation. Following an hour-long pursuit, officers have cornered his coconspirators in a Seattle fish factory. Janelle Lafayette, mastermind behind the Golden Gate Bridge bombing, is believed to be among those inside. We now bring you live coverage."

On the broadcast, the studio was replaced by a scene on the tipping point of chaos. The deep blues of Puget Sound were indistinguishable from the night sky. A trio of circling quadcopters shone spotlights from above. The hymns of Poseidon could be heard intermittently between their whirling blades. From below, freshly surfaced submersible drones illuminated the seascape. A processing plant stood alone on the planked pier as a beacon in the blackness. In the absence of an avenue for escape, the drones tightened the noose. They slowly shrank the perimeter, sharpening the holographic clarity for viewers in the process.

In thick green block lettering, "Earthly Foods" jutted out from the brick facade of the three-story building. Rectangular windows made up the top floor of its north and south sides. Rows of bricks separated these multi-paned windows from the steel industrial doors and hydraulic dock levelers on the ground level. Bright yellow safety bollards bookended each of the loading areas.

A line of black Humvees raced toward the end of the wharf. With a single focus, they resembled army ants after immobilizing a meal for the colony. One at a time they stopped. Each trailing vehicle shifted to the right while doing so to form an armored wall.

"Thank the stars," Rodin gleefully said, "Public Safety has arrived on the scene."

Sergeant Bannister exited the leading Humvee. Malicious intent swam in his dark-brown eyes. He deliberately walked across the pier. Upon reaching the edge, he pivoted and his gaze moved to the building. Behind him the other vehicles' doors opened, forty guns on the chess board, ready to execute their commanding officer's orders.

As Bannister entered commands on his control pad, his

visor snapped into place. From left to right, his head moved like the typewriter of a steady-handed stenographer. When the carriage reset, his posture stiffened. Public Safety's situational awareness remained static. One after another, the electromagnetic spectrum filters he applied failed to expose the Praxis targets.

In a moment of reckless abandon, Bannister unholstered his weapon and marched toward the building. Reason prevailed a mere hundred yards from the doorway. He stopped in his tracks and unfettered a vociferous battle cry. The peak of this browbeating crescendo was picked up by the quadcopter microphones overhead.

While returning to the company of his men, Bannister barked orders to Benton. Violent hand gestures outlined the first stage in his plans to implement righteous justice. Binary digits were deployed over the communication channels at a breakneck pace. Two of the hovering quadcopters decreased their engine throttles and began to descend. When level with the factory's upper windows, the aerial vehicles each sharply tilted downward. They pitched forward, accelerating toward the windows before reversing their propeller angles at the last moment. Each flew parallel to the building face in a dexterous display that mirrored the motion of a pendulum. Payloads were released at the zero point of this maneuver. The inertia sent numerous hexagonal polygons crashing through the panes of glass.

The processing plant shook with the rumbling, tumbling

Ovid Blocks. A thin viscoelastic polymer protected them during impact. One by one the dodecahedrons came to life. Utilizing motors, hinges, and springs, they operated like multidirectional jack-in-the-boxes. Whatever side was flush with the floor popped open, setting the block in motion. Along jagged paths the autonomous modular blocks moved toward their counterparts. Once aligned, their powerful magnets catalyzed a coalescence. The blocks seamlessly assembled into a serpentine mass. Slithering in search of organic matter, the pair of robotic reptilians scouted out the top floor.

The telecast cut back to the studio. "To those just tuning in," Rodin said with an exaggerated lilt, "we are live in Seattle, where tensions are mounting in a standoff between Public Safety and Praxis. In a few moments, we will be bringing you inside the fish factory where the terrorists have taken refuge."

Live reconnaissance footage was supplied by the micro-cameras that dotted the Ovid Blocks. A three-dimensional map of the processing plant simultaneously unfolded in the upper corner of the broadcast. Worldwide, the vicarious thrill of the hunt ensnared the attention of men, women, and child alike. Driven by blind Pansophical chauvinism, the citizenry cheered on the protectors of the peace.

The mechanical serpents wriggled through a landscape of leather executive chairs, supercomputer towers, and holographic projectors. Despite the blind spots caused by these obstacles, only a single pass was required to generate a comprehensive floor plan. With each s-shaped movement, another hiding spot for Praxis was eliminated. Similar to their scrupulous search of the floor above, their exploration of the offices turned up nothing of note.

As they glided down the moldings of the central steel staircase, the building's function emerged from its form. For the salmon species, the processing plant was an infernal chamber of horrors, analogous to the public square for non-renouncing heretics during the Spanish Inquisition. Ominous electrodes dangled over conveyor belts, waiting to percussively stun schools of the unsuspecting. Blood-stained steel ramps were ready to transport the sea creatures into an automated processing line, where carcasses were eviscerated, cleaned, descaled, decapitated, and filleted. A plethora of pisces faced their demise and mutilation at the hands of these diabolical instruments.

Signs of life were absent from the heart of the fish factory. The robotic scouts exited the hygienically clean zone. They closed in on the plant's lone unexplored area, the staff preparation rooms. Light-beige, perforated lockers lined the walls. White aluminum benches, supported by black pedestals, were anchored to a cream tiled floor. The mechanical serpents reduced their speed for the final stage of the reconnaissance mission. They entered the equipment closet side-by-side, then split up to investigate.

Public Safety's primary objective, a robotic pack mule carrying contraband, sat in repose along the back wall. As one of the serpents approached, double-acting cylindrical actuators located above the knee and ankle joints of the mechanical quadruped expanded. Its hinged legs unfolded like an accordion. Oversized duffel bags hung off the sides of its stainless steel frame. A swallow-tailed, tangelo-colored, Praxis flag dangled from the robo-mule's rear end. A silhouette profile of a man was at its center. Painted in white, the Greek letter Ω filled the portrait's cranial cavity.

Meanwhile, the other serpentine scout meticulously examined the plant's invisible workforce for traces of the perilous outlaws. Clothing racks of lab coats, aprons, boots, and gloves were arranged by size for the seafood processing staff. Seemingly innocent crimps and creases within the wardrobe demanded extra attention from the onlooking officers. Undoubtedly, Praxis was nearby, but Public Safety sought to lure them out of hiding. The tedious sleuthing process continued unimpeded until midway through the third garment rack.

A restrained rustle penetrated the soundscape. A rubber boot rose from the ground, then stomped on the robotic reptilian. The impact disrupted the magnetic fields connecting the Ovid Blocks, scattering them in all directions. Unperturbed, they relaunched the clumsy somersaulting movements of their primitive forms and gathered intelligence individually.

Wearing a hyper-realistic mask of Chairman Fields, a man intrepidly emerged, tossing away the lab coat he was concealed within. "The pages of history will recount the seeds that we've planted on the barren grounds of oppression. It's with our blood, our sweat, and our tears that the tree of liberty will germinate and reach the heights of day's past. Men naturally indulge in illusions of hope, but the forests of freedom I speak of do not exist solely in folklore, nor in the visions of idealists. The canopy peaks out from under the cloud cover! Gentlemen, this is not a time for ceremony. Today, we—"

Rodin reappeared with a charming smile. "Sorry, we're experience technical difficulties. The ravings of a dangerous madman, no doubt about that. Quick recap for those just waking up: We have major developments in Seattle, Washington. Public Safety has surrounded a fish factory. Inside, four heavily armed Praxis terrorists have been rooted out. The game of hide-and-seek is over. We return to live coverage from the standoff."

Halfway down the pier, Bannister digested the influx of surveillance information. As he scanned the processing plant, his fingers clinched the pistol grip of his assault rifle. Preparing for the firefight, officers unfolded their inflatable ballistic shields upon the pier. Ripcords were pulled in turn. Carbon dioxide filled the pneumatic frames of the synthetic spider silk protective barriers. In a modernized phalanx formation, the flexible shields were interlocked. Shoulder to shoulder, in a crouched stance, they marched forward as one. Trailing the fortification, Bannister intuitively dictated their movements like a masterful maestro.

The plant's central shipping door opened. The sound of rolling steel commenced the symphony of destruction's opening sonata. Current flowed through the parallel rails of the squadron's assault weapons to produce a low hum. An acoustical apex was reached when thunderous cracks of electricity arched as ballistics exited rifle barrels. A storm of projectiles bombarded the processing facility's facade. The striking of the brick face and interior metal walls penetrated the air like percussion instruments. The blitz received no return fire; there were no signs of the fugitives.

From an upstairs window, two Praxis members peered down at the firestorm below. A thin man masked as the board secretary mounted a rocket launcher upon his shoulder. Masquerading as Camille Rodin, a woman loaded the anti-tank weapon from behind. As he knelt down and leaned into the window frame, friction caused the infrared-signature-matching layers on his jumpsuit to peel. The disguised couple would shortly be betrayed by his radiating body heat.

Bannister immediately recognized the slight shift in the building's thermal profile. With the bend of his right index finger, he unleashed several rounds in the direction of the temperature change. Traveling at thousands of meters per second, a bullet penetrated the cranium of the female figure. It severed her brain stem before exiting the other side of her skull. The fates had spun the thread of her life; now the deities closed their abhorred shears. After her final agonal gasps, the lifeless mass collapsed onto its former ally. In a frantic state, the man pushed his ill-fated friend aside, popped back up onto his knee, and fired his weapon. Urgency eliminated the luxury of utilizing the rocket launcher's iron sight. The explosive warhead soared over the officer's heads and struck one of the parked vehicles to their rear.

Turbulent flames were expelled every which way. The Humvees were transformed into abstract expressionist sculptures of mangled steel. Before long the fire engulfed parts of the pier. The rapid oxidation from the exothermic reaction released billows of dark smoke into the skies.

A shockwave radiated outward following the concussive blast. The outer columns of the Public Safety formation, along with their inflatable shield, were hurled into the water. All remaining officers were sent sprawling to the planked platform. Replicating the surroundings, their awkwardly positioned bodies flickered in yellows, oranges, and reds. The decided advantage once held by the law enforcement arm of the Pansophical Corporation dwindled in the pandemonium.

Thirty seconds later, the leader of the small band of outlaws strutted out of the open shipping door. His short, stout companion, masked as the board's chief financial officer, trotted closely behind. Trailing in the rear with an ungainly gait, the robo-mule obediently joined its masters in the chaos. The pair of men fired indiscriminately into the darkness. Defenseless Public Safety officers fought the disorienting effects of the violent shockwave under a hailstorm of tungsten. Slow-reacting members of the squadron were littered with holes before they could free themselves from the state of utter confusion. Over the proceeding minutes, the donnybrook claimed lives on both sides of the ledger.

At the conclusion of the fatal fray, the Praxis threat was neutralized. Coinciding with the termination of the gunfire, the submersible drones ramped up their emergency response efforts. Earlier they had been ordered to stand down due to the risk of disrupting the tactical operation. Now in full force, the maritime emergency drones introduced the flourishing blaze to its eternal elemental adversary. Gallons of water were pumped from the sea to nullify the fiery advance.

With both elbows firmly planted on the ground in a prone position, Bannister released the assault rifle from his unerring grasp and returned to a vertical stance. He placed his hulking hands on opposite sides of his helmet, extended his palms to crack his knuckles, and removed the headgear. The overhead spotlights reflected off his massive, lumpy, shaven skull as he sauntered in the direction of the processing plant. His head swiveled with arrogant impassivity while he surveyed the carnage. With a patronizing smirk, he kicked down a rope ladder to his water-treading subordinates. Aside from Bannister, these men were the only individuals fortunate enough to escape the battlefield unscathed.

Between two shipping doors, the leader of the Praxis cell sat slumped against the building. Slanted to the left, his ear was flush with his shoulder. His crimson palms faced the heavens. The toppled robo-mule lay beside the fugitive.

The illegal contents of the transport were scattered on the ground. Above a heap of books, the fluttering Praxis flag staked an ideological claim on the area.

The sergeant stared blankly into the symbol of resistance. Praxis's existence threatened everything Bannister swore to protect. The rebellious silhouette ridiculed his authority; it mocked all virtuous citizens who lived first and foremost for their fellow man.

Ire boiled in Bannister's heart. He reached down into his sock and drew his handgun. Rotating his torso, he blindly unloaded its magazine into the corpse.

CHAPTER FIVE

ntony's eyelids trembled. Underneath, his optical organs bounced around their sockets in the final stages of sleep. A navy-blue cotton sheet covered his battered physique. A cloud comprising the fluffy underbellies of waterfowl delicately braced his cranium, setting the three curves of his spine in neutral alignment. Internally, his neurons chattered away via electrical impulses, taking the form of alpha and theta brainwaves.

Midway through the transition from slumber to wakefulness, Antony's eyes opened. Awareness seeped into his arena of experience, prematurely terminating his last REM cycle of the night. The evolutionary mechanisms designed to protect humans while frolicking in the playground of the dreaming malfunctioned. Sleep paralysis deprived him of nearly all movement. It trapped his consciousness within an incapacitated voiceless meat bag.

Antony mentally tussled with these freaky feelings of atonia. He quickly discovered that the simple act of kicking off his bedding was a preposterously insurmountable undertaking. His eyes darted around the apartment. These ocular movements were apparently all that was permitted. When the perimeter turned up nothing of note, his irises settled upon the ceiling fan. The wagon-wheel effect provided him with a temporary distraction. The optical illusion slowed down the blades, momentarily held them stationary, and then abruptly reversed their direction. Following a few rapid blinks, the fan reverted back to its original clockwise rotation. Bored of the misleading motion reversal, he shifted his attention elsewhere.

A sweeping nefarious aura defined his second appraisal of the surroundings. This menacing presence permeated the gaseous elements that naturally filled all corners of the room. Triggered by chronic stress and compounded by the traumatic altercation twelve hours earlier, inwardly generated sensory stimuli produced a hypnopompic hallucination. Then and there, visual and aural illusions manifested before him.

In the quietude, an adumbral figure lurked. The towering, ghastly silhouette raised its gaunt forearms. It extended its elbows and broodingly rubbed its palms together. Upon ceasing this foreboding gesture, it hunched over and reached into the cherry red toolbox beside the coffee table. A prolonged deranged laugh was discharged as it removed a rust-covered backsaw. A tapered file followed. Without delay, the latter was put to use on its jagged assistant. The abrasive notes cast Antony into a state of panic, a state of panic devoid of a tangible outlet.

What have you done to me? What do you want? Why can't I move? Let me go. Please let me go. Please. Answer me! I demand that you answer me this very instant. Help! HELP! Somebody help ... HEEEEEEEEEEELLLPPP!

The stream of consciousness feverishly flowed down inquisitive hills, through caverns of commotion, over despondent rocks, into a beseeching creek bed. Like a panhandling mime on an empty street corner, Antony's internal pleading was met with the frigid sounds of silence.

In sheer futility, Antony thrashed against the paralysis. His eyes hopped from extremity to extremity in the hope that attention alone would infuse life. Beginning at his right arm, they jumped to his right leg, then to their symmetrical counterparts. Lamentably, his limbs failed to respond to these desperate requests for assistance.

Across the living room, indifferent to his stampede of consternation, the adumbral creature confronted its unknowing creator. A frayed white cloak was draped over its shoulders. A tattered black dress shirt and slacks presented glimpses of its cadaverous physique. Underneath its hood, the specter's atrophied features seemed to be perpetually veiled in a supernatural shade. After releasing the file from its angular fingers, it gawkishly moved toward the sliding sofa bed. Each ungainly step was accompanied by an exaggerated swing of its freshly sharpened tool.

Trapped within the cerebral cell, with the executioner approaching on the green mile, Antony's eyes completed a final survey in search of an escape. Liberation from the bondage of the mind was nowhere to be found. The inanimate objects of the apartment offered no aid. He was powerless. Unable to look away, yet lacking the fortitude to visually accost the specter outright, he directed his squinched horror-filled eyes at the looming threat.

The malicious creature leaned over and gently whispered, "I've been waiting for you." The granulated syllables echoed throughout Antony's auditory canal.

Preceded by an outburst of demented laugher, the specter relocated to the bottom of the bed with an elongated stride. It overextended its bony digits, then curled them tightly around Antony's right ankle and considered incision sites. Calculatingly, it lowered the handsaw like an artisan butcher preparing to make a primal cut on a prized carcass. Without applying pressure, it dragged the serrated teeth over his thigh, opening up minor lacerations along the way.

The physiological reaction to the tactile hallucination activated Antony's hypervigilance response. Mere seconds away from threat level midnight, his internal doomsday clock went off. Adrenal glands injected waves of epinephrine through his circulatory system. The increase in blood flow to his dormant muscles shattered the illusionary fetters of subconsciousness. Reality crashed through the doors of perception.

An empty room materialized in Antony's now fully aware mindscape. The shadowy specter and its unthinkable torments were no more. He sprang up into a seated position.

The rush of adrenaline sped up his heart and consequently the need for oxygen. Breathing heavily, he hastily threw off the thin sheet to assess the damage to his appendage. He rolled up his jeans, then frantically rubbed his hands up and down his right leg. The cherished limb was unharmed, free of the vile amputation preparations. Grateful for being able-bodied, he heaved a sigh of relief. The purplish oblong contusion that enveloped his opposite knee was momentarily immaterial. With the threat removed, his sympathetic nervous system tempered its output. Gradually, his mind and body transitioned to a state of calmness.

Antony allowed himself to fall back into the contoured cushions of the sofa. He focused on his respiratory rate and closed his eyes. He counted each steady exhalation. A natural seventeen breathes per minute was his target. Five minutes passed, and the mental exercise permitted the hormonal cascade to run its course. Internal stability reappeared, expelling the mechanisms of fight-or-flight to their sentinel posts.

Rolling over, Antony reached his clammy hand under the bed in search of his diary. Upon retrieval, he scrunched the pillows up against the sofa's back support and readjusted his body with a shimmy. After propping himself up onto his forearms, he untied the chestnut-brown notebook's leather closure and plucked a writing utensil out from its spinal quiver. Both were gifts from his therapist, whose information was engraved into the fountain pen's barrel: "Elizabeth R. Winfield, PhD 625 Eastlake Ave. Seattle, Washington 98109

(206) 938-3103." He thumbed through the book. Pages upon pages of congested scratch passed over his visual field. The first blank sheet appeared three-quarters of the way through. Before placing the nib to the paper, he twirled the pen around his fingers as he gathered his thoughts.

2/3/84

The unimaginable horror that haunts my sleep returned this morning. I once again woke up paralyzed, unable to move anything except my eyes. A sense of evil foreshadowed the creature. One minute the room was empty, the next it was lurking at the edges of my peripheral. It appeared out of nowhere! The maniacal laugh, the terrifying sound of the saw being sharpened—I can't get these sounds out of my head! The creature's identity remains a mystery. I can't determine whether it's human or something from beyond the grave.

What's it waiting for? Time and again I'm saved at the last moment by a surge of consciousness. The vividness of these hallucinations continue to intensify. For the first time, I felt the saw's teeth. For the first time, I felt the blood dripping down my leg. I fear that this trend of realism will continue.

The breathing exercises recommended by Dr. Winfield were effective. They lowered my heart rate and prevented a full-fledged panic attack. During our next appointment, I'll ask her whether there are visual cues that could be of use. Whenever these episodes occur, I need to remember to wiggle my fingers and toes. These small movements are the key. Waking up is the only escape. We're always at the mercy of the mind. Our vulnerability in this regard gives me goose bumps.

The words were carefully conceived but scribbled onto the paper in haste. Antony perused his nearly illegible synopsis of the phantasmagoria before returning the dream diary to its designated spot. He heedfully swung his legs to the floor. Concurrently, he pushed off his elbow and opposite hand to elevate his torso to an upright position. When his weight was transferred from his resting buttocks to his faulty lower limbs, he grimaced. The hours of stagnation left the muscles within his battered leg rigid.

While holding onto the sofa for support, he started to perform his physical therapy routine. These morning exercises had become a vital part of his life post-reattachment surgery. At the time, they instilled much-needed confidence into his self-doubting mind. First he executed a standing quadriceps stretch. His hamstrings were next. He started on the left side out of necessity, then switched to the right side out of habit. Lateral lunges and calf raises capped the workout. These few minutes of physical activity reinvigorated his limbs.

The wake-up regimen stopped him from incessantly worrying over the horrid recurring illusions. After hallucinogenic episodes, journaling helped him disconnect from the experience, limiting the post-traumatic hangover. Hallucinations blurred reality's unsparing lines of demarcation. Fear-laden mindless thoughts drowned the unaware. Only months prior, Antony had found himself on a coastline ill-prepared for the debilitating tsunamis created by tectonic shifts within the dreaming realm. During those drab days, each of his passing hours possessed the same utter lack of significance. The calendar was inconsequential; Monday drifted into Friday. His throne of attention was persistently occupied by dreadful replays of the nightmare. Today, however, he walked with relative calm to the bathroom as he prepared to embark upon the new day.

The modernized eco-friendly lavatory was the epicenter of the Sartoris' condominium remodeling project. Completed over three years ago, the renovations represented the first phase of the couple's ten-year plan. All excitement corresponding to the amenities had disappeared long ago. Freshness faded away; eternal novelty was a commercial ploy that was unable to keep pace on the hedonic treadmill.

Driven by the urge to urinate, Antony approached the foldable toilet. On many inebriated nights, he had penitently knelt before the porcelain priest. He deliberately tapped the ball of his foot twice on the slate-colored tile adjacent to the confessional. The bowl swung down from its space-saving position to accept the excretory sins of the confessor. Now was not the time for sacramental rituals, however. Antony unzipped the fly of his faded blue jeans and emptied his bladder of waste. Upon completion, he double-tapped the floor sensor. The bowl rotated back to its previous hidden position. Before being flushed away, his excretions entered a miniature medical laboratory, where they were tested for biomarkers.

Pivoting away from the toilet, he took two nonchalant steps in the direction of the bathroom vanity. He clutched the white ceramic counter with both hands and leaned forward. While postured on his left leg, he slid off an earth-toned argyle sock using his right big toe, then repeated the act on the opposite side. Once barefoot, he sidestepped onto the bathroom's built-in health-assessment platform.

He examined his reflection in the smart mirror. "What have I become?"

Gazing back through the looking glass stood a stone-faced man, clothed in the wrinkled attire from the previous evening, with his head wrapped in first-aid bandages.

"I can't go on like this." His facial blood vessels opened at the sight of his overcoat's fastened wooden buttons. He averted his eyes from the inescapable reminders of another drunken night. "Something needs to change."

An augmented display covered the left half of the mirror. Behind the transparent pane, organic light-emitting diodes presented a mixture of public service announcements and personalized information. A Pansophical Corporation logo appeared at the top of the display. There was an image of a shining sun peeking out through a gray cloud. Underneath the weather forecast was a collection of global metrics charting positive trends related to climate change. These environmental measurements included everything from carbon dioxide readings to charts on biodiversity and glacial maps. Antony disregarded these esoteric Anthropocene attributes. His eyes gravitated down to his monthly calendar. A single event in bold red font prominently filled the square for Thursday February 3, "Tembakoo Vaccination: Eastlake Immunization Center 16:35."

Antony apprehensively raised his field of vision to the digital clock on the opposite end of the mirror. Unless in a hot zone, he rightfully realized that the perils of the virulent virus were secondary to the dire secular repercussions of missing an inoculation appointment. A deep sigh of relief exited his lungs as the chrono-confusion was lifted. His appointment was still hours away, and the immunization center was well within walking distance.

With time to spare, Antony's concentration shifted from the immediate to the long term. Before his accident, he was not the least bit health-consciousness. That all changed following his first visit to the replantation specialist. Vital signs that previously failed to warrant a second thought now incurred daily monitoring. Perspective was gained when the scales of probability tipped from hypothetical impairments to palpable hardships.

Basic bodily functions were measured by bio-sensors within the health platform. Antony's vitals were outputted along a wellness timeline near the bottom of the mirror. He inspected the colored lines that represented his health metrics. Each one glided unwaveringly along the thirty-day-long x-axis. Body temperature, pulse rate, respiratory rate, and blood pressure — he exhibited them all within the range of a healthy man in his fifties. Underneath, an extensive disease risk summary was generated from his urine and stool as well as data collected by imperceptible cameras.

The absence of change to Antony's wellness profile was a source of comfort. With a half-smile, he unbuttoned his overcoat and draped it over the bronze freestanding towel rack. Then he carefully unwrapped his gauzy turban. The curative nanobots had performed masterful work. The wound's inflammatory phase had passed, and new tissue proliferated. After nodding in approval, he discarded the bandages. It was time to cleanse himself of the filthy ignominy amassed over yesterday. He took off his clothes. One by one, he tossed each piece of apparel through the open door into the hall.

"Earth to Unis. Earth to Unis."

The activation phrase produced no result.

"Where are you?" He raised his voice. "Earth to Unis."

Another minute of inactivity passed before he recalled the late-night struggles with his robotic domestic assistant. He could not help but laugh at himself as he stood there stark naked, agitated with arms folded. For now the task of transporting dirty clothing to the hamper was relegated to members of humanity.

As Antony's focus returned from the brief gadget-centered interlude to his hygienic routine, he spun around and approached the stand-alone shower. Using his index finger, he pressed the up arrow bordering the engraved thermometer icon on the decorative shower door. Under a steady stream of water, he found a tranquil refuge away from the responsibilities of reality, away from phantasmal tormentors, away from any apprehensions of extinction. The absent-minded respite was short-lived. A worldwide conservation initiative dynamically adjusted water levels to fairly limit wasteful consumption. Four minutes and eighteen seconds into his leisurely wash, two high-pitched beeps originated from the aqua management system's showerhead. One minute later, the water ceased to flow. Antony switched gears as the final moments of ablution ticked away. He vigorously massaged the shampoo into his scalp, then rinsed off the viscous liquid as time expired. The mid-shower disruption evoked feelings of solidarity, not annoyance. Elevating the community's needs above his own brought him delight.

Through the steam, Antony blindly extended his arm out of the shower. Upon snatching a plush baby-blue towel, he patted down his body to remove the excess water from his skin. He briskly walked down the hallway, drying himself en route to the living room. Before sifting through his partially folded wardrobe, he wrapped the towel around his waist. Clothes were selected strictly on a criterion of minimal wrinkledness. A midnight-blue roll-neck sweater, black relaxed-fit jeans, a red undershirt, plaid boxers, and two unmatched socks—he gathered the ensemble and carried it back to the bathroom.

Mechanically, Antony proceeded to check items off his hygienic to-do list. The sequence of grooming and wellness tasks had not changed since late adolescence. Teeth were brushed, face was shaved, deodorant was applied, vitamins were ingested, and body was clothed.

On Antony's way out, he reached toward the locomotive-themed key rack adjoined to the doorframe. A respirator dangled from the nearest hook. Based on its spotted filters, its last use was between six and twelve months ago. He slipped the harness of the half mask over his head. Prior to tightening its straps, he hesitated. His gaze dipped to the lofty stack of academic journal articles below.

In his search for answers during the weeks ensuing the loss of Dominique, he learned everything he could about the Tembakoo virus. Methodologically speaking, Antony found studies on transmission prevention to be riddled by design flaws and statistical fallacies. Nonetheless, on vaccination days, when the new normal temporarily upended the newest normal, large swathes of the population clung to their respiratory comfort blankets. Overriding appeals to emotion, Antony opted out of the pandemic security theater at least for today.

CHAPTER SIX

A stiff northwestern land breeze smashed into Antony's exposed epidermis upon exiting the apartment complex. He ambled headfirst into the sustained winds. Heat escaped from his body as the colliding air molecules complied with the laws of convection. His skeletal muscles trembled rapidly in an effort to maintain homeostasis. The overambitious aspirations of Phaethon remained unfulfilled. The god's chariot sat in a state of disrepair behind a thick mountain of cumulonimbus clouds. The meager warmth provided by the sun could not counteract the frigid winter temperatures. Antony brought his overcoat in anticipation of the return trip, but he was forced to call it into service prematurely. He slipped his upper appendages through its snug armholes. To further shield himself, he concurrently lifted his shoulders while lowering his head.

Fifteen minutes into his unhurried journey, the cherry-colored newsstand on the corner of Alexandria Street and Eastlake Avenue came into view. Although jaunts were typically appreciated, he bemoaned the decision on this afternoon to utilize his legs. His knee hematoma required rest and ice more than anything. The prolonged strain on his injured joint sent ripples of discomfort through his anatomy. Bedecked with a visage of displeasure, he hobbled to the back of the socially distanced line that had formed around the automated kiosk. He braced himself against the exterior of the newsstand, then transferred the bulk of his weight to his pain-free leg. Relishing repose, a deep breath was expelled from his lungs.

"Ridiculous, absolutely ridiculous!" A short tubby man in a royal-purple porkpie hat turned to face Antony. "How long has that newsstand across from our building been out of order? I've called the Department of Information each and every day. Nothing has been done. Nothing! If it's not fixed by tomorrow, there's going to be hell to pay."

A veil of obliviousness bound Antony. Near the end of this unprompted tirade, he raised his field of vision from the cracked concrete. "Hi. How are you?"

Ahead of Antony within the queue, stooped over like a petulant Atlas burdened by a self-centered world, stood his building superintendent. Luis Herrera's perpetually evolving collection of headwear served as his prominent feature. In spite of his flamboyant cries for attention, admiration was annulled once his outfit was perceived as a whole. Few could rationalize complementing the man's fashion sense upon seeing either his soiled overalls or perspiration-stained undershirt.

"How am I? Antony, did you hear one word of what I just said? Our newsstand has been broken since forever. How many more times am I going to have to walk to Timbuktu for a damn paper? It's ridiculous!"

Luis's exclamation triggered a hydrological event. Like the turbulent ejection of a watery plume from the earth's surface, droplets of saliva erupted from the oversized gap in his front teeth. The unintended discharge of spittle glided through the air. It eventually found a home on the right cheek of his fellow apartment dweller.

Antony's lips compressed to form a thin line. He wiped away the physical traces of the spit-talker's bacterial storm with his woolen sleeve.

"Hurry it up, will you?" Luis shouted over his shoulder.

"Yes," Antony agreed, devoid of tone. "Please, hurry up."

Remaining amiable when interacting with Luis was a challenge for all who crossed his path. Antony's patience was already approaching depletion. Within the walls of Sanctuary Village, he employed a strategy of avoidance, combined with a rolodex of excuses, to release himself from Luis's chamber of chronic complaints. At the moment, eager for a breather, he had no choice but to endure the intolerable bellyaches.

A half-minute passed, and Luis threw up his hands in frustration. "Come on now! Could today get any worse? Seriously!"

"Doubt it," Antony said curtly.

"I spent my whole morning waiting for my miracle jab. And now I'm going to end up wasting my afternoon on this line. It's ridiculous! Do you have any idea how much work I have to do?"

Antony responded with a subtle eye roll.

Tact, however, was an ineffective tool when communicating with the socially unaware. The mistakenly interpreted social cue induced a concordant smile by the pudgy almond-skinned superintendent. Although he often encountered nonverbal hints of an annoyed nature, he foolishly attributed the perturbed behavior of others to external factors.

"All of this makes you want to scream, doesn't it?" From under Luis's medial cleft, his diastema flickered into view. "Staying up to date shouldn't be so hard."

Unfortunately for Antony, the soothing of Luis's frustrated temperament was short-lived. An androgynous figure wearing a boysenberry button-down shirt with tight black trousers casually exited the kiosk alcove. In one hand they held a rolled-up newspaper, in the other, several multi-chromatic periodicals. At the front of the line, a pair of teenage girls, both inappropriately dressed for the weather, filled the void in the ordering station. Fixated on the departing ambiguous character, Luis slid into the on-deck circle.

"No consideration," Luis said while crossing his chubby arms. His fuss-fueled foot taps served as an aggravated metronome. "Some people, you know, only think of themselves."

Hair cells nestled within Antony's cochlea converted the acoustic vibrations arising from his posterior into electrical signals. Neural impulses were decoded within his auditory cortex. The formation of thought instantaneously followed; the sound was classified as the rustling of a potato chip bag.

He rotated his head in the hope that the source would take the form of an acquaintance. Any familiar smile capable of graciously ending this irritating conversation would be welcomed. Much to his dismay, his eyes washed over a faceless family. A masked mother tensely stared ahead while rocking her twin stroller. Each bassinet was encased within a plastic bubble. Under her nose, her older toddler squeezed snacks under his nacho-stained neck gaiter.

"Common courtesy, where have you gone?" Luis asked.

Antony shrugged without making eye contact.

"Speaking of which," Luis continued, "when did people stop throwing away their own damn trash? Our building has turned into a pigsty! No one pitches in. No one cleans up after themselves. Someone left a half-eaten sandwich in the game room last weekend. It's ridiculous! And I've had enough! When the time comes, you and your neighbors are spraying for the roaches."

"Sure," Antony said, gesturing in the direction of the youngsters exiting the newsstand. "Well, you're up."

Luis dismantled his posture of impatience. While cramming his stubby fingers under the upturned brim of his vintage headwear, he stepped inside the kiosk.

Tranquility permeated Antony's essence as the perpetual spouter of discontent disappeared from sight. His wait on this line was experienced as a life immersed within a timeless state. Perceptions of time were distorted; its mystical flow had been dammed by a gap-toothed bothersome beaver. As he exhaled deeply through his nostrils, chronological awareness returned the pace of experience to its customary rate. At long last, he was permitted to bask in the relaxation he sought.

Conceived to entice consumption, creative magazine covers floated past his peripheral vision on the newsstand's animated digital menu. First a one-point perspective of a Martian ice cabin passed by, then a surrealist image of a pensive model fused with a paintbrush. Finally there appeared a genetically resurrected woolly rhinoceros with a geometric gradient overlay. Antony reflexively closed his eyes in order to free himself from these distractions. His appetite for information revolved strictly around current events, specifically those within the Zero-G Basketball Association.

For the first time that afternoon, Antony's mind wandered into the cognitive desert of the star-crossed gambler. Woebegone thoughts stemming from yesterday's stroke of misfortune overtook rational evaluations. The tragic flaw penned by the blind poet in the days of antiquity was replicated over two millennia later with Antony's monetary well-being stranded on the Aegean Sea.

In his experience as a sports handicapper, bankroll management was a recurring problem. Intervallic-sized bets based on statistical confidence levels were often trumped by emotion. Spurred by unsubstantiated belief, he exponentially increased wager amounts during prolonged win streaks. This set the stage for inevitable ruination in a single defeat. Last night's heart-wrenching loss at the hands of the Berlin

Hippogriffs exemplified his self-destructive behavior.

For Antony, egregious miscalculations of this sort were compounded by a lack of accountability. His present quagmire of indebtedness was attributed to a dereliction by Lady Luck. Awaiting a mystical reversal of karma, he instated an arbitrary break from his venturesome activity. Despite this self-imposed recess, his urge to see the day's betting lines remained.

Antony banged his skull against the newsstand to quiet his doubts over controlling the whims of fortune. Without thinking, he repeated the action again and again. The triad of thuds sparked a conniption fit from within the ordering station. "Don't get your panties in a wad! I waited for my damn turn. Now you have to wait for yours!"

All within the queue transferred their focus to the boorish asperity. Moments later, Luis hopped out from the alcove, mad as a hatter but more like a March hare. Multiple magazines stuck out from his canvas duffle bag.

"No respect, no consideration, for anyone whatsoever!" Luis's plump nostrils flared. "When did common courtesies become so uncommon? Ridiculous, all of it, all of you! Who was it?" He pointed his accusatory finger at young and old alike. "Tell me! Which one of you was pounding on the walls?"

No one in the line moved.

"Seriously," he carried on, "how long was I in there for? Two, three minutes? I wasted half my damn da–"

"Ahem," Antony said, popping out his elbow from his

reposed stance. He nudged the outside of the kiosk with an arm triangle to return his frame to an unbraced position. Liberation from the raving nuisance was mere footsteps away. He had suffered in silence, but the charade of quasi-politeness had reached a level of exasperation. With his central incisors sunk into his bottom lip, he moved to end Luis's blatant hypocrisy. "Perhaps you can conduct your sermons on the failings of the human race elsewhere?"

"The nerve of this guy," Luis yelled back. "And where do you want me to go?"

"Away from the entrance would be a start." Antony employed the same attention-drawing openhanded gesture he used earlier. "In case you hadn't noticed, there's people waiting."

The realization of the social faux pas cast a rosy hue over Luis's complexion. He gave a muffled apology in Antony's direction, then waddled back toward Sanctuary Village Apartments. After years of obnoxious encounters, Antony reveled in toppling the sanctimonious tower of refined civility. Watching Luis's stubby legs scurry away more than made up for the delay. Antony tittered with satisfaction as he entered the newsstand.

Arctic-white panels filled the modest-sized recess. Its right interior wall was transparent, providing users with an up-close look at the intricacies of the printing process. Customers were identified by a radio frequency proximity sensor mounted above the arched entryway. A tweaked version of the Jungian Lens assessed emotional states in real time. Shopping habits were invasively zeroed in on like a neurosurgeon moonlighting on an infomercial. Within fractions of a second, data siphoned from all walks of Antony's life were loaded into a machine learning algorithm to psychologically target consumption motives.

Based on Antony's financial worries, his personal atmosphere was crafted around frugality. Up-tempo electronica music was played to keep the queue moving and to minimize his inclinations to indulge. On the holographic interface, a bright orange background communicated affordability. An image of the latest issue of *The People's Voice* floated in the center of the display. The worldwide newspaper of the Pansophical Corporation featured a live-action aerial photograph of the waterfront firefight from the small hours of the morning. Beneath the graphic snapshot was the headline "United We Stand: Seattle Public Safety Thwarts Barbarous Praxis Plot."

At the sight of the corpse-strewn pier, his smile dampened. Placing his hand over his heart, he acknowledged the sacrifices made to oppose radicalism. Failing to extol these bulwarks would be downright impiety, but his gratitude went beyond the superficial. Deep down, Antony sensed that this struggle against the scourge of terrorism would decide mankind's fate. He shifted his attention away from the woes of society, then dragged the publication into his shopping cart.

Antony slid his hand into his back pocket and removed a lint-covered wallet. A ragged 50฿ bill peeked out from its rustic leather folds. He emphatically flicked his wrist in a downward motion to jostle free the clinging fiber bundles. Akin to the inoperative stubby wing of a dodo bird, the corner of the currency flapped in vain. When he opened the wallet moments later, he discovered that those bancor shares were the last of their kind. A disheartening dose of reality flushed through his physiognomy like an ornithologist visiting the island of Mauritius.

Fantasies of limitless amounts of discretionary income had abandoned him. Purchasing *The People's Voice* bordered on splurging considering his deteriorating financial well-being. His dejected gaze followed his pointer finger as it sluggishly proceeded to checkout. Subsequently, as if completed by proxy, the shabby cotton and linen composite bill was taken from its tri-fold container and inserted into the currency validator. These actions unfolded before his eyes without conscious command.

All bancor bills featured a microchipped Pansophical Corporation seal along with an image of the company's founder, Andrew D. Fields, posing before an industrial backdrop. Authentication of the medium of exchange was determined through a series of tests. The smart bill's magnetic ink and fluorescent properties were validated. Following these legacy anti-counterfeiting measures, its public key was verified to prevent double spending, then cross-checked against a dirty-money blacklist. Without complication Antony's money was accepted. Change was dispersed in the form of two crisp 20₿ bills. Ownership rights were updated once the transaction was added to the permissioned ledger.

The latest issue of *The People's Voice* was downloaded from the Department of Information's secure intranet, stored within the printer's random access memory, and then transcribed onto newsprint. Antony blankly stared into the leathery void of an empty wallet. His trance was interrupted by a cacophony of spinning rollers, grinding gears, and faint clicking noises. He rotated his head to watch the printing operation. At its conclusion, his eyes fell upon the running counter below the typographic machine. The yellow numbers sped by in an indecipherable blur like a stopwatch laced with methamphetamines. Adjacent to this rapidly growing nine-digit number was a black plaque with "The People's Voice" written in blocky white font. With the average household supporting a paper-a-day habit, circulation exceeded a billion copies on most days. The global polylingual newspaper was updated continuously throughout the day. Its transient product cycles ensured never-ending demand from the populace.

Languidly, Antony bent at the waist and extended his arm through the newsstand's delivery bezel. Hot off the press, the periodical literally warmed his chilled fingers. After snatching his change, he glanced once more at *The People's Voice* sale tally before exiting. Sentiments of acceptance eased the resentment he felt toward his financial failings. Social proof of his purchasing decision was unimpeachably established by the sheer magnitude of the numerical figure. The wisdom of the crowd had spoken; the social connection that he shared with his fellow citizens was reaffirmed.

Down Eastlake Avenue, Antony lightheartedly strolled toward the immunization center. Within his cranial walls, a cognitive map of the environment assisted with wayfinding. Hippocampal place cells served as spatial beacons. They activated at familiar locations to form the basis of his neural mapping system. Antony passed these reference points on autopilot. One block from the newsstand, he walked by a forest-green fire hydrant with chrome-yellow valve covers. Here, weeks earlier, he had participated in a digital purging ritual that had escalated into an old-fashioned book burning. A quarter mile later, there was the sweet-toothed temptress outside of Little Miss Muffin's Oven. Praying on unhealthy passersby, the wide-eyed caricaturized statue wore a fuchsia floral dress, a white pastry apron, striped leggings, and a cupcake-themed chef hat. Three hundred feet away from his destination, there was the nondescript office complex that housed Dr. Winfield's practice. Each landmark corresponded to the firing of a distinct place cell within his brain.

Meanwhile, in Antony's neighboring entorhinal cortex, his grid cells measured the movements of their fleshy host through complex computations. Unlike their navigational counterparts, these unique cells eschewed location-specific details. Mirroring the first aviators to take to the skies, they operated through dead reckoning. Their hexagonal firing patterns signaled distance displacement as well as direction traveled. With each footfall, his spatial coordinate system was updated. His lead left heel landed squarely on the concrete [South – 25 inches]; he pushed off his rear toes and swung his right leg forward [South – 26 inches]; pausing to cross the street, he pivoted, then repeated the gait cycle [West – 23 inches]. The combination of the interconnected brain cells guided him through the three dimensional landscape.

The double-saddle-shaped facade of Eastlake Immunization Center was distinct among the high-rises in the Seattle metropolitan area. Its elegant curved glass membranes were supported by a lattice of stainless steel cables and a trio of massive concrete columns. Atop its central support, a Pansophical flag fluttered in the stiff wind like a cyclopean sentinel.

In admiration of this visually striking edifice, Antony lifted his head. His pupils met the omnipresent optic before gradually descending the structure's transparent exterior. At the same time, streams of citizens entered and exited the building, blind to the architectural marvel.

The moment was fleeting. A gorgeous woman endowed with golden proportions jostled Antony from his wonderment. In each of her hands, a lime-green tote bag pendulated. The mesh side-pocket of her upward swinging bag grazed Antony's elbow. On its way down, it forcefully struck his thigh. "Pardon." She glanced back at Antony through her rhinestone cat-eyed sunglasses without breaking stride.

Along with this half-hearted apology, she left an intoxicating fragrance trail. As the zesty sensual notes of jasmine, honeysuckle, and rosewood enchanted Antony's olfactory bulb, the perfume wearer raced into the building. He fully recognized the exigent nature of vaccination days, so he excused her impoliteness. Besides, attractiveness had inherent privileges. Prompted by her sense of urgency, he ceased dillydallying and stepped into the automatic revolving doorway.

The narrowly spaced glass panels within the cylindrical enclosure slowly spun around their axis to record pedestrians. In the center of the Grand Appointment Hall, anchored by rows of vertical I-beams, there was an enormous video board. It featured an alphabetized list of incoming patients and their station assignments. Thousands of citizens restlessly scurried in all directions. Some wore face shields, many opted for masks, and a few encased themselves in bubble suits. Palpable dread circulated through the enormous open-plan structure.

Ordinarily, the psychodynamic epiphany that hairless apes were mortal beings was uncannily suppressed. The primary pillars of the newest normal were built upon a desensitized bedrock of inoculations. Loss was commonplace. Cultural norms emphasized letting go and pressing forward. Urges to mourn for Tembakoo's victims were overridden by first-order values revolving around communal prosperity. In the face of ubiquitous death, the Pansophical Corporation glorified the resilience of the human spirit. Compulsory visits to immunization centers restored the vision of the blind majority. Blissful ignorance was confronted by the antipodal reality of a species striving to stave off extinction.

The emergence of these fearful revelations was not lost on Antony. Unfortunately, he was not afforded the luxury of a blindfold. He was routinely accosted with the harsh fact of Tembakoo's existence. When a single soul inhabited two bodies, the absence of one's better half constantly reminded the survivor of the executioner's identity.

Antony apprehensively moved through the chaos of the Grand Appointment Hall toward the queuing display. Among the unvaccinated, frayed nerves took the shape of guarded postures and incessant fidgeting. All within the congregated mass waited for the unassigned dash next to their respective name to be replaced by a station number. Anxious about the crowd, in search of a distraction, Antony's attentional field strayed. He extended his cervical vertebrae like a parched child caught in a rainstorm.

Through the heart of the Escheresque structure, escalators and transparent walkways challenged the notions of architectural feasibility. Zigzagging moving staircases connected some floors while omitting others. Meandering glass passageways linked opposite ends of the building, at points incoherently crisscrossing at dizzying heights. Peering up at the ostensibly physics-defying pedestrian pathways, Antony's eyes briefly latched onto traversers of the deconstructivist maze.

To pass the time, he arbitrarily selected individuals, then conjectured upon their destination floor. His sightline dipped to the building directory. Twenty-four floors meant that his probability of success by random chance was 4.17 percent. Laws of probability came second nature to those who possessed the gambler's mindset. Pedestrian prediction was underway; zero-for-one in a flash became zero-for-nineteen. While this childlike challenge quelled his uneasiness, he began to grow frustrated at Lady Luck's refusal to serve as an accessory in this time-wasting pursuit.

The string of defeats led Antony to change his intuition-based strategy. Conditional probability was incorporated and perceived urgency was considered. He stroked his chin while he hypothesized that scrambling individuals were more likely assigned to an upper floor, whereas those who dawdled were presumably heading for a lower-level destination. Any floor that experienced an influx of patients was temporarily eliminated from the selection pool due to occupancy limits. Armed with these new techniques, floor ranges were effectively narrowed. Shortly after, pay dirt was reached, then again in succession.

"Boomshakalaka," Antony said with chuckle. "Let's make it three in a row."

Before he could identify his next unknowing participant, time expired on the amusing guessing game. The digital queue assigned Antony Sartori to station B.

A metallic palette coated the Grand Appointment Hall. Partitioned booths with robotic receptionists lined the perimeter of the ground floor. These glossy-aluminum life-sized humanoids appeared as seamless extensions of the minimalist structure. Each stall included a chair, a pewter desk, and a multicolored lettered designation overhead. These conspicuous polychromatic labels mirrored an alphabet line within a kindergarten classroom.

Antony briskly walked through the throng toward the corrugated outer walls. Below a burgundy B, he plopped his tuckered frame down. A patient scan was conducted to confirm that he was at the proper location. Suddenly, the android assistant came to life.

"Hello, Antony Sartori, I'm B1-26. Please make yourself comfortable. I have some questions for you when you're ready."

The android's voice emanated from behind a chrome waffle grill within its torso. Despite its ventriloquist-dummy-styled jowl, it spoke with the syntax and prosody of a native speaker. B1-26's vocal characteristics were selected from a vast linguistic database, trained by autoregressive language models. For Antony, the congenial robot presented itself as a well-educated, middle-aged female. In contrast to the unnerved citizens all around, B1-26 emitted a soothing vibe. Awaiting confirmation, it rotated its palms upward while looking at Antony with its enlarged computer-generated eyes.

"Hello, B1-26." Antony crossed his legs and interlaced his fingers neatly on his lap. "Ask away."

"Great. Please answer the following questions both honestly and to the best of your ability. At any time over the last three days have you experienced severe headaches?"

"Regrettably, yes. There was a drunken incident last night." Antony lowered his head. "I took a misstep while walking home. It left me with a splitting headache. And a bloody scalp as a souvenir for my clumsiness."

Reflexively, he separated his hands and combed his fingers through the shaggy spiked protrusions that covered his skull. As he raised his sight line back to the questioner, an engorgement of subpapillary vessels caused his cheeks to flush. B1-26 identified his physiological response. It delayed asking a follow-up question to allow his abashment from the bungling act to pass.

On vaccination days, the immunization center was a tinderbox of tension. Within the distressful walls of the Grand Appointment Hall, keeping citizens calm was a priority on par with gathering health information. B1-26 and its robotic brethren monitored nonverbal communications, both to facilitate pleasant interactions and to detect deception. Words were vehicles for manipulation, easily misconstrued, but nothing could prevent the body from divulging subconscious truths.

The Tembakoo virus had no cure. A one-way ticket to a quarantine camp awaited the infected. Medical screenings were plagued by falsehoods. The virtues of honesty were compromised for even the most scrupulous of individuals. Lying represented the desperate recourse for all symptomatic citizens who dreamed of remaining in society.

Antony's petty shame was replaced by the disconcerting realization of disclosing a Tembakoo symptom within the present setting. He understood the futility of attempting to conceal truths from the mechanical polygraphist. Nevertheless, one inevitably questioned the prudence of voluntary self-incrimination when facing the direst of repercussions.

In the protracted silence, he wondered how he would react if he suspected that he himself harbored the virus. Did he possess the courage to sacrifice his life for the greater good? Or would the sight of B1-26's confined range of motion activate his survival mechanism of flight? Upon escape, how would he navigate the looming threats that awaited the exiled?

Shepherded by curiosity's charm, Antony's attention shifted away from his immobile inquisitor. Immersed within this hypothetical scenario, his pupils grazed over the unvaccinated herd in search of the nearest exit. His field of vision moved deliberately through the alphabet designations of the screening stations. A lemon-yellow L, a midnight-blue M, a neon-orange N—the image of the fourteenth letter inexplicably enslaved the murky depths of his psyche. The urge to avert his gaze was overridden by the onrush of a foudroyant flashback from 366 days prior. Winding threads of memory spun within his unconscious mind. The terminal panel of his neural tapestry series on elation was recreated. With his eyes open, the visual memory was woven on a loom of generalities. As the thin folds of skin sluggishly closed, the scene was projected on the back of his eyelids with a vivid clarity only surpassed by enlightened awareness.

Antony's voice fluctuated as he slipped off his respirator. "Hello, Qo-58. Please give me a few seconds."

With feet firmly on the floor, he scooted forward, then depressed the suction valve on his microprocessor-controlled prosthesis. The negative pressure differential was eliminated. Accompanied by a pop, the airtight seal between the carbon fiber socket and the gel liner that stretched over the remnants of his right leg was broken.

"Ahhhhhhh! One more month of dealing with this aggravation before I'm made whole once again. Take it from me, being a cyborg isn't all it's cracked up to be. I'm counting the hours until my return to the ranks of mankind."

All robotic receptionists were programmed to observe gaze as a deictic cue to foster social connection. Qo-58 distinguished Antony's pupils from his sclera and followed his sightline. Its pseudo optical organs locked onto the artificial appendage without comprehension. Antony's physical disability was on record, but interviewing a man while he removed his limbs was uncharted territory.

"Just another minute, and I'll answer all your questions," Antony continued. "It's been a long morning. Our orders got mixed up over at Buzz's. By the time my wife and I finished our breakfast, we had to jog over here. This is the first chance I've had to sit down comfortably, away from everybody."

"No harm done," Qo-58 said. "Take your time."

"Despite my complaints, the truth of the matter is, this thing has been a lifesaver." Antony carefully placed his bionic companion under his chair. "It took me a few weeks to become acclimated, of course, but moving around is more or less natural now. Only real issue is that us humans tend to sweat."

Using both hands, Antony manually maneuvered his stump. He rolled off its protective liner, then meticulously inspected the residual limb for signs of swelling or friction burn. During his trial period with the prosthesis, he had learned firsthand that seemingly harmless red pressure patches could develop into ulcers. Now a seasoned professional, he recognized the importance of practicing impeccable hygiene. Preventing epidermal breakdowns took precedence over questions about his medical history.

"Sorry, Qo-58." Antony reached into the pouch of his windbreaker. He removed a charcoal-colored hand towel followed by a travel-sized tube of lotion. "Ordinarily I wouldn't do this in public. But I couldn't risk the possibility of having my number called while I was in the bathroom."

Starting at the tip of his stump, he wiped away the perspiration that had accumulated throughout the early portion of the day. In a similar vein, he dried the socket of the artificial limb, then slid his sweaty liner onto the armrest inside out. His routine concluded with the application of a smidgen of antiperspirant and a light massage to stimulate blood flow.

Antony sat back, relieved. "Ready when you are."

Midway through Qo-58's series of rote questions, a

tingling sensation compelled Antony to wriggle his hips. To and fro he moved in an effort to suppress the unpleasantness. The chair failed to provide the firm level surface his residual limb required. In the midst of resituating his disabled frame, he accidentally dislodged his airing-out liner. When he bent down to retrieve his pliant secondary skin, he rotated his head in the direction of the booths on the rear wall.

In front of station N, Dominique stood as a Middlemist Camellia in a prosaic garden of dandelions, creeping butter-cups, and morning glories. Among the solemn expressions of the crowd, her faultless crescent of pearly whites shone like no other. The essence of Antony's being blossomed in the presence of her resplendent smile. For twenty-seven years, the simple arousal of her facial muscles supplied him with all the nutrients needed to engender euphoria. She wore a gray-and-purple-patterned scarf over a half-zippered black leather jacket, a pair of navy skinny jeans, and tan ankle boots. Slicing through the pandemonic masses, her protruding sapphire irises landed amorously on her kindred spirit. Through Antony's eyes the universe dematerialized, the contents of the Grand Appointment Hall bit by bit blended into obscurity. For a moment, there was only his inamorata; there was only his Dominique.

On rare occasions, the significance of the present was enigmatically betrayed by a flash of clairvoyance. During this instance, Antony was not presented with a privy glimpse of an omniscient storyboard, but he intuitively felt the gravity

of the moment. Visceral perturbations of the paunch operated outside the realm of logic. With gazes locked, he and his
wife possessed a shared understanding of the importance
of the here and now. Only in hindsight would the veridical
significance be revealed to Antony. The spellbound couple
visually consumed their complement. Each refrained from
blinking. The notion of being away from the other, even for
milliseconds, was unbearable.

In silent adoration, Antony studied the features of
Dominique's warm, tawny, kite-shaped face. Pale golden-
blonde finger waves softly draped over her forehead before
running down her prominent cheekbones and tapered jaw-
line. These thick, glamorous strands framed her exquisite
profile like the leafy cartouches of a master baroque crafts-
man. Age had deprived her of the smooth supple skin of her
youth. The lower portions of her face appeared marginally
deflated. The years had erased the delicate symmetry that
originally ensnared Antony's unsuspecting heart, but her
beauty endured the trials of time.

Dominique unlocked the mesmerizing manacles that
bound the couple's sightline through a prolonged blink. Tinges
of wistfulness without warning saturated her profound sentiments of affection and veneration. The inner corners of her
thick eyebrows rose. Her upper eyelids drooped. Emotional
energy followed gravity's pull, slowly traveling through her
body. Over the subsequent seconds, Dominique's ectomorphic
anatomy constricted. Her pristine posture slumped. Antony's

countenance replicated her pensive undertones. Their affective states of consciousness escalated in rapid succession. Seeing the reflection of her own melancholic musings on the face of her dearest vanquished her last vestiges of courage.

Tears welled in Dominique's eyes. Salty droplets of sadness flowed over her curled mascara-coated eyelashes. Streams of blackened tears daubed her dewy foundation like the smirched parchment of a ham-handed calligrapher. On the brink of descending into a full-fledged sobbing fit, she forcefully tensed her facial muscles to impede the waterworks. For an instant, her composure was regained.

Dominique's long, thin lips parted, each syllable deliberately mouthed to ensure understanding: "I will always love you, Antony."

Once more, Dominique flashed her ineffable smile. The one she reserved for the only man capable of infusing her life with bliss. Then she turned away and walked resolutely toward the nearest escalator without allowing her gaze to stray.

In her departure, Antony's consternation multiplied. All was awry, anguish afflicted his amore. The world rematerialized before his eyes. The couple's surreal intimate moment was replaced by an impersonal reality teeming with humanoids and nameless organic beings.

"Dominique," he frantically shouted into the discordant babblings of the Grand Appointment Hall. "Dominique!"

Antony hysterically popped up onto his leg while clutching his artificial limb. Desperate to alleviate Dominique's dolor, he jammed his stump into the prosthesis. His pupils tracked her through the labyrinth. Simultaneously, he rocked back and forth, shifting his weight between appendages in order to expel the excess air from around his residual limb. By the time he regained his bipedal mobility, she had disappeared. Dominique was gone, gone forever. Never again would Antony bask in the presence of the woman who completed his existence.

"Antony?" B1-26 said. "Antony?"

Upon hearing his name, he returned from the recesses of his mind to the present.

"Are you feeling okay?" B1-26 asked.

With a glazed-over expression, Antony stared back at the android.

"Can we proceed? It's important that I collect all your relevant health information before a doctor administers your vaccine."

"Huh?"

The repressed memory rattled Antony's processing capabilities, leaving him cognitively incapacitated. Reliving the sorrow-stricken remembrance drained him of his life force. If not for the seat supporting his limp muscles, he would have collapsed helplessly onto the ground. The weight of the past was too much to bear. Yearning for yesteryear, despondency consumed his physiognomy.

"Please take a minute to collect your thoughts," said B1-26. "Whenever you're ready, we'll finish going over your medical history."

Antony acknowledged the humanoid with an apathetic nod.

"Vaccination days are difficult for everyone." B1-26 rotated its elbow joints. It positioned an open hand upon its chest cavity in the place where a human's heart would reside. "Too many have lost their lives to that horrible virus."

The presence of the embedded camera in the middle of B1-26's bulging cranium reminded Antony of the inherent disconnect between the two of them. Blood flowed through one, electricity through the other. Whereas experience produced indescribable subjective mental states within the man, sequences of elaborate algorithms, free of qualia, defined the robot's existence. More precisely, from an anthropocentric perspective, the android was lacking any subjective experience at all.

A removal from the woes of the living precluded the inorganic entity from understanding the profundity of death. The object before Antony was unaffected by the countless casualties left in Tembakoo's wake. B1-26's overt displays of compassionate empathy were a sham. Antony's feelings of emptiness intensified upon dissecting the illusionary nature of this sympathetic behavior.

After several minutes of brooding silence, his urge to separate himself from the haunting memories of his surroundings compelled him to action. "Please continue."

"Thank you. We at the Department of Health Services appreciate your cooperation. Earlier you mentioned that you've been experiencing headaches. How are you feeling today?"

"I'm ... back ... to ... normal now." Antony's drawn-out intonation reeked of aloofness.

"Great to hear. And at any time over the last three days, have you felt nauseated?"

"Yes. But that was also alcohol related."

After the incubation period, the prodromal symptoms of Tembakoo mirrored the classical symptoms of an acute infection. Body aches, fatigue, fever, and malaise — each could be attributed to a myriad of viral genomes. One could not differentiate between Tembakoo and a mild case of the flu at their onsets. When symptoms appeared, people confidently ascribed their afflictions to relatively benign bugs. Forgotten by the average man, nightmarish images of Tembakoo's victims were stuffed away into individualized jars of fear. A week following the initial symptoms, the defining characteristics of Tembakoo manifested as hypersensitivity, orificial bleeding, hematemesis, and skin discoloration.

Antony dispassionately rejected B1-26's subsequent inquiries into the more telling signs of Tembakoo with a headshake and a series of noes. His responses were conveyed without any thought given to the connection between the words and the grim maladies they represented. Matter-of-factly, he had not bled from the eyes, nose, or ears, he had not projectile vomited, and his olive skin remained unchanged. There was no reason for him to provide verbose responses. He had no desire to engage in superficial blather. Beyond short-lived symptoms explained by excessive amounts of alcohol, Antony was keenly aware that he was free and clear of the signs associated with the virus.

B1-26 gestured with a thumbs-up. "And that will conclude the first portion of our medical screening."

Without providing a verbal response, Antony sat up.

"Just a few more questions before I can send you on your way. Have you recently been in close contact with anyone who has exhibited the aforementioned symptoms?"

"No," Antony replied.

"Have you recently traveled to the Atlantic Territories of North America?"

"No."

"To the best of your knowledge, have you been in close contact with anyone who has recently traveled to the Atlantic Territories of North America?"

"No."

"And lastly," B1-26 said while steepling its hands, "I'd like to take a moment to remind you that public health is our shared responsibility. We cannot win our war against Tembakoo if those among us ignore symptoms. Citizens who fall behind on their immunizations put us all at risk. Day in and day out, we must remain united as one. Are you aware of anyone who has been neglecting their civic duties, Antony?"

"No one comes to mind."

"Once again, thank you for your cooperation. Please head up to the eighth floor, room number 840." B1-26 pointed upward. "There you will be administered your vaccine. As always, if you develop Tembakoo symptoms, immediately visit the nearest immunization center or call the Department of Health Services. Unless you have questions, please report to room 840 at this time. Have a great day."

CHAPTER SEVEN

ntony traversed the maze of translucent passageways and vertical conveyors with the urgency of a lab rat pumped full of sedatives. On the sixth floor, he lethargically stepped from the escalator's comb plate onto the cleated moving staircase. This careless half-stride left his heel hanging precariously off the edge. His body temporarily tarried in an inter-floor limbo, as if unwilling to commit to the next phase of the vaccination process. As the escalator ascended, a stern-looking gentleman on the step below murmured while nudging the suede backstay of Antony's sneaker with his khaki-covered shin. Antony nonchalantly glanced over his shoulder. He gripped the rubber handrail and dragged his foot forward.

Two floors up, Antony lackadaisically followed a circular corridor. Cooper room number signs were fastened to the egg-white walls by silver standoffs. At the eastern end of the building, he arrived at his destination, "840 Russel Hooke, MD PhD."

Odoriferous molecules of cleanliness stormed out of the room as he cracked open the rosewood door. His nose crinkled. He bent his head away from the barrage of medical disinfectants. The foreboding smell was a stark reminder of the public health imperative. At its core it symbolized man's impotent efforts to stamp out the nonliving infectious agent. Even a passing whiff of this distinct scent could elicit trepidation. Antony paused. He allowed the smells of purification to pass before fully opening the door.

"Welcome, Antony Sartori." The metallic announcement was emitted from a ceiling-mounted speaker opposite the entryway. "Please take a seat. Your name will be called in the order in which you arrived."

In the middle of the variegated waiting room, there was a group huddled around a holographic projection platform. The acoustic intrusion briefly drew their attention. Eleven agitated expressions greeted the incoming patient. A medley of narrowed eyes, pursed lips, and exaggerated sighs were directed at the newcomer. Bewildered by this reception, Antony softly closed the door behind himself, then tiptoed to the point of attraction. At the base of the tabletop display, multi-hued laser beams shone through diffraction gratings to create a collection of vibrant three dimensional images.

A pastel-lavender and pink-winter sunset injected the backdrop of the hologram with color. Behind a curved black wooden podium, branded with the optic insignia of the Pansophical Corporation, Chairman Fields stood with his head bowed, eyes closed, and hands clasped behind his back. Exquisite standing floral sprays on oversized wire easels bookended him. These ornate tributary arrangements of white chrysanthemums, carnations, and Asiatic lilies were each accentuated by emerald palm fronds and decorative lush. As was customary, Fields was clothed in the illustrious formal attire of a Pansophical board member. Overlooking the tranquil expanse of Puget Sound, he appeared larger than life. In his motionless presence, the body of water entered the doldrums. It seemingly refrained from rippling as if under an aquatic decree. Arriving cargo vessels on the peripheral of the wharf were stonewalled in observance of the quietude. External motion was restored as Fields's thick-whiskered upper lip separated from its glabrous lower counterpart.

"Thank you. Moments of silence will not bring back our fallen citizens, but the memories of their heroic actions will persist through the annals of history. Today we honor the courageous Public Safety officers who lost their lives along this very waterfront hours ago. These brave citizens gave their lives in one last act of devotion to worldwide safety. Our collective hearts ache for the two dozen virtuous souls who are no longer with us. In the aftermath of this tragedy, let's take a minute to reflect upon the auspicious futures that won't come to fruition. Think of the lives that could have been. Think of the mother who will never hear her son's first words. Think of the father who was deprived of the opportunity to attend his twin's graduation. Think of those left behind, the husbands, the wives, the children, who today return to lonesome households. We at the Pansophical Corporation express our deepest sympathies to the friends and families of those directly affected by this calamity. Together, we as a global community grieve for these causalities of the war on terror."

Antony dipped his chin and lowered his eyes in respect of the innumerable sacrifices that have shaped mankind.

"On one hand," Fields said, "we commend the valiant acts of our fallen heroes. On the other, we pay tribute to the lionhearted citizens who carry on their legacies. Right now, there are men and women across the continents who are fully aware of the dangers that accompany service. Yet, without exception, they put on their Public Safety uniforms and defend us against unknown peril. These loyal protectors of the peace set the foundation for our civilization. To our Public Safety officers, your dedication reminds us all of the importance of upholding our societal obligations. Each and every day, your service inspires me to elevate myself to become the best citizen I can be.

"The Pansophical Corporation extends its sincerest gratitude to Sergeant Leroy Bannister, whose leadership was integral to the counterterrorist operation. In foiling Praxis's noxious scheme, millions of innocent lives were saved. And a significant blow was dealt to the savage terrorist organization. Four Praxis anarchists were killed in the firefight thanks to Sergeant Bannister's tactical acumen. The deaths of these traitors bring us one step closer to our longstanding goals of ubiquitous peace and prosperity. Finally, we commend the selfless actions of Nikola Fedorovich, who sustained grave injuries while administering medical aid. By honoring Sergeant Bannister and Officer Fedorovich, we honor the dear memories of their brethren who now rest in eternal slumber."

At the completion of the panegyric, the austere Fields took a deep breath. He calculatingly swiveled his head from left to right. As his visual field panned the twilit skyline, five miles away, the sightline of his holographic likeness fleetingly crossed Antony's troubled gaze. Upon hearing the news of the wounded officer, taut sensations developed within Antony's chest cavity. Tribalistic sentiments underscored by sympathetic distress reinvigorated his listless pith.

Nikola Fedorovich. Antony internally repeated the officer's name while pondering questions of courageous acts grounded in brotherly love. Without Nikola Fedorovich's heroism on the battlefield, how many more lives would have been lost? Without Nikola Fedorovich performing the duties of a combat medic, how would Public Safety have fared in this bloody skirmish? This was the same kindhearted officer who spoke up during his own judicial proceedings. On an insensate terrene, a selfless action conspicuously stood as a mountain on the vast flatlands. Bannister's portentous gavel would have stripped Antony of his precious freedoms if not for Nikola's interjection. Bannister would have permanently branded Antony a danger to humanity if not for Nikola's compassion.

Meanwhile, poised above Puget Sound, Fields's deliberate panning movement was replicated in reverse. From right to left, his indomitable gaze scanned the Seattle skyline like a pair of searchlights stymying an airborne assault. The elongated pause that coincided with these gestures initiated a tonal shift away from consolation. Fields eliminated the distance between himself and the podium. He hunched over and clenched the slanted top of the lectern with his powerful hands, then resumed his worldwide address.

"As externalities threaten to plunge our world into darkness, we naturally look to normalcy with envious eyes. Only in solidarity will humanity be able to continue its progressive charge toward transcendent prosperity. Today, united as one, we shine the light of truth on the evils that lurk in the shadows. Today, we take a stand against the immoral brutes who target our communities and torment the innocent. We will not sit idly by as Praxis jeopardizes our way of life. The onus does not rest solely on the men and women of Public Safety. We share in the responsibilities of bringing these perpetrators of terror to justice.

"Prevailing threats to our society take many forms. While our civilization endures in defiance of Tembakoo, radicalism festers under the surface. Praxis revels in fostering discontent among our prosperous people. Our enemy's deception knows no bounds. The distorted views and lies they peddle seep into our daily interactions. Their evil resides in even seemingly innocent denouncements of the Pansophical Corporation. We have all seen them slithering under the cover of night; we have all heard their fictitious whispers in the wind. Responses of silence embolden their wicked quest to usher in an era of death and destruction. I have implored you in the past to remain vigilant, but today's tragedy is proof of our shortcomings.

"Citizens of the world ... I speak these words to each and every one of you. Now is the time to intensify our efforts. Praxis and its sympathizers will find no safe haven on our earth! We will hunt them down. We will eradicate their poisonous doctrines from history. Humanity will prosper in the ashes of their failed revolution. Long live Pansophical!"

The sunset-tinged scene gradually disappeared. The bold letters of the Pansophical slogan filled the void.

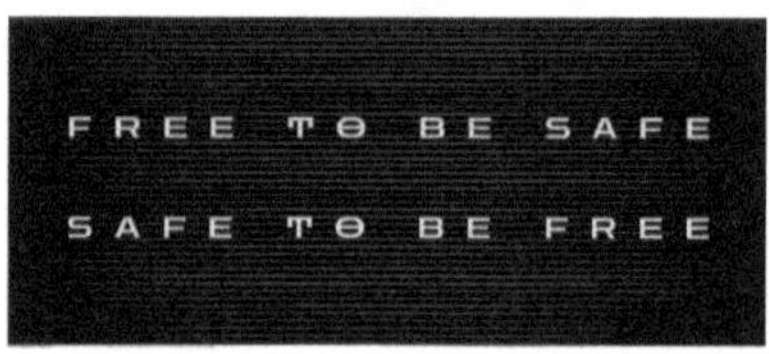

In unison, Antony and the members of the waiting room raised their forearms. "Free to be safe, safe to be free." They vigorously pumped their fists while repeating the eight syllables. Their larynxes synchronized, bestowing the immunization center with a singular voice. Resoundingly, the zealous maxim of the people pervaded the soundscape. Seconds later, the building was once again voiceless.

As the corporation's motto faded out, the holographic platform turned off. Antony promptly surveyed his surroundings before making himself comfortable in a burgundy upholstered chair abutting the saltwater aquarium. Everyone else similarly settled into empty seats. The crux of the chairman's admonitory words loomed over human action. Leery eyeballs bounced around the waiting room. Praxis, their sympathizers, could be anyone, could be anywhere. Suspiciously, Antony examined the strangers occupying the modular five-seater on the opposing wall.

On the leftmost end, a bulbous woman wearing an olive-and-white-striped turtleneck reached into her quilted pocketbook. While applying her spherical lip balm, she acutely studied the contents of the unzipped rustic knapsack at her feet. Simultaneously, its owner, a middle-aged man peppered with freckles, peered askance through his face shield into the folds of the handbag that hung from their shared armrest. Beside these snoopers, a dimple-chinned bundle of winter clothes hid under a maroon pom-pom ski hat. She frighteningly clenched her mother in the neighboring seat. The youthful parent beamed with a maternal protective glow. She assessed the room's occupants through squinted eyes while embracing her dear child. On the rightmost end, a pruny senior with a skull smattered with untamed white hairs pretended to adjust his surgical mask. All the while he furtively appraised Antony. His mistrustful glances were soon abandoned in favor of conspicuous staring. Antony followed suit. After numerous awkward seconds of sizing each other up, they exchanged hostile expressions and then each transferred their focus to other patients.

"Achoo, Achoo, Achoo, A-A-choo!"

Uncovered successive spasmodic sneezes dislodged the grade-school girl from her mother's loving grip. The full-body convulsion unrooted the child from the comforts of her seat. Her aqua high-top sneakers thumped down upon the golden trellis-patterned carpet. In response to these involuntary air expulsions, Antony reflexively turned his head and shielded his orifices with his hand. Patients across the room hysterically put up barriers. Those nearby recoiled in avoidance of the spray zone. Superficial visual sweeps may have ameliorated the atmosphere of treacherous distrust, but the specter of disease persisted.

A female voice with an unsettled inflection spoke up. "This is one of the healthy waiting rooms. Why are you and your daughter in here?"

Peering through the colorful marine habitat, Antony discerned the refined facial features of a nymphet. The worriment she articulated belonged to herself alone, but it echoed the repressed challenge that had formulated within his own mind.

"Please relax," the girl's mother said. "I promise you that there's nothing to worry about. It's just her allergies acting up." She knelt and extended her arms, then beckoned to her startled daughter with both hands. "Amanda, honey, come here."

Overwhelmed by the attention, the bashful child pulled her winter hat down over her face, then dashed into the solacing clasp of her protector. As the fresh-faced mother hugged her little darling, she smiled to mollify the concerned collection of peepers. This gesture, however, proved to be fruitless.

An accusatory reply sprung from the twisted lips of the mottled man who was seated next to the daughter.

"Allergies? These waiting rooms are vacuumed, sanitized, and scrubbed top to bottom every single day. How do I know, you ask? Well, that just so happens to be my job!" He pompously tapped the embroidered "Department of Public Works" patch above his chest pocket. "If you can find so much as a dust bunny in this place, I'll fork over 500฿. So tell me, lady, what's she allergic to?"

"It's seasonal allergies. I'm sure that many of you suffer from them as well." The mother flashed a closed-lip smile. "It's nothing more. It's nothing less. Everyone, please put your minds at ease. There's absolutely no need to worry."

A labored wheezing exhalation punctuated the mother's assertion. A raspy coughing fit followed. Over the unpleasant sounds of her respiratory struggles, the pitiless clamor of the other patients was ramped up to full volume.

"Are you going to blame that cough on allergies too?"

"Of all the waiting rooms, it's just my luck that I'd be stuck in here. It's not just the girl, they're both sick!"

"Nothing to worry about? You're a liar!"

"How can you calmly sit there with that grin while placing us all in danger? Get out before you infect us!"

"Yeah! Get out of here!"

Panicky condemnation sprouted from all corners of the waiting room. In the emotionally charged climate, the denunciatory remarks served as spring-loaded clappers intermittently striking the communal alarm bell. Logical judgments were dismissed by the poignant persuader of primitive fear. Antony remained silent as the tension mounted. Neither sneezing nor coughing were ever identified as definitive symptoms of the Tembakoo virus. Nonetheless, any harbinger of illness roused precarious thoughts. Within the confines of the immunization center, these thoughts were irrationally magnified.

Inside Antony's cranial vault, deathly ideations similarly seized control. A fear of death was paramount to survival. It was encoded within the biomolecules of conscious beings blessed with a sense of selfhood. All men feared the fathomless unknown, even the enlightened who purported to have lived each day to its fullest, even the tortured souls who mired in misfortune. Antony reflected on a figmental universe where he was another faceless notch on the baneful belt of the Tembakoo virus. The harrowing thoughts of meeting his end by the same infection that expunged his beloved from existence exacerbated his dread. His entire frame shuttered. Steered by morbid angst, his mouth opened, and he joined the unnerved posse.

"Look," he shouted. "There's no use denying the truth. Both you and your daughter are ill. I won't dare speculate any further. You'll be diagnosed properly soon enough. Until then, your presence is putting everyone in here at risk."

From Antony's disharmonized mind, these trepidatious observations were articulated at a rapid pace. As the knowingly fallacious statement exited his lips, self-reproach blossomed within the pit of his stomach. Moments later, his qualms about speaking up were internally reconciled. Modes of transmission for the blood-borne pathogen included sandflies, contaminated surfaces, and bodily fluids. A mutated strain of Tembakoo, however, could theoretically be spread as an infectious aerosol. Prior studies were only valid for older variants, after all. Reducing the likelihood of disease transmission by even a minuscule amount was in his own self-interest. More importantly, it was for the good of the community. Under the precept of maximizing well-being, his behavior was interpreted as the advisable course of action. He was grateful to serve as a conduit for the Pansophical Corporation.

Antony's words served as the final straw in the series of collective judgments. The mother's patience buckled under the weight of groupthink. Confronted by the growing opposition, she no longer possessed the fortitude to defend herself against the encircling barbs.

"Come along, Amanda." The mother lovingly cupped her daughter's cheeks and kissed her forehead. "Let's wait outside."

"But I'm not sick, Mommy."

"I know, honey. But these people don't believe us."

"Why not? Mommy, I'm telling the truth."

The mother sluggishly rose to her feet. She stared down each of the aspersion casters with an expression suffused by sullen resentment. Raising her voice, she addressed the room. "If any of you fine citizens can bear the risk, please let us know when Joann and Amanda Somerville are called. Of course, that's if it's not too much trouble. Thanks."

Without waiting for a volunteer to acknowledge her sarcastic request, the parent-offspring pairing, hand in hand, stormed out of the room. Free of the ailing disturbances, the patients' priority shifted toward lingering germs. One by one they ritualistically approached the wall-mounted sanitation station to cleanse themselves. A few hastily rubbed their palms together after a single pump of antibacterial foam. Others exhibited painstaking techniques, transitioning back and forth from interlacing fingers to rotational rubbing. The senior of the group spent a full minute lathering up his face. Antony sat patiently while everyone else eased their hygienic anxieties. Impelled by social pressure, persuaded by proverbs revolving around exercising caution, he parroted the actions of his fellow patients. When his turn came, he extended his hands one at a time to activate the sanitation station. Foamy blobs were dispensed upon his palmar creases. As he slathered around the froth, his field of vision rolled over the room's decor.

Nonrepresentational canvases hung from the teal walls. Their creamy pastel brushstrokes juxtaposed the excitable ambience of the waiting area. A bubbling water cooler was the sole sound to penetrate the strained silence. In the opposite corner, under the triangular speaker, a magazine-strewn laminated table caught Antony's attention. Wary faces popped up from behind periodicals and copies of *The People's Voice* as he ambled in that direction.

"Wonder if there's anything over here worthwhile. Let's take a gander." Antony amicably declared his intent to address the dubious expressions of the group. They analyzed his physical movements. Their stares seemingly possessed a tactile quality. He turned away, but he could still sense their steadfast gazes from the fringes of his awareness. Lengthening his hip flexors, he bent slightly at the waist and gathered the scattered jumble of magazines from the table-top. After aligning their spines, he leafed through the stack. The publications epitomized a tranquilization by the trivial. There were magazines revolving around leisurely lifestyles, home and garden tips, and several featuring the hottest celebrity gossip. Nothing within the tidy pile was deemed enticing enough to warrant a second glance. He chuckled at his own hopeful ignorance while placing the ho-hum assort-ment of readings back down. In retrospect, the probability that he would uncover one of the obscure publications he sought was minute at best.

Above the table, behind an egg crate grille, microwaves beamed through five equidistant walnut-sized holes. Clocking in at a few gigahertz, these low-frequency waves reflected off the walls, efficiently heating the enclosed region. Contact with the energy produced from the non-ionized radiation gently warmed Antony's skin. As his thermal core shifted from toasty to unpleasant, he gripped the lapels of his single-breasted overcoat and shed his outer layer of clothing. Using his index finger as an improvised hook, he raised the garment. He reached into its interior pocket and removed a ruffled copy of *The People's Voice*. Before taking a seat, the woolen article was tossed over his chair's backrest.

Antony stretched out the creased groundwood newsprint over his figure-four crossed leg and began to skim the headlines. Halfway down the front page, his concentration was disrupted. The door leading to the examination rooms swung around its hinges. Its acceleration was halted by the corridor wall, resulting in a heavy thump. A short burst of air subsequently displaced Antony's reading material. Passing through the doorway, a teenager wearing a flat-brimmed Martian spelunking baseball cap strode toward the egress. His raised cheek muscles and wrinkled nose disclosed a demeanor of disgust. Being in the presence of the unvaccinated generated unmistakable revulsion within the inoculated adolescent.

Dispassionately, Antony returned to browsing the headlines. The cockeyed newspaper that rested on his makeshift table slid back to its prior position with the tilt of his knee. A story on the Waldo outbreak was selected only to be abandoned after reading its lead paragraph. In the inner workings of his brain, typed letters combined through phonemic awareness to formulate words, yet comprehension was absent. Preoccupied by his surroundings, articles were deserted over and over again, not for a lack of interest but as a consequence of a fractured focus. Before his distracted physiognomy, the composition of the waiting room continually changed. New people arrived, others were discharged. Announcements accompanied the steady pedestrian flow. Unable to tune out these unremitting interruptions, Antony read on and off for over an hour without truly grasping the content of a single article.

"Antony Sartori, please report to exam room C. Antony Sartori, please report to exam room C."

The blaring directive was a delightful sound to his restless ears. Anxious to complete the final leg of the immunization marathon, he tucked *The People's Voice* under his arm and snatched his overcoat. Concealed floor readers scanned the patient as he hurried down the nondescript hallway of locked doors. His identity was cross-referenced against the appointment database to ensure proper placement. Upon confirmation, the deadbolt of his assigned room retracted to grant entry.

"We at the Department of Health Services thank you for your patience. Please take a seat in the treatment chair. Instructions for using Healthbot will appear momentarily. If you have any problems, press the call button for assistance. Dr. Hooke is currently seeing another patient. He will be with you shortly."

By the conclusion of the mechanically toned message,

Antony was seated comfortably with his belongings resting neatly in the corner. Inside the three-sectional treatment chair's base, compressed pressure sensors set the room's venipuncture system in motion. On cue, the mood-soothing light panels dimmed, the door closed, and the pole-mounted LCD monitor was imbued with digital life. Directions for the blood draw were conveyed via a series of cartoon illustrations.

Step-by-step, Antony followed along with the animated instructions. He spread his fingers out atop the armrest. Disinclined to limit the range of motion of his dominant limb, he tapped the start button using his left thumb. Overhead, the mechanized phlebotomist swiveled into place. The transparent rectangular appliance slowly descended. It stopped when level with the patient's chest. Antony reached his supine forelimb through Healthbot's circular opening, then laid his extended arm onto the machine's grooved foam base.

Unmindful compliance steered Antony's physical movements. However, as he initiated the procedure by grasping the first aluminum relaxation rod within reach, jitters crept into his state of mind. This tinge of apprehension stemmed not from an irrational fear of needles but from the mortiferous repercussions of producing an infected sample. Whereas well-executed duplicity during the medical questionnaire provided a form of superficial amnesty, there was no escaping the judgment of an infallible biochemical analysis. The probability that Antony's body served as a refuge for the Tembakoo virus was infinitesimal, but it was not zero. His worrisome eyes bore into the machine as it collected the crucial evidence that would be used to adjudicate his fate.

Inches above Antony's elbow, an influx of air filled the latex bladder that lined Healthbot's circulation control cuff. With the inflated tourniquet restricting blood flow, an infrared light illuminated his antecubital area. A topical anesthetic with disinfectant was applied to prepare the puncture site. Images of his vascular map were analyzed like a scout contemplating routes for a reconnaissance mission. Utilizing Doppler ultrasound technology, circulation levels were approximated by reflecting high-frequency soundwaves off his passing red blood cells. When an optimal vein was identified, a channeled stabilizing bar was lowered to immobilize the vessel.

At a fifteen-degree angle, a hypodermic needle with an upward-facing bevel punctured Antony's skin. His bodily fluids flowed through the hollow slender metal spike and combined with anticoagulants upon entering an attached test tube. Once an adequate volume was collected, the specimen was labeled with his identification information. The laboratory glassware was then whooshed away through the building's pneumatic tube network.

While Antony lifted his head to follow the sibilant sound, the tourniquet cuff around his upper arm deflated. The needle was withdrawn, and a sterile gauze was applied to the wound. In accordance with the final illustrated step portrayed on the monitor, he raised his limb off the cushioned support. Healthbot secured his medical dressings with a self-adherent wrap. Less than two minutes had passed since the start of the blood-drawing task. Now complete, Healthbot returned to its unobtrusive elevated home base.

A meretricious game show replaced the instructions on the screen. Antony dismissed the program with an aloof glance. Despite an absence of bodily discomfort, he instinctively coddled his punctured appendage while he shimmied down the vinyl treatment chair. With his opposite hand tenderly cupped under the azure bandage, he sauntered around his diminutive environment to fritter away his idleness.

The examination room was hardly a fount for amusement, yet these foreign surroundings activated Antony's inquisitiveness. He removed an ophthalmoscope from the integrated wall diagnostic station. While looking through the instrument, he fiddled with its refraction wheel. Inside the viewing window, the physical world was transformed into an ambiguous reality by the rotating lens of differing diopters. The room's lone piece of decor waned out of focus. He squinted to compensate for the onrush of blurriness. As he spun the optical power wheel back to zero, the framed poster on the opposite wall once again became clear. Inescapably, the observer's perspective rested at the mercy of the one who controlled the dials.

Antony returned the instrument to the charging cradle and approached the abstract image. It featured a collection of magenta convex polyhedrons, with asymmetrical sky-colored protrusions, superimposed over a black backdrop. With his toes facing outward and his feet hip-width apart, he lowered his center of gravity to read the fine print on the poster's border.

> Mature Tembakoo viral particles: Belmopan strain
> Recorded with 3D Structured Illumination Microscopy
> Image courtesy of Russel Hooke
> (Institute of Molecular Virology at Santa Clara University)

Unsettled by the beauty of the pernicious pathogen, Antony rocked back onto his heels. Over the past year, he regularly visualized the microscopic culprit responsible for Dominique's demise as a shapeless evil. Here, for the first time, he laid his eyes on the exact variant of his incalculable abhorrence. The fatal inanimate single-strand viral genome within its protective protein shell was paradoxically geometrically dazzling. He inhaled deeply through his nostrils as his subjective nightmare confronted objective existence. Squatting in silence with his eyes closed, these incongruent conceptualizations clashed. The clunky noise of an unlocking deadbolt disrupted his attempts to instill a sense of harmony upon his mental landscape.

Dr. Hooke entered the examination room wearing a fully buttoned white laboratory coat and pleated dress pants. His tender facial features were in a perturbed pinch. Under a golden tumbleweed mane, an unmistakable sheen of sweat coated his furrowed brow.

"Excuse me, Mr. Sartori, what are you doing out of your chair?"

"My apologies. Nice to meet you, Doc. It was only moments ago that I realized what this photograph was. How can something so minuscule, something so beautiful, be the cause of so much devastation?"

The doctor's glacial irises locked onto Antony's naive smile. "That's not something I, nor anyone else, can answer."

"I suppose, but I wish someone could." Antony paused. "Tembakoo stole everything from me. My wife, my love, my Domini—"

"The past is the past," Dr. Hooke interrupted. "For the sake of our future, all we can do is move on. Now please return to the chair, Mr. Sartori."

Choked up, Antony heedlessly disregarded the doctor's command. He steered the conversation away from the emotional minefield while his attention gravitated back to the poster.

"Wait a minute ... thought I read that viruses were colorless. Is that not true?"

Infused with an impatient intonation, the doctor repeated his request. "Return to the chair, Mr. Sartori."

At the impasse, Antony's microbiological inquiries collided against the task-oriented Dr. Hooke. Despite the brevity of their interaction, it became readily apparent that a day of doling out vaccines had drained the baby-faced doctor of any vigor he possessed. Antony took a final look at the deadly pathogen's portrait and begrudgingly complied.

Dr. Hooke unfolded his scraggy arms. His rigid posture

slackened as he walked over to the white ash cabinets on the opposite wall. He systematically gathered supplies and dropped them into his lab coat. "Good news, your blood work came back clean."

"So," Antony said, glancing over nervously, "no measurable levels of the virus?"

"None at all," Dr. Hooke confirmed. "I'm now going to recline your seat to administer your vaccine. Please roll over, facedown. And hold still."

Before Antony could voice his consent, the treatment chair was in motion. As its back support gradually declined, he uncouthly twisted his body. The pressure on his knee hematoma caused him to wince. A short groan verbalized his pain.

"Please, Mr. Sartori, I haven't even begun. And when I do, it will be completely painless. Now stay still. And stay quiet."

Dr. Hooke washed his hands, then yanked two blue nitrile gloves out from the wall-mounted cardboard dispenser. After thrusting his hands into these sheathed protectors, their cuffs were stretched and released. The snapping sound of synthetic rubber prompted Antony to plant his face snugly into the contoured horseshoe headrest.

Weathered bamboo planks filled Antony's visual field from this restricted prone position. Through treatment chair portals around the globe, citizens of Pansophical stared at similar patches of flooring in anticipation. From underneath the cabinetry, Dr. Hooke dragged out a stool. Its clattering wheels apprised the patient of the doctor's movements. As the source of the rattling drew near, its pace slowed. Into the fringes of Antony's peripheral vision entered the swivel caster of a spherical wheel.

"For the sake of my sanity, can you talk me through all this, Doc?"

"This may surprise you," said Dr. Hooke, "but this isn't my first rodeo."

"I never said it was. It's just that, lying here defenseless, in the dark, is nerve racking."

"If only you people would keep your questions and comments to yourself." Dr. Hooke released a prolonged sigh. "Fine." He stomped off to retrieve the examination room's tablet control panel, then placed it on the floor within Antony's inhibited purview. "Now don't move, we're about to start."

Connected to the security system, the tablet provided Antony a birds-eye view of the procedure. The doctor extended a tiny retractable platform from the treatment chair's armrest. After unloading the inoculation contents from his lab coat, he put on the binocular loupes that had been tucked away inside his front pocket. Remaining on his feet, he leaned over to inspect the domino-sized microchip implanted within the nape of Antony's neck. The foreign object was examined for signs of an adverse immune response, then its integrity was tested. Applying gentle pressure with his outstretched index finger, he outlined the rectangular subcutaneous silicone substrate. The chip's numbered titanium reserves were subsequently jabbed in succession. With the fastidiousness of a miserly jeweler, he scrutinized over each facet of the micro-electrochemical system.

Distressed by the prodding, Antony's facial muscles tensed.

Presumably satisfied by the implant's functional performance, the doctor slipped off his magnification spectacles and plopped down onto the stool. The maintenance phase of the examination ensued. He opened a bottle of isopropyl alcohol and submerged a cotton swab. To and fro, the saturated wad of cotton was moved in horizontal lines across the microchip. Imperceptible specks of debris begrimed the unblemished spindle of downy fibers. He discarded the soiled swab into a recessed waste receptacle, then fanned his open hand to facilitate evaporation.

Assembling the injection contraption followed. The doctor snapped a cylindrical power bank onto a modified syringe, then inserted its tip into the female Luer lock of a multi-pole needle. A series of clockwise rotations secured the needle hub. Preparing to fill the contraption, the doctor opened a single-dose vaccine vial. He drew the syringe's plunger back, stopping at its red target line. In a fluid motion, he flicked its plastic needle cover into the trash and penetrated the vial's rubber center with the sterile steel point. The plunger was depressed. The vial was flipped upside-down. Air was steadily exchanged for viscous antigenic material within the syringe barrel as its plunger reversed course.

Pushing his stool aside, the doctor rose. The empty vaccine vial and its metal lid fell to the floor. At ground level, remnants of the vial's potential energy were converted into rotational kinetic energy. Slowly, it rolled into Antony's view. Disobeying the doctor's request for silence, he bumbled through the esoteric chemical nomenclature written on its label.

"Tembakoo virus vaccine (Waldo strain). D-2-Amino-5-Phosphonopentanoic Acid & N-[(1-Butyl-2-Pyrrolidinyl) Methyl]-4-Cyano-1-Methoxy-2-Naphthamide."

As Dr. Hooke groped around on his hands and knees, Antony detached his face from the headrest. He propped up his torso using a tucked forearm. "Hey, Doc." He pointed through the facial window. "It's right there."

Ignoring the assistance, Dr. Hooke continued his search.

Antony cleared his throat to increase audibility before reengaging. "It's about four feet to your left."

"Don't you think I know?" Dr. Hooke barked back.

"Of course. But I figured you'd benefit from some redundant information." Antony capped off his snarky reply with a phony laugh.

Upon finding the lid, Dr. Hooke snatched its accompanying vial, then disposed of these materials along with his now-contaminated gloves. Once on his feet, the grumbling began. It continued as he strode across the room to replace his hand protectors. In an effort to defuse the awkwardness, Antony ruptured the unintelligible grousings with a question. "Out of curiosity, what's the purpose of all those ingredients? Inside the vaccine that is."

"Preservatives, stabilizers, adjuvants. They're all

necessary chemical additives that I don't have the time nor desire to discuss with you. This is your final warning. Any more insubordinate outbursts, and you will be physically restrained."

Antony lowered his frame to its previous recumbent position in response to the brusque chiding. Feeling anxious, he racked his imagination for cerebral sanctuary, yet only thoughts filled with anguish percolated to the surface. Equanimity eluded him. His hopes of suppressing the outside world soon fizzled as rubbery protrusions cupped the base of his skull. Dr. Hooke jammed Antony's face into the padded headrest. These tactile sensations bound Antony to the present moment despite his divertible intensions. A deep breath served as the only viable refuge.

The doctor inserted the needle into the refill port of Antony's drug delivery system. As the transdermal multi-pole spike pierced the resealable polymer septum, it split longitudinally. A pair of electrical interconnects emerged from within the insulated needle. Inside the implant, these exposed interconnects made contact with their electrode counterparts to form a conductive path. Electrical current flowed across the needle, through the compressed metallic springs on the baseplate, and into the microchip's battery. A blinking green light on the injector indicated that recharging was underway.

Holding the injection contraption steadily in place, the doctor depressed the syringe plunger. Polysorbate-coated nanobots flooded the implant's main repository. Rotating flagella moved the nanomachines to their preprogrammed reserves. To ensure a controlled forthcoming release, a membrane sealed over each reserve upon reaching capacity. Ten seconds later, the plunger bumped up against the barrel's ribbed stopper. The doctor scrunched the stopper with one final thrust to expel any remaining nanobots.

The simultaneous transfer of electrons and inoculation substance was an utterly unpleasant experience. Throughout the procedure, patients endured a spinal strain akin to an inept masseuse performing a deep tissue kneading. Antony's mastication muscles involuntarily clenched. His teeth gnashed together, paralleling the hands of time grinding to a subjective halt.

Eventually, the injector's charging light turned solid. The doctor withdrew the needle from the refill port. Instinctively, Antony's jaw relaxed as the tension on his cervical vertebrae eased. The doctor knelt down to discard his gloves as well as the used needle. He grabbed the tablet off the floor, then hustled over to the cabinets to return supplies. The procedure had reached its conclusion. The treatment chair's upright position was restored, and the examination room's door gradually opened.

Dr. Hooke rotated his shoulders to squeeze through the partially opened doorway. He blurted out a valediction from the hallway: "Exit to your right. Have a good day."

The room was empty by the time Antony had spun around. In appreciation of this solitudinous moment, he bowed his head and took an opportunity to reflect.

Preservation for the human race had been attained, but was this merely ephemeral? How long before mankind would face its next existential threat?

Antony rhythmically ran his middle finger back and forth across his cervical spine while mulling over these questions. Beginning at the base of his skull, his finger traveled down the left perimeter of the microchip, over its edge, and then down his last two vertebral ridges. His finger moved horizontally upon reaching his thoracic spine junction. Reversing course, he traversed the right side of the implant on his way back to the starting point. As he ruminated over the elaborate game of immunological cat and mouse, humanity's ever evolving defensive blueprint was deployed internally. Inside his drug delivery system, current was applied to the membrane of reserve number one. When its seal melted, the first wave of nanobots was released into his anatomy.

"Another mutation," he muttered aloud. "How many has it been?"

Previous visits to the immunization center blended together within his mind. Efforts at enumerating all the prior appointments proved to be a fruitless exercise. More than five, less than fifteen—he established the range with little confidence and without further attempts of refinement. Rising from the treatment chair with a shrug, he dismissed the musings as inconsequential.

All that mattered at the present was that there was a

viral barrier being forged by his immune system. Fortunate feelings flushed through his core upon conceiving of an alternative reality. Devoid of medical advancements, infectious agents would have ravaged the population without clemency to the point of extinction. In this parallel universe, life existed in a persistent state of suffering. Blessed were the beings sheathed in scientific safeguards during these hazardous times. His facial muscles contracted, tugging the corners of his lips upward, rumpling the skin that covered the outside edges of his eye sockets.

Propelled by a jaunty gait, Antony descended the immunization center's collection of pedestrian pathways adorning a Duchenne smile. Unruffled by the crowd, his pupils bounced randomly from the people passing by into the chaos below. Cheerfulness permeated his steps as he traveled across the translucent walkways.

On the final escalator, he blew blithe whistles through his puckered lips. His roving sightline settled on a couple several steps ahead. The young lovebirds had their hands affectionately tucked into the other's back pockets. They picked up on Antony's tune and chimed in with musical accordance. Only upon hearing their harmonious hums did Antony recognize that he was the source of the impromptu vocalizations. He carried on whistling. The couple spun around baring grins of approval upon disembarking the escalator.

On the ground floor, Antony glided across the Grand Appointment Hall. Roughly a hundred paces from the revolving egress, a black-and-white striped Z entered his visual field. His forward motion ceased. As if self-administering a sobriety test, he recited the alphabet in reverse while his eyes swept over the multicolored station labels. Midway through, triggered by the sight of the neon-orange N, the mental dexterity exercise came to an abrupt termination. Transfixed by the Latin letter, his hazel irises traced the sharp contours of the consonant.

Antony's joyous, unconcerned state was impaled by inexplicable forlornness. Incipient tears developed as he tantalizingly grasped at the underlying memories inducing this ambivalent condition. Within his mind's eye, the scene from a year prior was replayed with the clarity of a vastly overexposed film. Mnemosyne bathed him in the river Lethe, cleansing the painful past with the waters of forgetfulness. He lacked the details necessary for comprehension. The hazy recollection failed to provide insight.

Unable to trace the emotional causation, Antony's intense gloom drifted away. The serenity he derived from safety returned. With a sanguine disposition, his departure from the immunization center resumed. Each step was a privilege. Once outside, the water molecules within his exhalation condensed upon colliding with the cold air. Each breath was a blessing. He turned around to once more admire the marvelous facade of the Eastlake Immunization Center. All thanks given to Pansophical.

CHAPTER EIGHT

Antony peregrinated through the city with a delighted countenance on this chilly February evening. In his post-vaccinated state, a sense of hope freed him from the psychological hold of the Tembakoo virus. The world was born anew. Extinction concerns were reclassified as overblown paranoia. Travails arising from the pestilence were recognized as a collective burden to bear. Optimistic in the face of this communal struggle, he moved with his head high. The interactive adaptations that emerged from group living roused the social animal. He smiled and nodded politely at his fellow citizens as they passed by.

A tug of war between distrust and the innate desire for inclusion was on display during these fleeting interactions. More often than not, Antony's newfound affinity for mankind was reflected back through a carnival mirror. The affable grins he flashed were seemingly scrutinized for clues of treason. Masked strangers contorted their bodies away while appearing to study his warm demeanor for signs of infection. Again and again, his benign salutes were distorted by cynicism.

In contrast to the mistrustful majority, the mirthful minority reciprocated his acknowledgments of a shared existence with various pleasantries. Although few and far between, these congenial responses deepened his jollity. Each tiny gesture served as a spindle within his web of perceived connectedness.

Sprightly steps moved Antony down paved footpaths on his return to Sanctuary Village Apartments. A half hour away from his destination, the scrumptious aroma of a brick oven pizza activated his odorant sensory cells. On the following block, the delectable scents of smoked barbeque entered his nasal cavity. The smorgasbord of savory smells continued. At the journey's midpoint, across the street from the newsstand he had patronized earlier, sweet briny odors wafted out from the kitchen of the highly lauded restaurant Tidal. These irresistible aromas elevated his desire for food beyond the inactivity threshold. The bombardment of his orthonasal olfactory pathways incited a faint tingling sensation within his stomach.

In front of Tidal's recessed storefront, Antony changed his trajectory. Along the cobbled entryway, his path split the brass posts that supported the eatery's aqua-colored, half-barrel awning. An illuminated menu case was attached to its elegant wood-planked exterior. Inside, on vintage parchment, a list of dishes that epitomized freshness was presented to patrons in flowing cursive. Through athirst eyes, he browsed the catches of the day.

"Sambal honey-glazed king salmon with a cucumber watercress salad." Antony's salivary glands were stimulated as he subvocalized the entrées. "Tortilla-crusted halibut with Portobello mushrooms and wilted arugula." Each mouthwatering option sounded more appealing than the previous. "Garlic butter–roasted Dungeness crab with grilled asparagus."

Near the end of his perusal of the literally priceless menu, he removed his wallet to assess his financial situation. The paltry pecuniary sum that remained from his purchase of *The People's Voice* had been consigned to oblivion. Two bancor bills. Antony glowered at these tangible experiential impediments. He put his wallet away. His visual field moved into the temple of gastronomy.

Crustacean-inspired light fixtures casted the interior of Tidal in a bluish glow. Dressed in dapper royal-blue satin vests, the waitstaff bustled through the restaurant at the epicurean whims of the diners. On a raised private alcove, the sommelier primed the stemware for a party of Pansophical regional directors. These esteemed men and women conspicuously advertised their positions within the corporate hierarchy through their black double-breasted blazers, white-and-black-striped dress shirts, and solid-white ties. The sommelier beamed with satisfaction while completing the sophisticated ritual of seasoning their crystal glassware. Before she filled their glasses with proper pours, smidgens of wine were swirled and subsequently discarded. Antony's sightline floated away from the premier table. Low-level bureaucrats wearing Pansophical lapel pins filled the main dining area. Atop crisply ironed tablecloths, polished steel dome plate covers were lifted to reveal decorative displays of culinary perfection. Demeanors of delectation packed all corners of the luxurious establishment.

"Tasty temptations," Antony said with a snicker. He turned to face the aquiline-nosed maître d' who stood at the outdoor host station. "Promise, I won't pester you with questions about prices. But if you had to choose among the entrées, what offers the best bang for your bancor?"

"Sir, this isn't a place for bargains. But I can personally attest that all of our chef's creations are divine." The maître d' enthusiastically flipped open the reservation book with a pen in hand. "Would you like to make a reservation? We have lunch openings at the end of next month. And we're accepting dinner reservations starting in May."

"Mmmmmm. After one whiff of those heavenly smells, I've decided where I want my last meal. Regrettably, I could barely afford the complementary breadbasket. To say that this place is beyond my means would be a—"

"Say no more. Allow me to recommend our sister restaurant. It's much more affordable. The Marine Room, located on pier 70. Have you been?"

"Nope, never heard of it." His voice tapered off as he returned his attention to the satiated expressions on the opposite side of the window.

"Oh, you must go. Same daily catches as here with a Mediterranean twist. The whole fusion concept was the brainchild of our master chef's protégée. Let me tell you, the food is absolutely to die for! Order the Valencian seafood paella, and I guarantee you won't be disappointed. Their menu this week is something else. See for yourself."

The maître d' exuded the genial mien of a quintessential hospitality employee. As he completed his bona fide sales pitch, he removed a leather casebound menu from inside the host station, then extended it in Antony's direction. Engrossed within a fantasy of a sumptuous feast, Antony only perceived fragments of the accommodating suggestion. Despite being unaware of the contents of the handoff, he graciously accepted the outstretched item.

Antony slowly dragged his fingertips over the branded logo that adorned the bill of fare's smooth natural grain. Before he had an opportunity to skim the menu of enticing comestibles, his focus shifted to the approaching shrieks of excitement to his rear. A pint-sized child in a patched denim jacket raced toward the restaurant. In lumpish pursuit, his family's matriarch followed him down the cobblestoned path.

"Geema, Geema, look! It's the chairman!"

The child's prominent faux hawk smashed into the restaurant's central window like a hapless bird hoodwinked by the reflection of alluring foliage. Foamy hair product residue bespattered the immaculate glass at the point of impact. The unexpected mishap ignited Antony's incongruity instincts. In ill-concealed amusement, he reflexively giggled. Meanwhile, inside the opulent eatery, visages of widened eyes and cavernous mouths probed the establishment's exterior for the source of the thwack. In the aftermath of the disturbance, the maître d' scrambled to pacify the guests. He faced the startled diners with an exaggerated smile, then formed a pair of circles by connecting his index fingers and thumbs in a gesture of assurance. Once normalcy returned, he crouched and began cleaning the mousse-splattered storefront.

The transparent obstacle allowed the lumbering guardian to catch up with her fleet-footed grandson. "Lew-bug, how many times have I told you not to run away from Geema?"

The rattled boy frantically sniffled to repress the onset of tears.

"Little troublemaker." The rugose woman removed her hands from her fur-trimmed down coat and affectionately tousled his hair. "Did you hurt your noggin?"

Soothed by the gesture, the discombobulated boy regained his composure. Seconds later, his shrill hysteria recommenced. "Holy moly! It's the chairman! It's the chairman!"

"Go easy, I remember. We saw the chairman on TV this afternoon."

"That was before, Geema. Now the chairman is here!" The child rapturously bounced up and down while pointing at the exalted Pansophical directors. "Can you believe it? He's right there!"

The hooded-eyed woman followed the emphatic hand signal of the young carrier of her lineage. At the sight of the dining party's alternating white-and-black attire, her hyperpigmented face unfolded in incredulousness. After a series of blinks, she turned to the maître d'. With dubiety, she replicated the pointing gesture and asked for confirmation.

"Excuse me, my vision isn't what it once was. Is that … the chairman?"

"No, madam, you're mistaken." The maître d' put down his rag. "Chairman Fields has only dined at Tidal on one occasion. And he's not here today. Is there anything else I can help you with? Would you like to book a res —"

"No, no, no," the charged child contended. "Look harder, Geema! It's the chairman. He's right over there! Do you see him?"

In an animated outburst, the youngster once again guided the sightlines of the disbelieving adults. This time, he left smeared fingerprints all over the window. As the maître d' contrived an expression of happiness, he picked up his spray bottle and directed his efforts at removing these fresh oily impurities.

Antony chimed in. "Contrary to appearances, that's not Chairman Fields."

"See, Lew-bug. That's not him."

"Those men and women," Antony explained, "are in fact the directors for the Pacific Territories of North America. Look closely. The color scheme of their clothing is the exact opposite as those worn by the executive committee."

"Well would you look at that?" said the grandmother. "It's so obvious when you know what to look for. The white tie should have been a dead giveaway." She paused, twinkles materializing in her eyes. "Even though it's not the chairman, I'd love to personally thank each and every one of those directors for all that they've done for our fine city. Where would the world be without the Pansophical Corporation?"

Accepting this displeasing reality, the child's fascination with the diners faded away. An energy transfer between the familial generations was sparked. While the younger was drained of his frantic excitement, an energetic buzz seemed to be incited within his ancestor.

The boy jejunely spun away from the untidiness he had spawned and reached for the hand of his guardian. "Come on, Geema."

Retreating up the cobbled pathway, the child yanked at the arm of his star-struck grandparent. In admiration of her corporate sovereign, she stepped in the opposite direction, toward Tidal's entrance. The human chain between descendants was severed as his youthful phalanges slipped through their withered counterparts. Seizing hold of the restaurant's coral-shaped door pull, she leaned backward, employing her body weight to gain entry.

The maître d' leapt to his feet and scuttled over. "Sorry, madam." He debarred the idolizing intruder by placing his palm flat upon the door. "Only guests with reservations are permitted in the dining area."

Resigned, the woman released the ornamental handle. The weighty barrier slowly shut. "Guess it's all for the best." She strenuously rose up on her tippy-toes and peeked through the door's porthole window. "I'd love to thank them for their public service, but I'd hate to bother them during dinner. We all deserve some peace and quiet now and then."

"Absolutely," the maître d' said. "Well, if you'd like to reserve a table for a future date, we have lunch openings at the end of next month. And we're accepting dinner reservations starting in May."

"No, thanks. I'm actually allergic to seafood. Have a great night."

The fortuitous encounter carved an elated expression on the elder's liver-spotted face. Before reuniting with her grandchild, she bid farewell to the Pansophical higher-ups with a wave. Then the pair disappeared down the sidewalk hand in hand.

Antony's sentiments walked the fine line between envy and admiration. Unpleasant covetousness was evoked when observing the waitstaff's palatial treatment of the Pansophical brass. Through envious eyes, their wealth and prestige served as a measuring stick that explicitly quantified his failings. These corrosive comparisons of self-worth were a stark reminder of his own unfulfilled potential. The grandmother's reverence presented this event through a contrary lens. In adopting her perspective, the notion of the self was nobly surrendered; no comparisons were executed. On this side of the complex emotion, the directors were venerated for their humanitarian contributions. From environmental conservation to rescuing humanity from Tembakoo, the accomplishments of the Pansophical Corporation's overseers were universally recognized as an inspiration.

Compelled by a diffusion of synthetic neurotransmitters, Antony's waffling came to an involuntary end. Emotional duality was vanquished. Of the two affective states, awe was all that remained. In fact, Antony could no longer think of an alternative to admiration.

With a countenance that matched that of the grandmother moments earlier, he peered at the prestigious diners as they dove into a lavish spread of appetizers. Visual and olfactory stimuli alone, however, were unable to supply satiation. Whereas sensations of appetite had lured him to Tidal, it was the biological mechanisms of hunger that mobilized his anatomy and drove him away. A day without ingesting nutrients had left him with an empty stomach, an empty stomach that demanded attention through the employment of gastric contractions. Roaring growls originated from his hollow organ. In the interest of acquiring an affordable meal, his peregrination home resumed.

Through the blackened eventide, Antony ambled forward while imagining his barren refrigerator. Indecision swelled as he considered the numerous eateries available on his route. He evaluated the restaurants he passed with an inverted touchstone founded on frugalness.

Along the sidewalk, the lowering of security trellises marked the end of retail business hours. As these deterrents of theft extinguished interior store lights, surveillance cameras throughout the metropolis gained prominence. Antony glanced upward. He smiled in acknowledgment of Pansophical's omnipresent vigilance. For the city's inhabitants, the blinking red lights provided an unceasing source of psychological comfort.

Reluctant to reverse course, nourishment options were whittled away with each of Antony's steps. Only two fast food restaurants remained from his original list of extensive possibilities. Outside the Asian eatery Silk Road, he caught a glimpse of the unmistakable headgear of his building superintendent through a row of bamboo stalks. He quickened his footpace. If presented with a choice between starvation and another interaction with the intolerable Luis, he would have enthusiastically embraced the famine. Irresolution along the journey placed him at the entrance of Om Nom Nom. Through the agency of time, indecision in and of itself was a decision.

Outside the restaurant, rambunctious children bounced around the solar system using augmented reality trampolines. Other youngsters chased haptic holograms of iconic cartoons through varicolored tubes in games of tag.

"Welcome, Antony Sartori."

The mechanical greeting when Antony entered was scarcely audible over the whimsical whoops arising from the playground. Fantastical creatures splattered the walls of the dining area. Depicted in a vibrant manga style, these anthropomorphized beasts shoveled food down their throats. Under a wondrous turquoise canopy of foxfire fungi-fashioned lights, customers duplicated the hoggish actions of the spray-painted characters that surrounded them. The outrageously successful franchise had monopolized the family-friendly restaurant market with its combination of thrifty meals, gigantic portions of 3D-printed food, and a playful atmosphere that appealed to all ages.

Antony's buoyant mood experienced an updraft as his quest to quell hunger neared completion. He sashayed across the room in the direction of an empty table. The posh environment of the highly-reputed Tidal was a distant memory; the bizarre pageantry that defined Om Nom Nom tickled the fancy of his inner child. He flashed delighted grins at families indulging joyously. In the far corner, away from the hubbub of the playground, he dragged out a rainbow-bespattered steel chair and gave his feet a rest.

Cameras along the perimeter of the smart table identified the placement of the seated diner. The size and orientation of the visual display then responsively adjusted. Under a resilient layer of alumina-loaded glass, outlandish cartoons frolicked around the textual jungle. They tempted penny-pinchers with discounts. Antony's field of vision scanned the comestible categories on the wafer-thin interactive tabletop. He playfully jabbed at a feathered critter yo-yoing a coupon from its talon. At the last moment, it dodged the incoming attack and ensconced itself behind the desserts heading. Several more attempts to secure a reduction in cost followed, all of which ended with the pad of his index finger probing unoccupied pixels. With the shrug of his shoulders, he brushed off his deficient reactionary speeds.

"Now," he rhetorically muttered, "what shall I eat?"

Cuisines from regions far and wide made up the restaurant's vast menu. When dining at Om Nom Nom, customers confronted the paradox of choice head-on. Patrons counterbalanced the subjective benefits of abundant options against analysis paralysis. Seeking assistance with the selection process, Antony surveyed the contents of neighboring tables. An appetence for a burger developed within him, rendering the self-contradictory phenomenon of over-choice immaterial. In a matter of seconds, he customized a bacon cheeseburger to his liking and added a combo meal to his shopping cart. He licked his lips at the sight of his culinary concoction. There it was, a high-resolution image of three medium-well beef patties slathered in sweet barbeque sauce, topped with smoked Gouda cheese and caramelized onions, and sandwiched between two toasted buns. Transferring his body weight to his left buttock, he removed his wallet from his back pocket, then inserted a 20B bill into the smart table. Once the order was placed, a live kitchen-cam popped up to provide him with a front-row seat to his meal preparation.

Through a rotating nozzle, a layer of laboratory-grown

beef was ejected from a stainless steel bio-cartridge onto a scorching flattop grill. After the production of the first patty, the additive manufacturing process was repeated. Simultaneously, gelatinous vegetable globules dripped from tapered tubes to form his french fry side dish.

Antony's agog stare drifted from images of systematized food assembly to the abutting timer. Three minutes and 47 seconds. His focus narrowed onto the ones digit of the display. In an illusion of chronostasis, the 7 appeared frozen. He blinked. He blinked again. The numeral failed to progress. In an effort to speed up the perception of time, he separated himself from the video stream and approached the pickup cubbies along the rear wall.

Sounds of sizzling meats, hissing deep fryers, whining stepper motors, and whirling fans seeped through the acoustic panels that lined the natural-wood cubbyholes. Antony peered into the automatized culinary workshop. In an exhibition of organized chaos, an array of ceiling-mounted robotic arms prepared and precisely combined ingredients. Raw materials appeared from seemingly nowhere before being transformed into palatable meals through the application of heat. Whereas the live stream supplied each guest with a step-by-step look at the creation of their order, the kitchen as a whole resembled the stream of consciousness of a gluttonous madman.

Spinning away from the dizzying demonstration of food fabrication, Antony espied a pair of diners near the entrance.

A frail senior citizen with a half-lidded look licked the tip of his index finger. He scrounged up potato morsels from a checkered cardboard tray utilizing his wet digit. Across the table, his younger chubby companion removed a cobweb of melted cheese from his ducktail beard with a disposable moist towelette. In unison, the two men breathed sighs of repletion. Antony took pleasure in witnessing these gratified expressions of humankind.

The chubby one performed a series of steady neck circles as if replicating the revolutions of a pileous planet. He then calmly rose from his chair to assist his older dining partner. In a single movement, he extended an elbow as a mobility aid while placing his opposite plump palm onto the yellow handprint at center of the table.

As the men stepped in the direction of the exit, electrical actuators within the table's legs were activated. The interactive tabletop split apart. Its corners were elevated and inwardly folded to form a funnel. Soiled napkins, compressed balls of insulated foil, and assorted rubbish slid down the inclining surface into a hollow square base. After leveling out and reuniting, the tabletop tilted to a position perpendicular to the ground.

Moments later, an automatic janitor was summoned. The disc-shaped robot detached itself from the bottom of the smart table's base. A damp towel affixed to a telescopic pole emerged from its crest. These concentric tubular sections expanded until the microfiber cloth was flush with the upper edge of the vertical tabletop. The robot shuffled to and fro, wiping down the surface while retracting its tidying extension. Cleaning the floor was next. In the process of spiraling outward, the robotic custodian devoured debris through its frontal opening like a filter-feeding Baleen whale. Once the vicinity was free of waste, the chamois cloth strips that lined its exterior flipped down. Mopping commenced as the robot's spiral pattern was reversed on its way back to the docking station.

Behind a centrally located desk, a twentysomething petite female in a tie-dyed uniform oversaw the establishment's automated operation. Upon noticing Antony loitering around the pickup cubbies, she left her post and approached. "Thank you for choosing Om Nom Nom, where we unleash the feast! What can I do to awesomize your day?"

Pleased to engage in a modicum of casual conversation, Antony brightened. He glanced down at her graffiti-styled name tag.

"Hello there, Mariah, I'm just waiting for my order. I couldn't bear looking at that countdown any longer."

"The waiting is truly the hardest part," she said with a chuckle.

"Indeed, especially when you're famished."

"So, what's the trouble?" Her mousey features perked up as she offered support. "Was your Nom Nom table acting up?"

"Trouble? No trouble at all. I'm merely waiting. If memory serves, there was slightly less than four minutes remaining on my timer when I stood up. Thus, my bacon cheeseburger should be ready ... right ... about ... now!"

Coinciding with the exclamatory punctuation, Antony turned and pointed to an empty cubby in anticlimactic frippery.

"Very impressive," Mariah said, sparking a brief laugh between them.

"Showmanship never was my strength," Antony said. "Anyhow, I anticipate that my food will be ready momentarily."

"If it's not out in the next minute or so, I'll jump into the kitchen and find out what's the holdup. Since we updated our software, we've had orders lost at random. But that wouldn't be your problem being that your cooking timer popped up." Her facial expression conveyed a genuine desire to assist, an unmistakable inclination to please beyond job expectations. "Hmmm, then your problem must have been with one of our apps. Which one was it?"

"Sorry. I couldn't tell you a thing about those apps. I browsed the food menu, then placed my order. That's about all. Personally, I've never experienced complications using anything here."

She slowly nodded, encouraging him to elaborate on the difficulties incurred. "If you weren't having trouble with your Nom Nom table," she said as her narrow brow furrowed, "then why are you waiting over here?"

"I'm merely anxious to eat. And truthfully, I grow weary of staring at screens."

"Come on now." She paused and broke eye contact to observe the behavior of the other diners. "Look how much fun everyone is having!"

"Every once in a while, it's best to distance oneself from the world of digital distractions."

"Pfffft. We offer way more than silly distractions. If I had to guess, I'd say that you're the type of person who enjoys a challenge. Have you played *Escape from Flatland*? The puzzles are super tough. But it's far and away my personal favorite."

"No, I haven't," said Antony. "Strange as it may sound, I've never been overly fond of video games. At the moment I'm more than happy to simply be in the presence of my fellow citizens."

Mariah's diminutive lips separated as she drafted a response. Gradually the corners of her speechless mouth broadened, leaving behind a quizzical smile. Before Antony had an opportunity to further impart his preferences, she took a short step away. A malfunctioning table at the far end of the dining room appealed to her sense of responsibility. Unable to return to its standard horizontal position, the furniture called for attention by way of a pulsating red screen.

"Surprise, surprise," Mariah said as she rolled her drab eyes. "At least once a day some practical joker jams something into a Nom Nom table during its cleanup sequence. It's only a matter of time before I catch one of them in the act. And when I do, they'll be on the wrong end of a gnarly scolding!"

Antony squinted. "Appears … from here … that a cup is the culprit."

"It could be. More often than not, though, it's a bundle of forks or spoons. Okie dokie, duty calls. Come back soon for another serving of awesome sauce!"

"Will do. Have a great night."

Following the farewell, Antony's sight line tracked Mariah across the restaurant. She knelt next to the crying piece of technology and used her bent forearm to prop up its tabletop. With her off hand, she reached for the obstruction. The device returned to operational status once freed of the blockage. Upon shuffling out from underneath, she smirked in Antony's direction and raised a fistful of beige utensils overhead. Antony acknowledged the gesture with a disapproving headshake, then turned toward the mechanized kitchen. A soft drink along with a meal box waited for him in cubbyhole twenty-eight. There was a sketch of a kooky creature popping though the variegated Om Nom Nom logo on the eco-friendly clamshell container. Thrilled that supper was within reach, he heartily plucked these items from the compartment and hustled back to his table.

Sensors on both the biodegradable bagasse container and the disposable cup communicated the meal's contents to Antony's smart table. A window popped up on the interactive display adjacent to each physical object. Inside, nutritional information and assorted tidbits about ingredients were provided. Antony inserted a straw through the paper cup's clear lid, then promptly applied a smidgen of pressure to the tab lock of his meal box. The irresistible aroma of salty deep fried potatoes escaped when the container sprung open. Instinctively, he consumed a handful of the starchy side dish prior to washing it down with his sweet carbonated beverage. He expelled a refreshing breath from his chapped lips. Cherry cola–related info reappeared once he placed the drink back down. His visual field skirted its nutritional content in favor of a list with pictures of antioxidant-rich fruits.

At the sight of a mottled Rainer cherry, Antony's irises drifted to the upper-left regions of their respective scleras. A memory of Dominique's most cherished achievement as chief transportation officer entered his mind. Snatched from the fringes of the recollection, he echoed her words in a mumbled trance.

"Dare to dream. Boldly believe. Today's opening of the Evergreen Line personifies these words for myself. Welcome aboard!"

Antony's chain of thought united disparate scenes from years prior. Ceremonial scissors snipped a red ribbon to kick off the inaugural trip through the foothills of glacier-capped Mount Rainier. Freshly laid Hyperloop tracks penetrated the pristine wilderness in a synthesis of resplendent technology and the paradisiac outdoors. An afternoon with Dominique had been spent wandering through the bountiful orchids of a quaint Yakima Valley town. Hand in hand they filled wicker gathering baskets with plump, ripe cherries. The remembrance concluded with an evening of cuddling while gorging on fleshy drupes.

Fractions of a second later, the fantasy from bygone days receded into nihility. The doors to the nostalgic factory were closed as internal insurrectionists spit cherry pits into the works. Mimicking low-density lipoproteins, nanobots within Antony's cranium circumvented his blood-brain barrier. They navigated through the hub of his central nervous system with the purpose of simulating retrograde amnesia. Antagonistic substances were precisely released at relevant NMDA receptors. These infused chemicals obstructed binding sites within the dorsal regions of his hippocampus and his posterior parietal cortex. Targeted neuroreceptors were deactivated. Memory reconsolidation stalled. The machinery of Antony's mind was mangled like the handiwork of disgruntled luddites. His episodic memories of that special day ceased to exist.

Coinciding with the onset of a yawn, Antony's transitory dissociation from his immediate surroundings came to an end. He stifled his body's temperature regulation mechanism by means of several gulps of fizzy beverage. Thoughts pertaining to the prelapsarian recollection became imponderable as the present was restored. Its dismissal from the mind extended beyond the reverie's content into the sheer occurrence of the daydream.

He gleefully observed the interplay of the other diners while satisfying his own biological requirements for survival. After relishing a final bite, he rose from his seat with a gratified countenance and initiated the Nom Nom table's cleanup routine. Unconditional satisfaction had been achieved within his truncated hierarchy of needs. Physiological necessities, belongingness, safety—all requisites were fulfilled; nothing more could be desired.

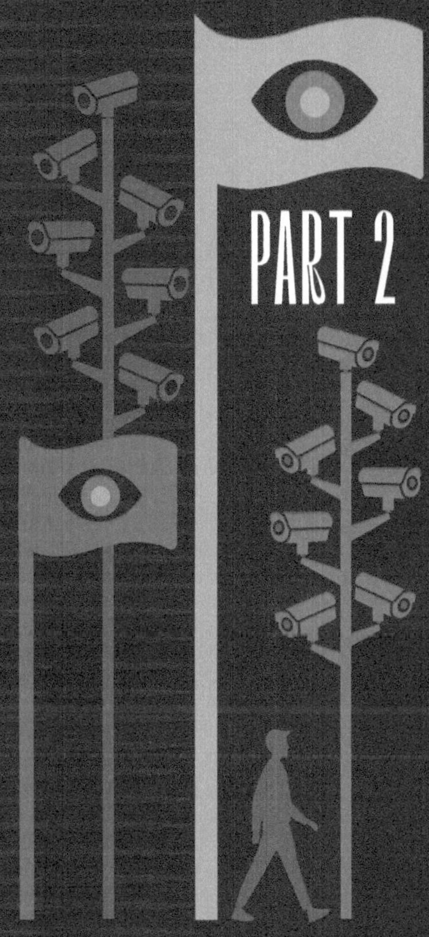
PART 2
MONDAY OCTOBER 9, 2084

CHAPTER NINE

A hangover scrambled Antony's wake-up routine. A greasy breakfast and a jaunt to the newsstand followed his belated start to the day. The afternoon awaited. At the moment, however, the sports section of *The People's Voice* was causing further delays. What began as productive multitasking now consisted of him chewing on toothbrush bristles while scribbling along the margins of preseason box scores. Hygienic tasks executed in concurrence with light reading devolved into a formulaic analysis of the upcoming Zero-G basketball season. After twenty minutes of model tweaking, a cramped hand forced him to relinquish his ballpoint pen. As the writing utensil rolled down his palm and across the bathroom vanity, he assessed the quality of his brainstorming session. Satisfied with these newly conceptualized independent variables, he tore out the page of scratch-work, tossed the newspaper into the wastebasket, then recommended brushing.

Glancing up from the spume-smeared sink, Antony located the date on the smart mirror's integrated calendar.

An appointment with Dr. Winfield at 16:30 today was his lone obligation for the week. His peeved expression reflected through the chronological register. A disconnect between himself and his psychologist had developed as of late. Identical topics were rehashed one session after the next. If Antony had his way, these appointments would have been terminated months ago, but his Prosperity Dividend was contingent upon attendance. Compulsion overrode disinclination. He strode down the hallway with his newsprint notes in hand. These jottings were added to the top of a kitty-cornered stack of similar quantitative adjustments, and into the streets he went.

Streams of juveniles, freshly discharged from scholarly captivity, appeared upon Antony's path. The gossiping boys and girls outside Gates Middle School seemed oblivious to the adult invading their territory. A pint-sized schoolboy with a crew cut and a braided rattail sprinted through the mass exodus. The boy waved his arms overhead in every which way like a weather vane within a capricious wind tunnel. Without slowing down, he ran through the upcoming intersection well after the traffic light had changed. Antony stopped on the corner. While awaiting permission from the pedestrian crosswalk signal, his gaze drifted to the commotion developing on the schoolyard.

Through ponderous footsteps, a freckled, fair-skinned youngster crossed the pitcher's mound of a neglected baseball diamond. Loosely held sand particles leapt into the air as his wheat-colored waterproof boots agitated the landscape. Laborious strides through the dandelion-and-crabgrass-encrusted infield were accompanied by frantic gasps for oxygen. From under his partially zipped, orangey-red sweatshirt, jiggling adipose tissue freed itself from the garment's taut elastic band. Rolls of fat frolicked in the open during his toilsome dash. He circled the backstop and peered through the openings of the rusty chain-link fence. His countenance blanched. Pulling himself as close as possible to the impending threat, his small snub nose poked through the woven threads of galvanized steel. From one classmate to the next, his eyes bounced. Hollering in derogatory discordance, twelve adolescent figures entered the outfield.

"Slow down, cream puff, we just want to talk!"

"Bwok bwok, bwok bwok, chicken!"

"Double-crossing pansy!"

"Climb, Kennard, climb." The alpha of the pack's sarcastic words of encouragement overwhelmed the offensive vocalizations of the others. Apparently unperturbed by the chilly day, the stout teenager wore a silver-colored T-shirt with a black double-pointed oval imprinted upon his chest. In the center of this eye-shaped ellipse, "Pan-Youth" exploded from the negative space in a stencil font. Potholes blanketed his forehead like a neglected highway. A dark, straggly mustache underlined his crooked nose. Among his peers, these telltale signs of puberty set him apart.

Kennard inserted his pudgy fingers into the holes of the

backstop. Lacking an alternative, he followed the derisive instructions and strenuously ascended the chain-link safeguard. While ideal for romping through puddly parcels, his cumbersome footwear impeded his evasive efforts. As the mob closed in, their ridiculing rhetoric turned to hysterical laughter. Near the top of the structure, the ostracized child hung precariously in the air, legs kicking wildly, unable to secure footing. Two beanpoles, identical twin girls in black-and-white striped shirts, tumbled to the ground in juvenile guffaw. Schadenfreude rippled through the pack of predators in the form of laugher. In a surge of strength, Kennard pulled himself onto the angled canopy. He crawled about while looking down upon his classmates with an expression of dread.

"Death to Praxis," the Pan-Youth leader bellowed, "the people are united!" The rest of the adolescent assemblage zealously followed suit. "Death to Praxis, the people are united!"

Once in harmony, the mantra resonated throughout the neighborhood. Drawn to the overt display of Pansophical flag-waving, a group of older teens in letterman jackets shed their skins of indifference. The generation of tomorrow congregated around the fenced-off school grounds. A few of the high schoolers observed in silence. The majority joined the chant in adherence to the underpinnings of global identity. Allegiances, forged by the subconscious human desire for acceptance, obscured the line between the individual and the group.

"Death to Praxis, the people are united!" The radius of intrigue on the streets expanded reciprocally with the chant's decibel level. "Death to Praxis, the people are united!"

Caught up in the excitement, Antony's legs incited locomotion. He moved to improve his view of the brewing hostile happenings.

Alarmed by the gradual swell in posterior voices, Kennard stood and turned his back on his antagonizing schoolmates. His corpulent face contorted with fear at the sight of the growing bellicosity. Clamors of condemnation arose from an unrecognizable mass of jingoes. Kennard's eyes shifted back and forth between these older spectators on the outskirts of the schoolyard and the fanatical hatemongers who were responsible for thrusting him into the perilous limelight. Around and around, he spun in place like a glassy-eyed top.

On the chain-link stage, the ancient rites honoring Dionysus were reproduced for all to enjoy. Kennard played the lead in the performance. When his circular motion ceased, he clumsily collapsed onto the overhang. The stress from his movements warped the checkerboard grid. Desperation chiseled the young boy's malleable soft features. Indecipherable pleas from the elevated perch fell on unsympathetic ears. His strangled cries for assistance were drowned out by the audience. "Death to Praxis, the people are united!"

Down below, three hooded schoolboys left the field of play. Pan-Youth logos adorned their silver sweatshirts. They exuberantly chanted while skipping in the direction of the oak trees that flourished along the fence line. Upon entering foul territory, the trio of rabble-rousers scooped up acorns like foraging squirrels preparing for a harsh winter. Each returned to the infield with overflowing pockets of leathery seed casings.

Kennard zigged and zagged in an effort to dodge the aerial assault of oak nuts. One after another, his classmates stepped up to home plate and partook in this carnivalesque competition. Hit the target, win the coveted prize of admiration. Acorns ricocheted off the latticework at all angles. Those embryonic projectiles that flew by unimpeded landed back near their barky creators. Sporadically, one reached its intended target only to bounce off his cotton polyester armor. His classmates soon became discouraged by their imprecision and abandoned their single-shot approach. They fired handfuls of acorns simultaneously in a rhapsodic shelling. Kennard's random movements were rendered ineffective. A hailstorm pummeled his unprotected face as the arbor armory emptied. He curled up into a fetal position and began to whimper uncontrollably.

Antony's pupils exited the stage and grazed across the pluralistic approval of the onlookers. Silence had replaced the uproarious shouts proclaiming in-group fidelity. The unblinking eyes of the bystanders feasted on the percolating tragedy. Captivated countenances capitulated to a culture of conformity. Responsibility was diffused, consent was granted through muted voice boxes. Antony took several slow, percipient steps away from the mesmerized flock. Intragroup and intergroup dynamics wrestled for superiority within the squared circle of his neomammalian cortex.

In anxious contemplation, his lips twisted as he nibbled on his woolen collar.

"Mommy and Daddy weren't terrorists," Kennard cried. "Public Safety took them away in the middle of the night. But they never hurt nobody. They never did anything wrong."

"Oh yeah," said the Pan-Youth leader, "then why were they labeled dangers to humanity?"

"Not so. Not so. That never happened."

"Sure it didn't. It must've all been in my imagination. Except ... that ... I remember their names. We all do! Janelle Lafayette, Marcus Lafayette, dangers to humanity, one and the same."

"I remember them too. Mommy and Daddy meant everything to me." Kennard's feeble, callow defense leaked out between snivels. "They were the best. Mommy and Daddy weren't part of Praxis. And neither am I."

The watery remonstration against the immoral characterization of the Lafayettes failed to convince the jury of his peers. One by one, the members of the Pan-Youth tribe set forth their indictments.

"Last week I caught Kennard giggling during a moment of silence for fallen citizens."

"This morning he didn't stand for the 'Hymn to Solidarity.'"

"Why does he always sneak off during the chairman's addresses?

"Why does he always wear orange after Praxis attacks?"

"Why else? The little traitor is taunting us!"

"Remove the mask of innocence, Kennard. It won't save you!" Akin to a budding athlete who mimics the mechanics and mannerisms of a Hall of Famer, the leader of the jingoistic troop aped the movements and piercing oration of Sergeant Bannister. He pointed at his hooded Pan-Youth deputies, then up in the direction of the helpless object of their hunt.

Following the orders of the alpha wolf, the three betas once again skipped into foul territory. With their obstinate eyes on their porky prey, they intermingled their fingers into the steel fabric of the backstop. On the count of three, they shook the structure with all their might.

Kennard buried his face into his knees. "I miss Mommy and Daddy," he squealed. "I'm lost without them. It's not fair."

"Let me tell you what's not fair. The life of Noriko." The leader turned toward his wolf pack and placed his hand on the shoulder of a scrawny girl with butterscotch skin. In sub-mission, the omega wolf raised her disproportionally large head to his eye level. "Every day after school, Noriko here returns to a home without a dad. A dad that was stolen away from his family while fighting for his fellow man."

"And what about me?" asked Kennard. "I don't have a home anymore. I now sleep on Grandma Honey's couch, all the way across town."

"Boo hoo. There's just one key difference. Noriko's dad was murdered by Praxis scum, murdered by people like your parents!"

"Not so. Not so. Mommy and Daddy never killed anyone."

Kennard unbowed his head and wiped the mucus away from his dripping nostrils. "No matter what, I'll never ever forgive you guys for today."

"No one cares about earning your forgiveness. Blood is on your hands, Kennard! The son will bear the punishment for the sins of the father."

As Kennard's bereaved demeanor rolled into resentment, he straightened his back and relaxed his limbs. "Stupid Pansophical is to blame for everything. It's all their fault. Stupid Pansophical." He pounded on the grated canopy with his fists. "Stupid, stupid Pansophical. I hate them! And I hate all of you!"

Gasps of disapproval arose among the crowd. Kennard's sacrilegious conniption fit cemented his verdict within the communal proceedings.

"There you have it," the Pan-Youth leader said. "Dead Praxis terrorists give birth to future Praxis terrorists."

Antony's innards churned as he weighed whether to intervene. On one side of the balance scale sat the underlying commonalties that flowed through the veins of global citizens. Life under the leadership of the Pansophical Corporation included norms that instilled a hatred of Praxis. He loathed the wicked treasonous organization for undermining society. He despised them for their murderous acts and for threatening Pansophical's prosperous reign.

Across the imaginary pivoted horizontal lever, compassionate arguments for Kennard piled onto the other weighing pan. The system was brought into equilibrium. Driven by empathetic cognitive heedfulness, Antony's field of vision gravitated back to the perilous performance within the theater of reality. Social responsibly called from the hilltops of civilized society. The outsider's unenviable plight gnawed on Antony's conscience.

A chain-link swing gate down the third base line caught his eye. He slowly walked in that direction. As more people assembled on the outskirts, the bystander effect was amplified, diminishing the probability of outside assistance. A feat was required, but Antony had hoped that another companionate citizen would answer the burdensome bell. Racing thoughts of entering the out-group galloped through his head. The need to love, to be loved, and to belong weighed heavily on the minds of Homo sapiens.

Action brewed on the field of play. The hooded threesome ended their pointless ruffling of the backstop and embarked upon their next phase of torment. One of them started to climb, and the other two followed closely behind. They nimbly closed the gap between themselves and their adversary. Upon arriving at the top of the galvanized structure, the blooming elements of rancor formed a semicircle around their cornered classmate. Kennard pushed off the steel lattice, elevating his body into a crablike posture. He scurried away as quickly as his chucky legs would permit.

Traumatic memories of Antony's run-in with Public Safety flashed within his hippocampus. Mirror neurons activated, intrinsically linking his inner emotional world with Kennard's precarious predicament. Onerous distress ended Antony's contemplation. Urgency transformed him from spectator of the melodrama to participant. He lifted the fork latch to the ballfield, swung open the gate, then in a shambled trot headed toward home plate.

Just as his foot crossed the chalky remnants of a foul line, a dull thud shook the infield. Gravity pulled Kennard's body back to the planet. The Pan-Youth pack howled in unison like an arena of boxing enthusiasts after a devastating knockout. While the hooded boys admired their savage handiwork from above, the ground force aggressively closed in on their wounded prey. The instincts of the herd replaced centralized instruction. Collective behavior came in the form of a flurry of punches and kicks. The inflamed youngsters hurled their blunt extremities with the sole purpose of inflicting physical suffering. Prepubescent fists and footwear pummeled the fetal mass. In the tumbleweeds of a primitive assault, Kennard's innocence was lost.

Antony raced across the pitching mound in a faltering sprint. "Stop! Break it up! Get off him, you animals!"

Signals originating from Antony's hypothalamus sent a surge of testosterone throughout his lean physiognomy. Like a rescue worker tossing aside debris upon detecting a feeble whisper, he disposed of the nearest assailants. The broomstick twins were the first to feel his old-man strength. In a frantic state, he grasped a handful of each girl's striped fleece from behind, then yanked the monozygotic pairing to the ground. The sisters fell backward in a twisting motion with their legs trapped under their body weight. Their entwined bodies mirrored the helical inheritance packed within their matching chromosomes.

"I said ... break it up!"

Antony emphatically took possession of the command through the nominative singular pronoun. "I" acknowledged accountability; "I" signified separation; "I" empowered the creator. His verbal mandate was dampened by the feeding frenzy of the "We."

Minus two members, the pack's trouncing of Kennard continued uninterrupted. Antony swiftly reevaluated the unpredictable malevolence. When odium obscured the channels of linguistic diplomacy, pacification required force. A two-handed push of Noriko transformed the top-heavy child into a peacekeeping projectile. Her asymmetrical face glazed over as she rocketed into her belligerent comrades. Paralleling the explosive pin action of a bowling strike, the initial impact set off a series of collisions through the fervid cohort. The abrupt appearance of a benevolent bystander forced the pack into an unfamiliar position. Unabashed protectors of Pansophical rarely encountered resistance when administering justice. On the school grounds, no student would dare stand up to Pan-Youth. The unofficial paramilitary organization existed unchallenged as the pyramidion within the school social hierarchy.

The onslaught of Kennard was suspended. A quasi-seventh-inning stretch presented Antony with an opportunity to catch his breath. He widened his stance and placed his hands on his hips.

The Pan-Youth members whispered among themselves.

"What the heck?"

"Who is this dude?"

"Why's he sticking his nose in our business?"

They laboriously returned to their feet, then brushed the sand, silt, and clay particles off their clothing. Stains of experience were embodied by these fresh patches of discoloration. Their eyes locked onto a man resolute on supporting the scapegoat.

"Go home." Antony filled his lungs to amplify his voice. "All of you! This ends now."

While Antony had mentally visualized the early stages of the conflict, he now descended into a maelstrom of probability theory. Incalculable variables swirled around his physical reality. The reaction of the bloodthirsty Pan-Youth tribe, the backlash of the crowd—both were innately complex unknowns that could snowball into personal ruination. Antony stayed silent in the hope that his confident display would dissuade reprisal. Age had provided him with a physical advantage, but legitimate authority was absent. In the shadows of his mind, he was keenly aware that a chain reaction, sparked by Pansophical chauvinism, could end with him being pummeled under a swarm of hatred.

The power grab of the spotlight had shaken the pack into a state of unrest. Overwhelmed by jitters, Noriko broke eye contact with Antony. She rubbed her forehead while turning away from the standoff. Abiding by Antony's decisive order, she sprinted toward an open school door. Resembling the foretelling first droplets to seep through a fractured dam, her departure served as the precursor for the water wall. In a full gallop, the twins erased Noriko's head start. They passed their escaping peer on her desperate return to refuge. As the surrenders mounted, spectator excitement evaporated. The crowd dispersed. In short order, all but one child had waved their white flag.

The alpha yelled to his fleeing wolf pack, "Where y'all going? We're just getting started." He faced Antony. His prickled upper lip curled in contempt. "Now, now, what do we ha—"

"Would be wise for you to follow your friends."

"Another member of Praxis slithers to the surface. The days for you and your fellow traitors are numbered, old timer. We, the citizens of Pansophical, won't sit idly by as we're slaughtered from within."

"That's all well and good. However, I'm no member of Praxis. And I don't sympathize with their treachery."

The precocious teenager rolled his eyes. "Yet here you are, putting your neck on the line to protect this worthless pond scum."

"Let's be clear, we live in a civilized society where rights are protected by the rule of law. Regardless of the crime, it's not your place to issue judgment, nor exact punishment. Now go home."

Moaning in misery, Kennard opened his defensive posture with a series of twists and turns.

The Pan-Youth leader's gaze dipped to the squirming corpulence underfoot. "Both of you make me sick." He took aim from above, then hocked a loogie squarely on the forehead of the helpless child.

The indignant action froze Kennard in his place.

"Leave him alone," Antony said. "Guilty or innocent, these show trials are not justice."

"That's where you're wrong. We live in a black-and-white world. Maybe you're part of Praxis, or maybe you're a spineless sympathizer. Either way, if you aren't with us, you're against us!"

Much to Antony's dismay, logic and reasoning were not remedies for the blindness of zealotry. Regardless of rationale, there would be ramifications for defending someone with ties to Praxis. The possibility of appearing on the Pansophical Corporation's radar crippled Antony's conviction. The prospect of another encounter with Public Safety entered his mindscape. Treading water in an ocean of uncertainty, he shifted his weight onto his heels.

"Go on now." The Pan-Youth leader mockingly waved as if shooing away a fly. "There's no shame in admitting when you're wrong. Walk away."

The bully's scoffing remarks allowed him to recapture

his place as king of the jungle gym. What he lacked in age, he made up for with an abundance of experience in the antagonistic arts. Emboldened, he returned his focus to the principal defendant within the people's court. Steered by unbridled malice, the young ruffian took a surly half-step toward the trembling Kennard.

Antony suppressed his internal revaluations as to whether he should have ever responded to the boy's despondent cries for assistance. There was no reversing the arrow of time; the present moment had been stamped by his empathetic intrusion. Abandoning Kennard at this stage of the rescue mission would have defied logic. In too deep to back down, he shifted his balance back to the balls of his feet. A peak on the moral landscape was on the horizon; its path was not paved with the battered bodies of defenseless children.

Leaping over Kennard, Antony inserted himself as a barrier between the assaulter and the assaulted. In this face-to-face standoff, he stood a full head above the Pan-Youth leader. Tangible enmity pervaded the space between them. The youngster puffed out his chest to artificially boost his physical stature. His agitated shallow breaths warmed the air surrounding Antony's throat.

Upon recognizing that a confrontation was imminent, Antony initiated preemptive action. He lunged forward with outstretched arms and bear hugged his foe. In the act of restraining the squirming adolescent, Antony caught a precisely timed head butt directly on his brow bone. Antony's head violently whiplashed. His interlocking hands separated. Following the jarring impact, he stumbled in reverse. Disoriented from the blunt force, unsteady from the backward locomotion, he plopped down in a seated fall. Several paces away, the alpha male remained standing. Akin to bighorn sheep battling for mating rights, the cranium collision ultimately established dominance.

A petite brunette woman walked toward the baseball diamond. "What's going on out here?" she said in an orotund voice.

Struggling through the half-daze, Antony's attention drifted to the approaching figure in the plum-colored dress pants and tweed peacoat. Her presence defused the situation. Antony's flexor tendons called upon his fingers. In completing this curling motion, grains of sand were wedged under his fingernails. He pushed off the earth's surface with his balled fists and returned to his feet. The power-hungry teenager snarled while he changed positions.

"Robert, Robert Owen, you stop this very instant!" As she neared the jingoistic aftermath, her purposeful walk hastened into a jog. "Kennard, it's me, Principal Diebler. I'm here to help." She squatted and spoke softly. "Try not to move. You're going to be all right."

"Help." Kennard groaned deeply and rolled over. "Please help me."

At the sight of Kennard's crimson mask, her angular face recoiled in disgust. She crept backward while appraising the damage to the disfigured victim of human brutality. Burst capillaries flowed without restraint. Kennard's identifiably plump features had been replaced by the irregular discolored knots of a fall gourd.

"Stay calm. Just stay calm." She spoke to her battered student yet simultaneously appeared to reassure herself. "Help is on the way."

From under Principal Diebler's chin-length layered bob, a pair of gold birdcage earrings with diamond-feathered inhabitants swung into view. Low-hanging autumn sunrays refracted through the carbon allotrope. Captivated by the scintillant gemstone, a quatrain bubbled up from the depths of Antony's memory bank and out of his mouth.

"The bars prevent a breakthrough,

yet the caged bird flaps its wings,

despite the scars of old and new,

forever the caged bird sings."

Principal Diebler raised her eyebrows, "Excuse me, sir. Who are you? And what are you doing on my school grounds?"

Antony struggled to access the information from events long forgotten. "Fifth grade, Mrs. Bennett."

"Okay. Let's try one question at a time." She rose to her feet. "How about we start with you telling me why you're here?"

"Fifth grade, Mrs. Bennett, second period, English. Poetry recitation final. 'The Caged Bird's Plight.'"

As he rattled off the association, the episodic memory

was fully recalled from the consolidated achieves of his neo-cortex. A brief scene was projected on his mind's eye with verisimilitude. In front of a dry erase board, behind a wooden podium, an eleven-year-old Antony Sartori stood overlooking his silent classmates. Tightly packed rows of chair-desk combos filled the room. Upon receiving a thumbs-up from Mrs. Bennett, he began his presentation. At its conclusion, the sweet sound of applause filled him with satisfaction. Lost in reminiscence, prideful emotions evoked from the past entered the present.

"Okay," Principal Diebler said. "I have no idea what you're talking about. But it appears you have a concussion." Her tender tone could not mask her frustration with the stranger's babblings. "I suggest you seek medical attention. I'm calling Kennard an ambulance."

Stepping away from the frozen battlefield, she reached into her coat pocket, removed a scroll-shaped smartphone, and then unfurled its screen. With the click of a button, its malleable display lost all pliancy and locked into place. She detached an earbud from the base of the columnar electronic. Before putting it to use, she wiped its mushroom-shaped tip on the inside of her blouse. "Of course, no service." She got up on her toes and fruitlessly swung her phone back and forth overhead.

With mobile networks perpetually under cyberattack,

smartphones in general were no better than a Citizen's Radio. After switching her telecommunication device into shortwave mode, she scanned the channels in search of emergency services. Over the airwaves, loyalists openly identified themselves, then took turns divulging their misgivings about friends and foes alike. The assistance Principal Diebler required was found on channel number nine.

"Finally ... Yes, one of my students needs medical attention ... He's breathing and conscious, but he's been badly beaten."

The stranger's spacey-eyes had wandered off into nothingness. Ten feet away, the Pan-Youth leader intently listened to his principal's account of the accident.

"The baseball field at Gates Middle School ... Yes, I'll be here waiting. Thanks." She put away the phone and shifted her focus to the third party of the scuffle. The witch hunts administered by the pugnacious Robert Owen and his Pan-Youth comrades served as a precursory attestation of guilt. She had deduced the gist of what had transpired but sought confirmatory evidence before handling disciplinary matters.

"Robert," she said, beckoning him over. "Tell me what happened to Kennard."

"We both know what happened, Principal Diebler."

"Of course we do. But I want to hear it straight from the horse's mouth."

"Justice has been served in the name of Pansophical. The child of Marcus and Janelle Lafayette lies before you. He is destined to follow in the murderous footsteps of his parents.

We will carry out our revenge through the bloodlines of every last terrorist until Praxis is no more."

Through a lens of consequentialism, the details evaporated into a mist of irrelevancy. Robert's self-incriminating account made no attempt to mislead. His deportment transformed from that of an unconstrained aggressor to a respectful pragmatist.

Principal Diebler nodded in acceptance, reluctantly appreciative of those who wielded an iron fist. Thoughts of condemnation clashed with her opinions regarding the societal need for security.

"Suspicious behavior is to be reported to the authorities." She uncomfortably cleared her throat. "We've spoken about this, have we not?"

"Yes. Yes we have."

"I understand your anger. I feel it too. But you should be concentrating on your studies, not disciplining your classmates. Who else was involved here with you?"

Robert grinned with self-satisfaction in response to her benign reproof. "If you think about it, we're all involved."

"How so, Robert?"

"Although Praxis is to blame, rooting out the traitors is our civic duty. It's my responsibly. It's your responsibly. It's the responsibility of all citizens. Only when we eliminate those who are disloyal to Pansophical will our world be free of violence."

"Right is right. And you aren't wrong on all counts. Tell me"—she lowered her voice—"what's he doing here?"

"Him?" Robert derisively pointed at Antony. "He's a spineless sympathizer who doesn't mind his own business."

"Something feels off about all this. He's not playing with a full deck, that's for sure. Have you seen him around here before?"

"Once or twice in passing. But he'll no longer be ignored."

"That will be all, Robert. Wait for me in my office. We'll discuss your punishment shortly."

"Yes, Principal Diebler."

Over the previous minutes, the outside world ceased to exist within Antony's mind. A phase transition was induced when Robert crossed his line of sight. Now the switch was flipped—down with reminiscence, up with life.

"Saved by the bell," said Robert, smirking with disdain. "Don't trick yourself into believing that this heroic act will go unnoticed, old timer."

Following several blinks, Antony's eyes deglazed as he watched the Pan-Youth leader strut away.

"Hi?" Principal Diebler waved at Antony to attract his attention. "Hello there?"

Antony vigorously shook his head to expedite his return to reality. "Huh?"

"I'm Megyn." She infantilized her speech. "The principal here. What's your name?"

"I'm ..." He ran his fingers along the sharp ridge of his

orbital rim. "Antony." His tactical exploration of the epidermal gash was gingerly executed. After inspecting his fingertips, he instinctually inserted them into his mouth to remove the crimson discharge.

"Can you please tell me what happened here, Antony?"

"I did all I could when the situation escalated."

"And who was doing the escalating?"

"I scared off an entire group of those little lawless monsters with the exception of that one over there."

"Really?"

"Yeah." Antony's pupils lingered on Robert as he disappeared into the halls of education. "That one has a special breed of hatred in his heart."

"I'm surprised. Robert is one of our best students. Is he the one who started this?"

"Impossible for me to say. But if it weren't for you, this fragile body of mine wouldn't be standing here in one piece." The corners of his mouth turned upward in appreciation. "Thank you."

Principal Diebler responded to this genuine gesture with an overstretched strained smile. Robert's assessment of the interloper noticeably weighed on her conscience.

"You're welcome. But it's my job to protect my students from harm." She pulled out a travel pack of tissues and tossed them over. "Here, clean yourself up."

As Antony attended to his injuries in silence, she recommenced her questioning. "So," she said with leeriness radiating through her words. "How do you know Kennard?"

Antony took a moment before responding. He recognized that her seemingly innocent query was a de facto probe into his cardinal motivations. While reflecting on the incident, he removed another tissue and pressed it onto his wound to facilitate coagulation.

"The first time that I saw the boy couldn't have been more than fifteen minutes ago. I watched him run, full of panic, away from those hooligans." He breathed deeply and stuffed one of the bloodstained tissues into his pocket. "Are we no different from our Neanderthal cousins? We mustn't submit ourselves to a state of lawlessness. If a crime was committed, the guilty must be held accountable, but not in this savage fashion."

"It's clear that Kennard was in harm's way," she acknowledged. "But let's not pretend that our society is on the brink of anarchy."

"A fair point. The truth of the matter is that I felt compelled to stand up for what was right. There's no justice in mob justice. Although I know nothing of Kennard's supposed wrongdoings, he's a fellow citizen, and a child at that."

"Hmmm. You confess to being ignorant. Yet you still chose to meddle?"

"I assure you," Antony said with conviction, "my decision to help was far from foolhardy. I've been wrongly accused under the presumption of guilt before innocence. And I've been bullied more than my fair share. There's a tragic lack of humility within the mob mentality, a sense of certitude that reduces us to beasts. When you've been on the receiving end, you start to see these situations differently."

Principal Diebler visibly relaxed. "I understand. But things aren't always straightforward. Praxis and their radical beliefs are dangerous. Are they not?"

"Life has always been about navigating dangers. We're fortunate that Pansophical protects us from m—"

Wee-ooh! Wee-ooh! Wee-ooh!

Both Principal Diebler and Antony diverted their focus to the ambulance pulling up outside the baseball field. Two burly paramedics jumped out of the vehicle. They wore fluorescent yellow-and-black fleeces with bands of silver reflective tape. The men swung open the ambulance's rear doors and removed its integrated patient transport. As they wheeled the stretcher down the sidewalk, Antony glanced over sympathetically at Kennard.

"When all this is over," he said while turning back to Principal Diebler, "what will happen to him?"

"I'm sure he'll be fine," she said. "Worst case scenario, he has some broken bones."

"His body will heal in all likelihood. The accusations of today, however, will leave permanent scars on his reputation. This place is no longer safe for him."

"That goes without saying. He'll be relocated after a stay in a rehabilitation center. I've had a handful of students who were troublemakers before they came here, but you couldn't pick them out today. Kennard is lucky."

"Lucky?"

"Well, not lucky right now. But lucky to be young. Molding future generations is easy. We've mastered the craft of building strong, productive children. Repairing broken adults, now that's a puzzle."

Advancing along the bumpy outfield, the rolling cot provided continuous clangorous updates on the paramedics' location. Every few feet the buckle from a dangling restraint strap clanked against the stretcher's metal frame.

Principal Diebler drew back her lips to reveal a friendly visage. She stepped away from their conversation to greet the approaching men at the edge of the infield dirt. In a few sentences, she briefed them on the incident. The paramedics rushed over to Kennard to establish communication and to evaluate the severity of his injuries. Once the victim was deemed responsive, they delicately transferred him to the cot's bolster, then strapped in his pulverized body. The transport was subsequently raised using its battery-powered hydraulic system.

The younger of the paramedics addressed Antony. "All right, your turn. Keep your head steady and follow my finger." After the first part of the concussion test, he detached a penlight from his duty belt. "Now look straight ahead." He shone the light into Antony's eyes. "Everything looks good. As long as you don't start having headaches or dizzy spells, there's nothing to worry about. Come with me. I'll get you bandaged up."

Behind the immobilized Kennard, he escorted Antony

off the recreational field. All the while, the other paramedic comforted the mauled child. Once the stretcher was loaded into the rear of the emergency vehicle, Antony was seated on the ambulance's aluminum bumper to receive the medical aid he required.

An antimicrobial solution was applied to Antony's gash. A sprinkling of curative nanobots and a sterile dressing followed. Crosswise his connectome, the events before his eyes jumbled together with a remembrance from eight months prior. The ruddy misshapen features of the paramedic morphed into the ladylike lineaments of his neighbor Norah McGregor. His surroundings transformed from a metropolitan landscape to the familiar confines of her apartment. His anatomy wilted as he attempted to make sense of it all.

Without memories, where would we ground our sense of self? Without a personal narrative, how could we form an identity? If we can't remember the past, who do we become?

CHAPTER TEN

nside the psychology clinic, recessed RFID interrogators monitored the waiting rooms. The radio waves they emitted encountered the antenna coiled around Antony's implant. His excited passive tag reflected back an altered signal through the air interface. Upon interpreting this unique backscattered wave, the system initiated its welcome program based on his preprogrammed settings.

The light levels gradually increased in intensity. From the speakers, the mellifluous extravagance of a Romantic-era piano concerto entered the auditory backdrop. Once the ambience was set, a motion microscope was activated to further tailor the surroundings. Infinitesimal movements were amplified through its complex algorithms. Magnified video pixels detected the patient's blood flow and skin moisture content. Imperceptible changes within his physique were analyzed to determine optimal thermal comfort levels. An external heat pump sent warm air into the ducts. A humidifier simultaneously infused these air molecules with water.

Antony settled into one of the two voluptuous chocolate-colored loveseats. He reclined against its leathery armrest and spread out his appendages. Only the grungy soles of his footwear dangled without support. Dr. Winfield's closed office door infixed within him the presumption that time was to spare. He welcomed the opportunity to unwind.

From the corner of his eye, he discerned a porcelain candy dish filled with sugary temptations. Resting his outstretched arm on the abutting console table, he reached in that direction. While retracting a fistful of treats, his hand passed through the light mist of an aromatherapy diffuser. Hints of eucalyptus imbued the atmosphere with tranquility. He drew the agreeable air deep into his lungs, then popped a fruit-filled bonbon into his oral cavity. His saliva dissolved the non-crystalline candy, releasing a strawberry-flavored glob. As the chewy filling perked his pallet, he stared at the watercolor painting on the opposite wall. Featuring a budding boreal forest viewed through a window, the canvas provided the cramped room with an illusion of depth.

One by one, his sensory modalities fell under the calming influence of the present environment. The harrowed happenings from the schoolyard faded from his thoughts. A half hour later, emergent movement from the office's lever door handle brought his state of placidness to an end.

He elevated from his reposed position. "Hello, Dr. Winfield."

"Good afternoon." She leaned against the doorframe.

"Please come in."

Dr. Winfield extended the invitation behind a mirthless smile. She wore a long-sleeved charcoal cardigan over an ivory scoop-neck blouse. Antony squeezed through the partially blocked entryway. Midway through this inelegant maneuver, he inadvertently brushed up against her shoulder-length curls. In response, the dwarfish psychologist flicked up her prominent mole-marked chin, tossing aside her caramel tresses to unveil a chiding countenance. All residual traces of peacefulness vanished as he navigated past the passive-aggressive obstruction.

Upon stepping across the threshold onto the hickory planks of the adjoining office, Antony wished to be elsewhere. Unfortunately, nothing could be done about this ill-timed desire. Behind him, Dr. Winfield flipped a set of switches to denote the beginning of their session. The present setting brightened while the waiting room music was replaced by obscurant white noise. She closed the door to ensure that they would have privacy.

Doused in a sundry of greens, Dr. Winfield's office was decorated to elicit affective harmony and inspire sentiments of rebirth. For Antony, the palette was perceived as bland, and the ambience induced boredom. He ambled alongside the window sill. An umbrella tree on the alcove ledge harnessed energy from the late afternoon sunrays. On a stonewashed olive-colored area rug, a pair of lime wingback armchairs stood face-to-face, separated by a glass coffee table.

Antony reclined his anatomy atop the velvety cushions of the neighboring jade chaise lounge. His eyeballs followed Dr. Winfield's shuffling ballet flats across the office. Her dragging footsteps halted in front of a wall-mounted writing desk. Above this floating furniture, visual evidence of her expertise adorned a pale-green backdrop. Framed beside a graduation tassel, enclosed by a baby-blue mat board, was her doctorate degree from Columbia University. In an adjacent frame, a certificate from the global professional board of examiners declared her special competency within the subdiscipline of clinical psychology.

Dr. Winfield transferred her focus to the lone adornment on the tidy desk, an acrylic block frame. A group portrait encased within featured a younger version of herself in Stockholm, arm in arm with Pansophical directors from the European Territories. She adoringly stared at the object, murmuring indecipherably. After an elongated moment, she slid the tangible remembrance aside. Professionalism redressed her demeanor. She removed a spiral notebook from the hutch's open compartment, then took a seat opposite Antony. While flipping through the notebook's scribble-filled pages, she rotated her pelvis, causing her upper body to angle forward.

"In light of our previous session, what's been on your mind, Antony? How's everything been?"

"Truthfully," he said, raising his vocal pitch to feign delight. "Things could not be better."

"That's pleasantly surprising. What's changed?"

"In a moment of self-reflection, the pieces fell into place."

"Hmmm. Why do you think this is happening now?"

"My revelation was presumably triggered by the hours and hours that we've spent together. Believe it or not, I was once skeptical of tales of transformation."

"So," she said while pulling on her earlobe, "this happened out of the blue? Nothing specifically brought about this newfound joy?"

"Nope, nothing in particular. That's the compound effect in action, I suppose." Antony deliberately paused. He fraudulently stretched the corners of his mouth laterally. "Who would have thought that radical change could be produced by such small, seemingly insignificant steps?"

"You know," she said, her gaze sharpening, "it requires enormous amounts of emotional energy to be inauthentic. Not only is it mentally exhausting, it's patently obvious to someone who has delivered psychotherapy to you for over a year and a half."

Awaiting a reply, Dr. Winfield clicked the top of her writing instrument in a triangular pattern against the open notebook. The nib passed in and out of its plastic barrel, composing an insufferable staccato sonata. For a minute and a half, speech was absent.

Irked by the compulsive clicking and the conspicuousness of his thwarted ploy, Antony flung his feet to the floor. He forced a dismissive snort through his nostrils while he sat up and adjusted his posture. The illusion of positivity he erected was designed to foster a congenial interaction. Its failings heighted his embitterment.

Dr. Winfield ceased her fidgeting and began to transcribe her musings.

"Mentally exhausting," he torpidly responded at last. "Tell me about it."

She stopped writing. "Let's start over. Normally our appointments begin with a recap of your week through a lens of emotional regulation. We discuss the importance of acknowledging the suffering of the past and go over strategies to deal with sleep hallucinations. We usually finish off with a homework assignment of attainable ways for you to move forward and contribute to society. I want to try something different today."

Piqued by the prospect of a novel conversation, Antony's frame relaxed. Any deviation from the customary agenda was preferable from his perspective.

Dr. Winfield nodded. "These appointments are all about you. My responsibilities are to diagnose, to fulfill the role of a counselor and that of a confidant. Over time you've become less responsive, and our interactions have suffered. I believe that your growth has stagnated as a result. At this point I'm wondering, how much are these appointments helping you?"

Foregoing spontaneity, Antony resisted the urge to crassly criticize these therapy sessions as superfluous. As he pinched the bridge of his nose, his sightline descended upon Dr. Winfield's opulent timepiece. His visual field raced around its rose-gold fluted bezel while he organized his thoughts. In search of the watch hands, his pupils intermittently hopped onto its diamond hour markers. The quantifications of the temporal coordinate eluded him. After the passage of an unknown period of time, he leaned backward with his ankles crossed. Introspection had mellowed his message.

"When I began coming here, I was mired in depression. The series of catastrophes that I experienced would've left anyone grief-stricken. In the aftermath, the sleep hallucinations would've placed most on the brink of insanity. You were an invaluable resource during those days. And for that, I thank you."

"It's been my pleasure. But that was then. What do you think is lacking in our relationship present day?"

"As I was saying, our weekly appointments at one point helped me cope with distress. Those days are behind us. These therapy sessions are of little use because I now have the tools to handle everyday life on my own. They persist as an obligatory relic fraught with repetition.

"We would have plenty to discuss if we touched base every few months. My life is hardly perfect. Scheduling, however, is beyond my control. Without destabilizing challenges to overcome, our relationship has grown stale. And as evidenced by today, occasionally contemptuous."

"The honesty is greatly appreciated." Dr. Winfield pressed her palm against her heart. "I can sincerely say that you've grown since we first met. Granted it hasn't been easy, change never is. But you've managed to eliminate nearly all the symptoms associated with your condition. I agree with your sentiments, cutting down on the frequency of our appointments would be beneficial. I'll file a petition with the Department of Social Services for a reduction in your treatment sentence later today."

As his anxieties were allayed, he activated his facial muscles to form a smile. "Thank you. Admittedly, I was hesitant to broach this subject. Instead of avoiding confrontation, I should've raised my concern months ago."

"There's no need to dwell on the past. Let's look forward. Ready for a hypothetical scenario?"

"Ask away."

"If I waved a magic wand and all your problems disappeared, what would your life be like?"

"Well, it's easy to construct fantasies, but life is inherently complex. Is not wishing away the troubles of the present only a temporary solution? Before long I suspect that I'd find something new to complain about."

"Astute analysis. Even when everything is going one's way, people have a tendency to find faults. Unfortunately, most of us manufacture problems out of nothing."

"Been there."

"I'm curious"—she pointed at his bandaged brow—"was it this mentality that drove your actions at the middle school earlier today?"

A nervous laugh slipped through his lips. He wondered

how she had found out. "I was by no means on the prowl for problems on my walk over here."

"Then why do anything in the first place?"

"Today was about protecting a child, a fellow citizen, from mob justice. Nothing more."

"So playing the part of the peacekeeper had nothing to do with political principles? Or sympathies for the Praxis cause? Remember, Antony, anything and everything said throughout our sessions stays between us."

The verbal assurance of confidentiality was complimented by the ocular dialect conveyed by her dark-brown irises. She clipped her writing utensil to the notebook's spiral binding. She maintained eye contact as she bent over and placed these reporting items under her chair.

In reaction to her potentially pernicious line of questioning, Antony's disposition grew austere. Following his schoolyard interposition, the repeated need to defend himself against blasphemous barbs had become tiresome. He sought validation, but in embodying Kennard's pleas for assistance, empathy was required.

His mind fragmented. A plurality of consciousnesses dynamically emerged within his psyche by virtue of the dialogical self. His inner chatter was expressed by interacting independent perspectives, one of which belonged to the patient, the other to the psychologist. The wetware production served as a testing ground for contrasting replies to the questions she had posed.

"Dr. Winfield, do we live in a society ruled by law or a society ruled by the whims of men? My loyalty to the Pansophical Corporation does not waiver. Never will I support the savage, subversive, activities of Praxis. The matter at hand, however, rests outside of tribal convictions."

Through scattered head nods, Dr. Winfield demonstrated her attentiveness. Antony viewed these nonverbal indicators of active listening positively. If for no other reason than a yearning to be understood, conveying his motivations without omission became his objective. Following a deep breath, he continued.

"A substantial divergence exists between a population that's vigilant of suspicious activity and one that silences and murders opposition. Initiating force against a fellow citizen is wrong. It is immoral, for it is a violation of their natural rights. In a just society, Kennard wouldn't have needed my protection. In a free society, he would've been able to believe whatever he desired?"

Skeptical of the corollary he reached, an upward inflection denatured Antony's final sentence of its declarative stature. The ambiguous punctuation was vocalized as a question-statement composite.

"I see," she said, shuffling restlessly in her seat. "And how did the act itself of standing up for this child make you feel?"

"The decision about whether or not to intervene was gut-wrenching." His field of vision sunk to the floor. "When I watched from the outskirts, I wished that the mob would abandon their pursuit. I hoped ... I prayed ... that someone would separate themselves from the hysteric mass to broker a truce. Regretfully, the onus of saving Kennard fell on my shoulders. And my shoulders alone. To put it mildly, it was an isolating experience."

"Few among us would have chosen to go down that path. What do you think this says about you?"

"I'll leave the psychoanalysis to those who are qualified. All I know is that sometimes, the only course of action is to confront convention and do the right thing."

"Of course, the right thing." She folded her arms. "Let's fast forward six months from today. How has this experience changed you?"

"That's a question to be answered by my future self. As I see it, the possibilities are nearly endless."

Before Dr. Winfield could inquire further into the enduring impact of his ordeal, a ringing telephone disrupted her concentration. She excused herself and sprung to her feet. Thereupon answering, she wedged the handset between her head and shoulder, then propped herself onto the corner of her desk. A sneer materialized on her face when looking in Antony's direction. After voicing a series of laconic acknowledgments into the receiver, she thanked the caller and hung up.

"I'm terribly sorry, Antony, but we're going to have to cut our session short. An emergency has come up with one of my other patients. Next week, same time, same place. We'll finalize your new treatment schedule then. Without making any promises, let's plan on meeting monthly from that point moving forward. Take care."

Dr. Winfield synchronized her farewell with the opening of the office door.

Reflective ruminations revolving around the appointment preoccupied Antony's thoughts on his homeward-bound peregrination. During the recollected sequence, he analyzed each of Dr. Winfield's reactionary gestures for connotative clues. Piece by piece, he deconstructed the verbal components of their conversation with the punctiliousness of an obsessive-compulsive linguist. Interpretations ceaselessly changed. His affective states swung in short succession. Whenever the memory replay reached its conclusion, the cyclic loop began anew.

What in the world was I thinking? As if she of all people wouldn't see through my childish charade. Why couldn't I have just been honest? Could have, should have, does it matter anymore? "Let's plan on meeting monthly." Those were her exact words. Thank goodness.

A surge of vitality quickened his footpace. Once a month he could do. Once a month was tolerable. Although, not if those appointments were anything like today. He wondered what she was thinking about right then.

Feelings of insecurity sapped the manifestations of optimism from his physical form. He began to doubt that she'd truly understood why he interfered on Kennard's behalf. His pace slowed, and his thoughts turned to murmurs.

"Once again creating unnecessary problems for myself. I

should have played up the sympathy angle. I shouldn't have said a word about societal values. But no, I opted for candidness, like an imbecile. I'm already dreading next week."

Transported by a gust of wind, an airborne leaflet curtailed his self-doubting blather. Blowing from the opposite direction, its trajectory intersected the path of his forward-striding shin. The inelastic collision would have gone undetected if not for the vivid contrast of the handbill's yellow background on his indigo jeans. Upon glimpsing down, he stopped walking, removed the piece of hitchhiking litter, and raised it to reading level.

A multicolored, nonbinary mass of silhouettes stood in the center of the glossy leaflet. One disreputable figure sat in the corner, disconnected from the herd.

Feeling alone?
Struggling to contribute to the greater good?
Questioning your sanity?
Assistance is only a phone call away.
1-800-SUPPORT (1-800-787-7678)

Antony's sightline bored into the numerals. He privately replied to the trio of questions in the affirmative. The sound of a barking dog seized his attentional spotlight. Putting aside his contemplations of alienation, he surveyed his surroundings. Apart from an energetic Jack Russell terrier pulling along its indolent owner, the metropolitan cross section was bizarrely deserted. Raising digits to dome, he lightly dragged his fingernails along his scalp.

Voices arose from inside the buildings all around him, inundating the soundscape. "Free to be safe, safe to be free!"

Antony jerked his head backward, startled by the rallying cry. His fingers fanned, and the handbill targeting disaffection was released back into the custody of the wind.

Citizens soon followed their words into the streets. Evidently, Antony had missed an address by Chairman Fields. Although the contents were a mystery, he apperceived that it would affect all those in his vicinity. Whether an environmental emergency, a Praxis plot, or a Tembakoo outbreak, he had faith that the citizenry would band together to overcome the odds.

Anxious to erase any signs of individualization, he yanked the bandage off his brow. His loneliness was dispelled as an onrush of people blurred the line of demarcation between the one and the whole. The validation he coveted earlier was sated by the innate similarities that defined members of the Homo sapiens species.

Each of these men and women had evolved from a common ancestor. Anatomically, they were similar. Cognitively, they were comparable. Internally, they were guided by subjective perceptions of free will. Every one of them was born; every one of them would die. Before Antony's eyes, experiential differences were washed away by the commonalities of the human condition.

CHAPTER ELEVEN

Peering into the lobby of Sanctuary Village Apartments from the sidewalk left Antony muddleheaded. Something was awry, but he couldn't quite put his finger on the source of the incongruity. An artificial flame from the fireplace entertained a pair of empty armchairs. A gleaming desk lamp showcased an impeccably polished coffee table. The spick-and-span lobby represented the palpable dividends of the building superintendent's incessant tirades on cleanliness. It was neither the spotlessness nor the orderliness that Antony perceived as amiss, however. There was an absence of sorts.

Seeking clarity, Antony allowed his eyelids to close. He performed an internal comparison of the three-dimensional common area on the opposite side of the glass and a visualization produced by his occipital lobe. One by one he inserted the lobby's furnishings into these contrasting mental tabulations. A minute later his eyes opened. He deemed the two inventories equivalent. Nevertheless, his gaze lingered on the empty space bordering the doorway.

"Must be the unfamiliar angle," he softly said aloud. "No other plausible explanation. Nothing in this building has changed in decades."

Following a shrug, he planted his prone palm onto the biometric security sensor. The intricate ridges and valleys of his phalanges were compared against the tenant registry. Once a matching handprint was located, the building's primary means of ingress was unbarred.

Across the lobby, inside the elevator shaft, steel hoist cables moved along a series of sheaves, raising the machine's counterweight and lowering its carriage. The elevator doors parted as Antony reached for the ladder-styled pull handle of the main entrance. A louvered metal door in the far corner simultaneously opened. Three figures converged on the lobby through these separate points of entry.

Shouldering a leather satchel, a dapperly adorned fellow with a yellowish-tan complexion and a pompadour fade emerged from the mechanical lift. An agile gait transported the man.

Antony's next-door neighbor, Norah McGregor, meanwhile surfaced from the basement stairs. In a Sherpa-collared sweatshirt and botanical leggings, she was cozily clad. Above a clear-contoured filtration mask, her honey-blonde wispy bangs draped over her forehead.

She faintly called for the exit-bound fellow. "Shirong. Shirong."

Seemingly oblivious to the verbal solicitations for his

attention, Shirong moved with intent. Without breaking stride, he fired off a phatic expression at the opposite-traveling Antony in the form of a "How's it going?" By the time Antony reciprocated in kind to the aimless social intercourse, the spry stranger was past him. A musky cloud of agarwood trailed his footsteps. The scent stood in stark contrast to his effeminate facial features.

After another fruitless hailing attempt, Norah cupped her hands around her mask and cranked up the volume. "Shirong!"

Halfway out the door, Shirong stopped in his tracks. He waved at Norah, then stepped back inside to reverse course.

Antony similarly gravitated in her direction. He was hoping to learn about the nature of the global address he had missed on the walk home.

With a glowing countenance, Norah floated past Antony to greet Shirong. Tear film accumulated above her lower eyelids, magnifying the intensity of the reflected corneal light to produce an unmistakable twinkle of infatuation. Shirong's cocky deportment crumbled. His confident gait was replaced by straggling steps devoid of conventional arm swings.

"Hiya," said Norah. "You almost ran off without saying hello. What's the rush?"

Shirong rested his palm on his opposite clavicle. Using his thumb, he plugged the hollow indentation below his Adam's apple. "Duty calls. The office."

"Really, Shirong? When aren't you at the office?"

"They need me back there. Called, in the middle of my nap. Woke me up. It's going long. I mean, tonight is going long. I mean, it's going to be a long night."

"If it weren't for those naps, I could sublet your apartment, and you'd never know. What's so urgent to—" She gasped. "Oh gosh, here I'm joking around when we're in the middle of an emergency."

He wrung his hands. "Are we talking a global state of emergency?"

"Heavens no! The chairman only elevated us over here to threat level yellow. It's a different story for those poor souls in Astara, though."

"I don't know." He paused. "I don't know anything. I mean, none of us, I thought, knew much of anything yet."

"Try and stay calm, sugar. We're all in the same boat. We're all waiting for updates."

"It's going to be a long night. What did Chairman Fields say? I mean, about the dead. How many so far?"

"Somewhere north of five thousand. Our citizens in the Caspian Territories need help." She tenderly sandwiched his hands between hers. "They need that big brain of yours. Please go."

"I'll do what I can to help," Shirong said. As he looked away, he appeared to regain his confidence. "There's probably a stack of epidemiological data sets already waiting for me. The faster we figure out the transmission vectors for this mutated strain, the better. Bye bye, Norah."

Antony loitered silently in the background all the while, waiting for an opportunity to politely interject. In overhearing their short-lived exchange, he had gathered all that he needed to know. Protected by a pair of oceans, the presence of the pestilence produced little personal angst. An upmost trust in the Pansophical Corporation further dampened his emotional response to the point of insouciance.

As the lobby's occupancy was reduced by one, the remaining parties acknowledged one another with a smile.

"This Shirong character, he lives here?" Antony asked. "Thought I was acquainted with everyone in our building."

"He moved in over six months ago," Norah replied. "Where have you been?"

"Wandering around in a world of my own, it appears. Whatever happened to those shindigs you use to organize?"

She rolled her eyes. "Take a wild guess."

"Has our friendly neighborhood super struck again?"

"Who else but Luis? We apparently broke one too many of his rules."

"What a shame." Antony shook his head. "Those get-togethers were a good time."

"Right? They were so much fun! Shirong would've loved them. And everyone would've loved spending time with Shirong. How could they not?"

"Oh, Shirong," Antony said teasingly. "I'll be sure to properly introduce myself the next time we cross—"

"Really you must," Norah said, uncharacteristically

effusive. "I have no doubt that you'll become fast friends. Come to think of it, you two are a lot alike. To start with, both of you are crazy about stats."

"Justifiably so, for the language of mathematics is the language of the universe."

"Shirong would say something like that. I wish he was around more. He spends every waking hour at that office, playing with those models. Guess we're all better-off when he's working to save mankind, though."

"Tembakoo suppression is the noblest of causes. I look forward to striking up a chat with him. Out of curiosity, what unit did he decide to purchase?"

"Pick of the litter, 1C. Not only was that place in perfect condition, its previous owner left behind some beautiful handcrafted furniture." She paused. "I'm drawing a blank. What was that guy's name?"

"I haven't a clue," Antony answered without thinking.

"Hmmm." She stroked her double-chin with her manicured fingers. "I'm positive that it started with a J. I can picture that woolly beard of his. Name is on the tip of my tongue. Jacoby?"

Antony chuckled. "Don't believe I've met a single Jacoby in my entire life."

"Well, whoever Jacoby really was, he was forgettable, unlike sweet Shirong."

Over the ensuing seconds, Norah was struck by one of her hot flashes. A subtle sheen of perspiration appeared along her hairline. The heatwave imbued her creamy beige cheeks with a warm shade of pink. Last time Antony caught her in the middle of a menopausal episode, she fabricated an outrageous explanation. Given her obsession with youth, he assumed that she was ashamed of the biological process that designated an end to her procreation potential.

"Is everything okay?" he asked.

She scrunched up her sleeves. "Everything is wonderful."

"Why don't we take a seat?"

"Why don't you stop being such a worrywart?" Repurposing her appendages into rudimentary fans, she set her hands into motion. "Good things come to those who sweat, as my yoga teacher says. We've been fall cleaning all day. And I must say, it's been exhausting."

"So," Antony said with a laugh, "that's why you suddenly look like a competitor in a chili pepper challenge."

"You know me too well." Norah yanked off her mask, then ran her hands through her disheveled hair. "Truth be told, if I hadn't wasted so much time begging Fritzy to pitch in, I'd already be relaxing. Us McGregors are a stubborn bunch, that's for sure. Try as I might, I can't spark real change in that brother of mine."

"Even a small spark has the potential to set our inner fire ablaze."

Extracted from a slice of the past, Antony reflexively quoted his erstwhile companion. The sapient words belonged to the man who had spent his retirement on a rocking chair, the same former resident Norah had disremembered moments ago.

"A spark won't do if we're talking about Fritzy." Norah tittered. "Put away the matches and break out the blowtorch."

Overwhelmed by a deluge of recollections, Antony missed the joke.

"Anyway," she continued, "you wouldn't believe how much stuff we've collected over the years. Or how many boxes of junk we're throwing away."

Antony pieced together the assorted clues of individuality that constituted the mystery of the nameless resident. He recalled flashes of the man's physical traits; he retrieved diverse snippets from the discussions they once had; the multifaceted components of the citizen's identity reverberated off the skeletal walls of Antony's cranial cavity.

"Jasper," he exclaimed. "Jasper Turner!"

"That was it. Jasper, the old man from the sea."

"Jasper was a treasure." Sorrow permeated Antony's tone. "After a man's heart stops, after a man's body decomposes, a terminal death occurs the last time his name is read or spoken. We serve as accomplices in the extinction of those we forget."

"Life isn't always so serious. Memory slips will happen more and more the older you get."

His eyelids drooped. "I suppose."

"By happy chance, I have something that will brighten your day." She stepped in the direction of the elevator. "I found a fancy wooden case when I was cleaning under Fritzy's bed. There's an anchor on the outside and a pipe of some sorts inside. We had no idea where it came from. But now there's no doubt in my mind that it was Jas—"

"Thanks, but no thanks."

"Awww, don't be like that. Jasper would've wanted you to have it."

"On the contrary, was it not bequeathed to you and your brother?"

"Come on." She took another step away. "It's sitting in a box to be thrown away as we speak. If we hadn't bumped into each other, it would already be in the trash. Please, Antony, it's all yours."

Under Norah's kindhearted goading, he agreed to accept the keepsake. Together they rode the elevator in silence.

Disquieted by the memory lapse, Antony wondered about the frequency of these forgetful incidents. His ruminations on the fallibility of the mind shortly shifted to his schoolyard episode. Was his unbidden reminiscence of "The Caged Bird's Plight" an incipient sign of cognitive deterioration? Was a neurological disorder responsible for that dreamlike transmogrification of his paramedic?

At the seventh floor, the elevator chimed. The passengers disembarked. Brooding away, Antony lagged behind on their walk over to apartment 7G.

A blockade composed of cardboard cartons impeded entry into the McGregors' residence. Norah pushed aside these obstacles with the sole of her slipper, carving a path through the foyer. On Antony's way through this crude passageway, he reached inside the largest of the boxes and pulled out a hand-painted porcelain camel.

"If I hear about the difference between the dromedary and the Bactrian camel one more time"—Norah snatched the Arabian trinket from his grasp—"I'm going to scream." She placed it back into the rubbish heap. "Why don't you wait here while I find that thingamajig?"

Browsing over the castoff collection, Norah's search radius narrowed. Back and forth she paced while wagging her finger. Along the way of retracing her housework, she provided updates via external self-talk. "And if those are filled with old work stuff, these must be from Fritzy's room."

She plucked a sky-blue cushion from the closet and dropped it onto the tile. She crossed her legs underneath herself as her derriere descended onto the insulated pad. Once comfortable, she leaned back against the grassy purification panels that lined the foyer walls, then propped one of the boxes against her shins.

As Norah rummaged about, Antony approached to assist. Attempting to replicate her cross-legged transition, he lowered his frame in a falter. Before touching ground, he backtracked. "Excuse me for a moment. Nature calls. When I return, you can remind me what exactly we're searching for."

Homing in on the whereabouts of the nautical memento, she mumbled her reply into the miscellany of trifles. Unable to decipher her suppressed response, he released an interjection of uncertainty on the way to the bathroom.

Overlaid on a jasmine backdrop, apricot-colored bulbous forms and rusty convex-diamonds peppered the walls of the hallway. Captivated by the undulating illusion produced by this geometric design, Antony dawdled in his efforts to void his bladder. A dozen baby steps later, a rising trill from the end of the hall brought his loafing headway to a halt.

The mellowed slurred whistles of a rose-breasted grosbeak followed the sharp swelling song of the worm-eating warbler. Antony had heard Fritz's beastly repertoire on innumerable occasions, at times in the flesh, at other times through the apartment walls. Be that as it may, complex birdcalls represented a newly acquired skill for his kooky neighbor. Antony lifted his heels off the floor and skulked toward the origin of the avian melodies. Through the barely open doorway, he peeked into the native habitat of Fritz McGregor.

Bedecked in bird-watching attire, Fritz quiescently gazed into a tripod-mounted spotting scope. He stood in the far corner wearing a smoke-gray thermal jacket, camouflage pants, and matching mud boots. One of his eyes was covered by a leather patch. With the other, he focused all his concentration into an angled eyepiece. Ten feet onward, a holographic projection of a coastal forest protruded from the floor.

On the brink of guffawing in response, Antony retreated to avoid detection. His laughter seeped through his sealed lips as a quelled snicker. Once he regained his composure, he moved in stealth for a second viewing of the comical curiousness.

Fritz remained stationary, enthralled by the three dimensional facsimile that teemed with winged wildlife. It was only after one of the blue jays flew off did he become animated. Beseeching it to return, he delivered a terse call. When this proved unsuccessful, he reproduced an elaborate mating serenade. His feathered friend was nowhere to be found. Fritz lifted his head. Coincided by a snarl, the hunchbacked elder dragged his eyepatch across his narrow nose. After swiveling the tripod handle several degrees, he reimmersed himself into the woodlands.

Eventually tedium depleted this lunacy of its humor, and Antony began to ponder Fritz's detachment from reality. Was happiness possible within an existence of perpetual escapism? Unmarred by the sinister realities of adulthood, Fritz knew nothing of the angst that arose from a pandemic; he knew nothing of the ubiquitous mistrust that followed an act of terror. Fritz lived with his head in the clouds while filling his days with playful pursuits. Many within the citizenry lived similar lives of unbridled indulgences. Sans productivity, their life narratives teetered on collapse. Facing an absence of meaning, corporate zealotry filled the void for most. Bliss, based on the Pansophical ethos, however, was reserved for those who sacrificed themselves for the common good.

Naturally, the question that begged to be answered was whether Antony himself was happy. Not at a superficial level but genuinely satisfied with his life. He challenged his perceptual blind spots. Yes, he'd made sacrifices, but why should altruism be the only criterion? Why should individualistic measures be ignored? Conflicted, he started to doubt that it was possible for him to assess his own happiness. And if he couldn't even do that, how could he be confident in his ability to judge his own sanity? What were the odds of a third party concluding that he, like Fritz, was delusional? Without validating mechanisms, how could he distinguish between his subjective experience and objective reality?

A sequence of enchanting flutelike notes from the aspiring birder snapped Antony out of his contemplations. His plunge down the deranged rabbit hole suddenly stopped. In a snarky monologue, he scoffed at these psychotic thoughts. He denigrated all concerns of a physical universe beyond his experiential point of view. He turned away from Fritz's preposterous exhibition.

The McGregors' bathroom embodied the passé ambience of their apartment. A trio of diamond-pointed globes disposed of the darkness. An eggshell chair rail separated the wood panels along the perimeter from a floral motif. There was a glitter popcorn ceiling overhead and a basketweave ruby floor strewn with band-aids underfoot.

Antony loitered no longer. He cleared away the disheveled medical bag that sat atop the tufted toilet seat. After expelling the liquid waste from his body, he approached the sink.

The smart faucet initiated its default user subroutine upon scanning Antony's outstretched hands. Beads of soap dispensed from one nozzle, water flowed from the other. A purple LED illuminated the tepid stream. Bound for the toilet tank, the cohesive molecules cascaded over his lathered fingers into the drain. White water was reprocessed as gray. The conservational plumbing architecture exhibited perfect reuse.

While the sudsy substance purged the germs from Antony's flesh, he nonchalantly inspected the dilapidated medicine cabinet mounted above the vanity. Manifesting as blackened blemishes, moisture had disintegrated the protective coating along its mirrored door. A sizable region of the cabinet was left exposed thanks to a missing lower hinge. An assortment of lotions, nasal sprays, and eye drops populated its congested middle shelf. Color-coded prescription bottles brimmed its bottom ledge. Among them, an amber pill container with an orange childproof cap stood conspicuously upside down.

Antony aimlessly scanned the contents of the run-down fixture. As visible information was transmitted along his neural pathways, salience was computed. Amid the clutter, his attention was deployed in the direction of the salient stimuli. He desisted from his hand washing. Using a tweezer-like motion, he plucked the inverted prescription bottle off its shelf. Soapy droplets reduced the friction coefficient at the points of contact. His fingertips skimmed along the container's circumference, sending it into freefall. Reflexively swiping downward, he nimbly nabbed the object in midair.

Astonished by this dexterous demonstration, he stared at his closed fist for several seconds before loosening his grip.

McGregor, Fritz

Sanctuary Lane 7G, Seattle, WA 98122

Naphthadopa 160 mg

Take two tablets by mouth twice daily

Qty: 60 | Refills: 3

He glanced over the primary components of the label without a second thought. Antony's scrutiny intensified once his sight line arrived at the drug's chemical structure. He phonated the scientific nomenclature to the best of his ability.

"N-[(1-Butyl-2-Pyrrolidinyl) Methyl]-4-Cyano-1-Methoxy-2-Naphthamide."

An eerie familiarity emerged as he stammered out the abstruse string of characters. The sensation slithered down his vertebrae, leaving a taut spinal column in its wake. While gazing at the incomprehensible jargon, he tentatively flexed his opposite elbow, then raised his quivering palm above the nape of his neck. With an extended middle finger, he absent-mindedly traced the boundary of his implant. Lap after lap, his trembling digit skittered along the edges of its silicon wafer. Molasses coated the sands of time; his temporal experience slowed as he attempted to untangle this peculiar phenomenon.

"For crying out loud, not now, Fritzy!"

If not for the sounds of the bickering siblings, Antony's withdrawn behavior may have continued indefinitely. In response to the external cue, he stepped away from the vanity. His bemusement persisted, but the time had come for him to depart. As he reached for the doorknob, he hesitated. Fritz marched down the hall babbling about kiwi eggs. In the interest of avoiding another neurotic encounter, Antony gave him ample time to return to his bedroom before exiting the bathroom.

The collection of boxes that had filled the foyer were no longer present. The slightly ajar front door led Antony to surmise that Norah was off disposing of unwanted belongings. He poked his head outside and directed his probing pupils to the trash chute. Seeing no sign of life, he retracted the anterior portion of his anatomy.

"Antony," Norah called out from the other room. "Is that you?"

Tracking her silvery voice, Antony shut the door and began to circle the asymmetrical shelves that divided the apartment. In spite of Norah's decluttering efforts, the partition remained abound with ornamental trifles and sundries. Formerly a decorative display, the structure today served as nothing more than storage. Gaps among the assorted items supplied Antony with irregular viewing windows into the rest of the residence. Between abutting bobbleheads, he caught a glimpse of an empty kitchen. A few footsteps later, he found Norah lounging on the living room's loveseat sipping lemonade from a striped straw.

"Are you done hiding?" She teasingly grinned. "If you didn't want to help, you could've just said so."

As Antony drew near, her line of sight dipped. Her relaxed facial features were rearranged into a quizzical expression.

"What's that in your hand?" she asked.

Following her puzzled gaze, Antony froze. "Oh. This." His eyes once more locked onto the agent of his unsettled state.

Norah leaned forward and squinted at its orange cap. "What are you doing with Fritzy's medication?"

"It fell," he said, his voice jittery, "from that chasm within your medicine cabinet. I had no idea that I forgot to put it back."

"Give it here." She extended an upturned palm.

"I'm sorry."

"Nothing to worry about. We're all good."

"No. No, we're not." He handed over the prescription bottle. "I haven't felt like myself all day. I've been experiencing inexplicable flashbacks. Nothing makes sense. It's becoming impossible for me to shake these misgivings about our reality. I'm starting to fear that these sentiments of self-doubt will only worsen with time."

"Come take a load off." She scooched over and patted the plastic-covered cushion. "We all get nervous when there's Tembakoo outbreaks. Those feelings will pass. You'll be freshly vaccinated and worry-free before long."

Despite being misunderstood, Antony was reassured by Norah's nonjudgmental response. He laterally stretched his lips in a contrived closed-mouthed smile. Readily confessing to qualms about the authenticity of the here and now could be dangerous under different circumstances. In the present setting, his admission was rationalized through her empathic eyes.

"What do those pills do anyway?" Antony asked as he joined her on the couch.

She peeked at the label, then tucked the container away into the mesh pocket of her leggings. "Naphthadopa. Just one of the antipsychotic drugs Fritzy takes daily. It's a minor sedative. They help stabilize his mood and prevent manic episodes."

"On a day such as today, a mind-easing sedative would go a long way," Antony said half-jokingly.

"This isn't a laughing matter. If you think Fritzy is a handful now, you wouldn't want to see him without his medication. I just wish they didn't kill his motivation."

"What a waste of potential. If only it were possible to eliminate those side effects. Undoubtedly, your brother could've been more."

Her reposeful frame stiffened. Antony's offhand comments had struck a nerve. "What do you mean, could've been more?"

"That didn't exactly come out right. I was referring to the mentally ill more in a general sense."

"Hmph!"

"Allow me to clarify." Building on his earlier musings, he embarked down the philosophical tangent. "Medication can serve as invisible manacles. Under the appearance of being humane, we strip those with psychiatric disorders of their dignity. We deprive them of the honor of being productive citizens. Have you ever wondered about the ethics? Have you ever asked yourself whether it was right to control your brother in this manner?"

Norah rose to her feet. She glared downward at Antony like a curmudgeon professor bestriding a student after an imbecilic challenge. "You know what? If you keep acting like this, it won't be Fritzy's sanity we're talking about, it will be your own." She spun around sharply and stomped away.

Antony was at a loss. He had never seen her display that level of indignation. Wavering between waiting and complying with her not-so-subtle insinuation, he shuffled positions before sensations of comfort could solidify. Every minute or so, he stood up to leave, only to reconsider and backtrack in short order.

Upon reappearing, Norah chuckled at the sight of his externalized uneasiness. "A wise man once told me that if you relax the body, the mind will follow."

Unsure how to respond, Antony looked over timidly.

After an uncomfortable pause, she continued. "How rude of me! Are you thirsty? What would you say to a glass of freshly squeezed lemonade?"

"I'd say yes, please."

"Figured you would. But before I forget, I found that thingamajig for you."

The vexation that spurred Norah's withdrawal had passed. She knelt down and pulled an envelope-sized wooden case out from underneath the loveseat. Preceded by a tender glance, she laid the keepsake on his lap.

"In remembrance of Jasper," Antony said with a smile.

She affectionately placed her hands on top of his. "Now you'll never forget the friendship you shared."

"I'll cherished this for the rest of my days. Thank you, Norah."

"You're very welcome. I'd love to sit here and reminisce, but I need to take care of Fritzy. I'll be back."

A rattling accompanied her swift strides as she went off into the kitchen. Medicinal masses ricocheted around the prescription bottles within her pocket. She proceeded to systematically gather the ingredients for her brother's medicated cocktail.

All the while, as Antony watched on, his fingertips explored the nautical pyrography that embellished the walnut case.

The synthesis of Fritz's stability tonic began with Norah lining up the five pill containers on the mottled countertop. She pried them open one by one, then set each atop its corresponding color-coded cap. Once she collected the proper dosages, she put the tablets into a paper soufflé cup in preparation for the automatic pill crusher. Next she rounded up the masking agents from the weathered cabinets. She poured twenty-two ounces of grape soda into a leopard-patterned tumbler. A tablespoon of raw cane sugar followed.

Antony redirected his focus to the token of companionship laying across his thighs. Savoring the moment, he took one final tactile examination of its maritime wood burnings. His tour began with a clockwise whirl around an eight-pointed compass rose. Wistful reflections of his departed acquaintance were elicited when he moved onto the rope-entwined anchor. Following a deep calming breath, he slowly unlocked the case's metal draw latch.

Inside, an immaculately polished boatswain's call rested within a velvet foam mold. Affixed to an ornamental keel, the two-toned whistle was composed of a narrow copper tube and a brass buoy with a topside hole. A chain lanyard hung from its underside.

Antony removed the boatswain's call from its case. He peered through its hollow tube, then probed its metal sphere using his pinky. Curious about its acoustic range, he puckered his lips and sent a steady stream of air through its mouthpiece. A pressure differential was created within the buoy, emitting a high-pitched note.

Twenty-five feet away, Norah flinched and jerked her arms upward. The dirty mixing spoon within her grasp struck one of the chairs and flew into the air. She picked up the stirring utensil and conspicuously dropped it into the biofuel recycling tank outside the kitchen. Without saying a word, she discountenanced Antony's action by means of a stare.

Dissuaded by her disapproving glare, Antony ceased piping trials at once. As he lowered the boatswain's call, something caught his eye. Through the case's tailored cavity, handwriting impressions protruded from the underside of a white backdrop. He carefully scrunched up the foam to create an extraction point. Using his opposite hand, he withdrew a crisply folded sheet of paper. After storing away his seafaring whistle, he inverted the paper's deep creases for further inspection.

Dated four decades earlier, the document was a cargo manifest for the *WPSC Mazu*. The freighter started at the port of Nagoya, docked in Shenzhen, then traversed the Pacific Ocean. Three weeks later it arrived in Long Beach. The manifest was filled with port codes, container identifiers, and categorical descriptions of goods.

Antony skipped over the logistic minutia of the supply chain. Halfway down the page, his visual field contracted on a collection of drawings. Within the cells belonging to container PANU 808637 3, bordering a typed description of "Pharmaceuticals," a graphite likeness of the Pansophical Corporation logo juxtaposed a poignant depiction of a teary eyeball. The former's simplistic features bluntly contrasted its intricate polychromatic counterpart. Consisting of a turquoise iris inside a sclera suffused with dilated blood vessels, the optical illustration captured the lamenter's spirit. Beneath these color pencil strokes, tears trickled onto a tombstone inscribed with a handwritten register.

In splendid penmanship, each entry on the tombstone listed a first and last name followed by a seafaring position and a set of dates separated by a dash. For the nineteen crewmen listed, the latter of these points in time occurred during the *WPSC Mazu*'s Pacific crossing.

Visceral distress was evoked as Antony read through the abridged obituary. On a day characterized by disquieting occurrences, the sorrow that seeped through the paper fibers overwhelmed him. All his feelings of depersonalization, all his perceptions of derealization, returned in a flurry. In a vain effort to silence the mental turmoil, he robustly rubbed his eyes.

The impulse to escape his physical surroundings roused him to action moments later. He stuffed the cargo manifest into his pants pocket while rising from his seat. Without bidding his neighbor farewell, he exited the apartment with his sights set on his favorite watering hole. With the resolute urgency of a thoroughbred galloping down the homestretch, he headed for The Emerald. Unable to cope with these dissociative disruptions, he sought the comfortable numbness of a drunkard's refuge.

CHAPTER TWELVE

nside The Emerald, a trendy tapster draped in denim aloofly attended to the pub's sole patron. Black steel gauges stretched out his earlobes. An oily man-bun served as his crown. Every few minutes, he peeked up from his mixology guide to monitor the status of a single pint glass. Whenever its harvest ale supply neared exhaustion, he separated himself from his studies to retrieve a clean piece of glassware and poured another round in silence.

"Thanks," Antony said. He swigged the remainder of his beer. "Keep 'em coming, Floyd."

Wonted banter typified Antony's visits to The Emerald, but given his frame of mind, the uncongenial nature of these interactions was ideal. Embodying the anxiousness amassed over the afternoon, shredded coasters littered his vicinity. He pushed his empty glass through the soggy scraps toward Floyd, who cleared it all away without making eye contact. Before dispensing Antony's replacement, Floyd tossed out a crisp coaster from the bar caddy. Time and time again, this simple exchange was recreated without deviation.

Along Antony's gastrointestinal tract, microscopic ethanol molecules entered the surrounding capillaries by diffusion. Through these tiny blood vessels, the alcohol flowed into his helpless liver. As the alcoholic intake exceeded his anatomy's metabolic capacity, the intoxicating chemicals accumulated within his bloodstream at an escalating rate. After the fifth frosty beverage, the inebriants began to assert their influence over the command center of his central nervous system.

In the goldilocks zone, between the distant worlds of drunk and sober, Antony temporarily reclaimed his composure. The imbibed alcohol assuaged the intractable disruptions that had plagued his consciousness. No longer was his sense of self detached from his perceptions of reality. The incapacitating tremors along his mindscape ceased, for now Antony was back on solid ground.

Midway through his next beer, the robotic greeter let it be known that he would no longer be drinking alone. "Welcome, Albert Pridgeon."

A sprightly senior wearing a plaid trapper hat strolled through the entryway. An elongated wrinkled neck with a tortoise-looking face protruded from his oversized parka. From across the establishment, he fired a finger gun with a snap and a wink at his fellow regular. Antony countered by moving his rigid hand in a semicircle inches above the bar top. Geniality aside, Antony wasn't overly fond of the old man due to his propensity to share long-winded tales peppered by forgotten punchlines. Although engaging, Albert was the human equivalent of an anthology with random pages torn from its spine.

"Neither rain, nor snow, nor sleet, nor hail," Albert announced with zest.

During an ice storm weeks earlier, Albert had received a smattering of drunken laughs upon proclaiming his indomitable spirit in the pursuit of spirits. Henceforward, he adopted this expression as his catchphrase in inclement weather and balmy days alike. Caught up in his new persona, he had recently started experimenting with clever ways to use his weather-centric intro as a jumping-off point.

"What's the good word?" he asked while bouncing onto his stool of choice.

Antony waved once again but now from a few seats away.

Floyd forced a smile. "Same old, same old. What will it be today?"

"Forecast looks grim," Albert said with a chuckle. "Today calls for a dark and stormy."

Floyd tentatively turned toward the liquor wall. Eyeing the bottles, his head swayed back and forth. Apparently unable to subdue his incertitude, he set his chukka boots in motion and headed for his mixology guide.

"Boy, oh boy, do I have a story," said Albert. "I'll have Clara in stitches when she hears what Rocko did." He placed his hat on his knee, then looked around. "Where is our favorite bartender?"

"Clara's not here," Antony replied.

"Don't be silly, she's always here."

Floyd unburied his nose from his book. "Not today. I'm flying solo."

"Are you ready for prime time, pal?" asked Albert.

"Not at all," Floyd said, his tone baring a hint of worry. "Let's keep this between us. Clara's been running a fever for the last day or two. Midway through the chairman's address, she hightailed it out of here."

Albert crossed his fingers. "Hopefully, it's nothing."

"Nothing but an overreaction," said Antony bluntly. "Unless Clara's been secretly vacationing in the Caspian, there's no need for alarm."

"Maybe you're right," Floyd said. He hesitated for a moment. "But still, better safe than sorry."

"Absolutely," Albert said. "Together we stand, if selfish we fall. Protect one another, or death to us all."

In accord with the popular nursery rhyme, Clara had answered the call to duty. The concerned expressions on the faces of Floyd and Albert were recast as pride for a fellow citizen. A minute passed in quiet.

"Anyway," Albert said, starting up again upon receiving his cocktail. "The funniest thing happened today."

The loquacious barfly proceeded to recount his puppy's latest skirmish with a robotic parcel carrier. His tale blended descriptions of canine hijinks with historical tidbits about the postal service. As was all too familiar, an abrupt conclusion was forthcoming, Antony tuned out story time.

Branching off Albert's weather-centric catchphrase, Antony privately speculated about the characteristics of a Monday evening bar-goer. He pigeonholed personalities while envisioning a typical crowd at The Emerald. Customers daunted by Tembakoo proliferation were expunged. Those remaining included a platoon of regulars, citizens afflicted by alcohol dependency, and the grief-stricken seeking a respite. Satisfied with these preliminary classifications, he turned his torso toward the doorway to amuse himself with an attribution challenge. He collected anecdotal evidence over the next half hour as foot traffic heightened.

"Welcome, Ivan Myshkin."

A goateed man in his thirties gave the environment the once-over. Austerity had been carved into his sharp facial features. A port-wine-stain birthmark trickled down the hairline of his shaved head. He threw a sketch-pad with a calligraphy pen down onto a small table next to the entrance. As he approached the bar, he unzipped his gray-scaled camouflage windbreaker. Standing equidistant between the other patrons, he sternly stared into the back of Floyd's skull.

"Scotch and soda," Ivan said, his gravelly words bulldoz-ing their way through Albert's ramblings.

Upon being cut off, Albert swiveled atop his stool. When he set his cheerful eyes on the source of the interruption, he sheepishly spun away. Antony observed through his periphery. The predictable nature of the rebuffed greeting provoked a snicker.

Within the confines of The Emerald, Ivan existed as a familiar stranger. Despite routinely occupying the same physical space, there was an unspoken agreement among him and the other regulars to avoid interactions. Whereas Antony knew innumerable intimate details about Albert, Ivan was virtually anonymous. The origins of his humorless temperament were unknown. The contents of his nightly writings were a mystery. The man simply savored his scotch in solitude and never in excess.

All things considered, Antony added a third mental tally to the regular's category within his devised taxonomy. Before boredom could dispense of this imputable exercise, the mechanical usher presented a batch of introductions.

"Welcome, Tabatha Pierson. Welcome, Tammy Pierson. Welcome, Talia Pierson."

A trio of shivering sisters scuttled away from the brisk twilight air in succession. From their dainty facial features to their delicate mannerisms, an uncanny resemblance coupled the siblings. They appeared as carbon copies time-lapsed over two decades with the youngest barely of drinking age. After placing down their purses, the eldest sister consoled the hollowed-eyed baby of the bunch. In short order, the middle-born followed suit by lovingly latching onto her relatives.

Antony constructed psychological profiles of the new-comers from his vantage point across the pub. Slowly, his impressions took shape. During a sisterly embrace, he recorded an incomprehensible jumble of tenderness and profanities. Before a round of shots, he overheard a toast of good riddance. The downcast expression of the youngest Pierson was a glaring constant throughout his information gathering.

A narrative around heartbreak was formed within Antony's imagination. His dreamed-up backstory centered on Little Tabatha, who was ill-prepared to have her sublime utopia transformed into a desolate expanse of hopelessness. Tonight, in spite of her reluctance, Tabatha had been persuaded to leave the comforts of home to cope with her heartache as a family. The veracity of these speculations were immaterial to Antony; the causal classification was conspicuous.

Unlike the Pierson sisters, less than ten seconds were required for Antony to assign a behavioral cause to the next entrant. Lorenzo Ruiz stumbled into The Emerald in a state of stupefaction. Every lurching step constituted an adventure. On each footfall, it was as if he was unprepared for the imminent collision between sneaker and ground. Antony attributed a carousing motivation immediately upon seeing this careening gait.

Lorenzo grew flustered when the robotic voice declared his arrival. "Who said that?" His glassy eyes searched erratically for the greeter.

Dissatisfied by the absence of a response, he clamored

again and again for answers. Lorenzo's agitation mounted. In futility, he sparred with everyone and no one simultaneously. He hurled accusations of using voice modifiers at the sisters. He decried Antony and Albert as unaccommodating eyewitnesses. He denounced Floyd for watering down the booze. When nobody refuted his ludicrous allegations, Lorenzo removed a flask from his tattered trench coat and emptied its contents via consecutive swigs.

Antony looked on smugly as Lorenzo's actions reinforced his snap judgment. While acknowledging the small sample, the fit of the model left him feeling awfully perspicacious. Each of its three categories contained at least one observation. None of the pub's patrons qualified as outliers. A sense of confidence brewed within him. He abandoned his people watching in favor of being antisocial just before his astuteness could be put to the test.

"Welcome, Ronald Hasslet."

The new arrival swaggered through the optical turnstile. After wiping his feet, he stepped toward Lorenzo. He placed a hand on his shoulder, pulling the drunkard into his personal bubble. The words he whispered left Lorenzo looking uneasy. The man slipped the inebriated mess a few bancor shares with a handshake, then sent him on his way.

With the scene diffused, the pacificator headed to the restroom. Everybody else in The Emerald reabsorbed themselves into their personal preoccupations. On his return, despite an abundance of unoccupied seats and tables, he settled onto the stool next to Antony.

"Voilà, the commotion has been ousted," the man triumphantly declared.

Gazing into the piquant product of fermentation, Antony ignored the stranger's comment. From nucleation sites etched into the bottom of the pint glass, he followed the life cycle of the bubbles. The carbon dioxide spheroids expanded as they ascended. At the end of their journey, they congregated at the surface to form the beer's frothy head. He lifted the laboratory and sent the liquid swirling with the flick of his wrist. Intrigued by the fluid mechanics, he possessed little interest in a superficial exchange.

"Great," Antony said with a tinge of sarcasm. "Now everyone can enjoy their drinks in peace."

"Indeed, enjoy we must." Undeterred, the man seized on the conversational breadcrumbs. "The question is, if we honestly examine this trivial disruption, where do we assign the blame? Most would jump on the bandwagon to criticize the social etiquette of that inebriate. But perhaps we shouldn't be so quick to judge?"

Antony engineered a prolonged pause. "Is that right?"

"As a matter of fact, it is," the man said with aplomb. "There's a biological component guiding this line of reasoning. Our behaviors, emotions, and thoughts are all dictated by neurochemicals and action potentials. At our core, it's these neurological communications that shape our identities and govern how we live our lives. Him, you, me, all of us.

Mankind is forever at the mercy of hidden forces."

Antony's sightline remained fixed on his bubbling beverage. "So, we're all absolved of personal responsibility?"

"Of course not. You misunderstand me, friend. I was merely pointing out that it's not difficult to fathom how one's conduct can be influenced … or even maliciously manipulated."

"Thanks a bunch for sharing," Antony said caustically.

"Think about the prevalence of drug usage. Whether we're talking about commonplace stimulants or depressants, narcotics or medication, isn't our entire society constantly under the influ—"

"Where you going with this?"

"Consider the wide-ranging effects of these substances. Do they not alter our moods? Modify how we act? Shape our perceptions? Distort our realities? The incident you witnessed a few minutes ago was a microcosm of a societal ill, not an anomaly."

Antony slouched forward. He planted his elbow on the bar top and propped up his contemplative cranium. While stroking his chin, he cognitively coalesced his earlier musings on medicine with macro-level maladies.

Beyond a shadow of a doubt, psychotropic drugs metamorphosed the mentally ill. Exhibit one, Fritz McGregor. In retrospect, Antony wondered whether he had ever met his bona fide neighbor. He now suspected that he had spent decades interacting with a pharmaceutical-suffused husk. Naturally this raised the question: were these individuals one and the same? Bifurcating these states of consciousness had never crossed Antony's mind.

From the self-evident case of Fritz, Antony's reflections shifted to his own experiences within altered states. He reviewed the inquiries set forth by the stranger. Moods? Actions? Perceptions? Chemical substances mutated each of these facets on the majority of Antony's days. He gained an appreciation for the extensive influence of intoxicants as he inwardly advanced through the essence of the argument.

Trickling out from the confines of the private speech realm, he asked a question under his breath. "Distort our realities?"

Curiosity refreshed Antony's standoffish demeanor. Opening his posture, he acknowledged the stranger for the first time face-to-face and was greeted by an expression of reassurance.

"Yes," the man whispered, "even to the extent of reality distortion. Now you're beginning to understand control on the grandest of scales." He cleared his throat and extended his hand. "The name is Paine. Nathaniel Paine. But my friends call me Nate."

Antony warily clasped hands. "Well that certainly wasn't your name when you walked in here."

A sly smile rolled across Nathaniel's lips. "Observant."

High-pitched squeaks emanating from a neighboring bar stool prevented any explanation. Both Antony and Nathaniel glanced over. At the sight of Albert conspicuously inching his way into their discussion, Nathaniel released a disarming chortle. The overly agreeable senior citizen replicated the act.

Once their laughter subsided, Nathaniel turned back toward Antony. When he picked up their conversation, he abandoned the provocative for the innocuous. "Delighted to make your acquaintance, Antony. What are you drinking, friend?"

"Tipsy Octopus, Golden Harvest." Antony instinctively took a sip. "I've yet to find a better autumn beer."

"Barkeep," Nathaniel said, motioning over to Floyd. "Two Tipsy Octopuses please."

"Coming right up," said Floyd. "What about some food? Hungry at all?"

"No, thank you. Drinks will do for now."

Three-quarters of the way through the first pour, foam sputtered out from the beer spigot. Floyd returned the tentacle-shaped handle to its upright position. "Kicked. Beers are on the house. But it'll be a few minutes. Sorry." He hurried into the back to swap the kegs.

People appeared to possess a predilection to please Nathaniel Paine. His alluring blend of features hijacked heuristic processing, kindling a response of exaggerated emotional coherence. Intelligence, benevolence, virtuousness—the most desirable of personality traits were attributed before he could say a word. A long stubble beard blanketed the high delicate cheekbones of his oblong physiognomy. Between striking green irises, a prominent nasal bridge produced a proboscis that resembled the beak of a bird of prey. A thick, wavy, dark-chocolate mane complemented his natural tan complexion. He commanded the halo effect with adroitness. Over a navy polka-dot dress shirt, he donned a golden-brown blazer along with a light-blue scarf. His suave outfit in this casual environment seemed to amplify cognitive biases.

During Floyd's absence, Antony quietly fixated on Nathaniel's enigmatic statements on the malleability of mankind. The other bar-side men similarly stayed mum. The melodic fiddles, flutes, and harps that played in the background gained auditory prominence. Lulls in the Celtic ballad were filled by the gossiping Pierson sisters. Nathaniel shifted to eavesdropping mode by parallelizing his shoulders to the sibling trio seated across the bar. Albert appeared to follow Nathaniel's lead. He put back on his hat and partially cupped his hand around his ear, fine-tuning his acoustic attention for the amorous anguish.

A few minutes later, the kitchen's aluminum door swung open, and Floyd reclaimed his proper post. He grumbled on his way to the draft beer tower. His mouth twisted into a grimace upon snatching a clean glass. Opening the tap, he set the dispensing system in motion. As the brew flowed from its stainless steel reserve into the drinkware, he glared at the fresh blisters that marred his smooth palms.

"Sorry about the wait," Floyd said as he walked over. "Lousy keg coupler was stuck fast." He tossed out a pair of coasters and set down the beers.

Nathaniel flashed Floyd an appreciative expression for his gesture of goodwill.

"Anything else you need, give me a shout." Floyd grabbed a first aid kit out from behind the bar, then returned to his mixology guide. While burying himself into his studies anew, he covered his hands with aloe and rubbed them together gingerly.

After sliding one of the complimentary beverages over to Antony, Nathaniel hopped onto the empty stool next to Albert, who appeared to still be snooping on the Pierson sisters.

"Love," Nathaniel said, annunciating the abstraction in a manner that conveyed its primal value. True to its nature as the glue of attachment, the word clung to the atmospheric elements. It uncannily lingered in the space surrounding the speaker. Following a pause, he poetically waxed on. "Humanity's transcendent virtue, yet an inexplicable mystery. In love's absence resides indifference. In the void, fear flourishes and hatred thrives. Some of us are fortunate enough to capture it. Others spend their entire lives in pursuit."

"Love," Albert chimed in with gaiety. "What more could you want in life?"

"Absolutely nothing, buddy," said Nathaniel. "Clearly you've been struck by serendipity. Clearly you've snared that unconditional affection we all desire."

Albert smiled broadly. "I can't deny it. I just may be the luckiest man alive."

"Here you are, living out a fairy tale." With a pat on the back, Nathaniel solidified rapport with the congenial barfly. "Consider me envious."

"Honest to goodness, it was love at first sight."

Antony groaned as Albert launched into reminiscence.

"Back when I was a child I used to have these repeating dreams of meeting an exotic beauty. Each night I'd sweep her off her feet with a different romantic gesture. Believe it or not, I used to pretend to plan out our wedding using my action figures and stuffed animals. Well, guess what? My high school sweetheart and I celebrated another anniversary last weekend."

"Good sir," Nathaniel said, "you are an inspiration."

"Sixty-three wonderful years we've been married." Albert fidgeted with his platinum wedding band. "But we've been inseparable since ninth grade. It all started on one special day, back in biology class. Some superhero movie had just come out. My lab partner was off playing hooky. Isiah caught a matinee just to spoil it for everyone. Pranks upon pranks—that kid was as immature as they come. Whoopee cushions, fake poop, you name it. Worse still, he smelled like tuna fish. Ha! Boy did I hate him."

Albert took a sip of his cocktail. With the thread of his garrulous account seemingly lost, he rubbed his forehead.

"And what about the object of your affections?" asked Nathaniel at last.

"Silly me, of course. So our teacher was in the middle

of taking attendance when the new kid from a world away walked into our class. Daluchi was the most beautiful girl I'd ev—"

"Now that's what I'm talking about," Nathaniel said. "How different would this story be without truancy? Sans the gift of clairvoyance, one knows not when they'll encounter their missing piece. We must be welcoming of our romantic destiny when it arrives."

"No ifs, ands, or buts about it. Only fools let love pass them by."

Nathaniel gestured toward the sisters. "Take a look over there. Sure they're young and dazzling, but unhealthy relationships have scarred each of them. Can you sense the embitterment that seeps into their words? Concealed under layers of cosmetics dwells disenchantment. Prince Charming himself would be shooed away before unraveling the riddles of their guarded hearts. I've come across cynics, but none have needed an injection of optimism more than those three."

Equipped with an arsenal of experience and a fondness for sharing, Albert appeared to revel in the idea of rescuing the disillusioned damsels. He stood exuding a gallant air. "Time to turn those frowns upside down."

Nathaniel gave Albert an approving thumbs-up as he walked away.

"Another disturbance dispelled," Nathaniel archly said while sliding back onto the stool next to Antony. "Now, where were we?"

"Huh?" Antony looked over, bemused.

"A trifling matter of displacing a nosy citizen. Nothing to concern yourself with. Anyhow, indulge my curiosity." Nathaniel pointed at the nautical-themed case bookended by Antony's feet. "What's that?"

"Who's nosy now?" Antony clutched the keepsake like a toddler coveting his favorite toy. "This right here is not your concern."

"My apologies, I didn't intend to intrude. I asked because it looks familiar. An acquaintance of mine had a chest adorned with similar wood burnings. Within it he stored a remembrance from his time at sea, a ceremonial whistle once used on naval vessels."

"How dare you." Indignation elevated Antony's reply by an octave. "What impertinence is this?"

"Please Antony, lower your voice." A quelling gesture complemented his appeal.

Antony nudged the barstool out from under his buttocks. "Who do you think you are going through my stuff?"

"I assure you," Nathaniel said, maintaining equanimity. "I would never touch your property without permission."

"Then how'd you know about the whistle?"

"If you compose yourself and give me a moment, I'll explain. The chest I mentioned belonged to a former acquaintance. I refer to him as an acquaintance, rather than a friend, because our time together was regretfully short-lived. He was a pillar of the community who attracted people from all around to his rocking chair podium on Sanctuary Lane."

"How …" Antony's frame sunk back onto his stool. "How did you know Jasper?"

"Gregarious, worldly storytellers tend to distinguish themselves from the banal."

"I'll drink to that." And so Antony did. "When did you two meet?"

"Jasper's notoriety spread through the grapevine. About a year ago, I resolved to form my own opinion of the man. It at once became clear that his lofty reputation paled in comparison with the genuine article. We strolled down memory lane on a handful of occasions. When Jasper reminisced, he did so candidly, with an authenticity that can only be acquired by firsthand experience. Have you ever noticed the latent disconnect when others recount the past? As if their personal narratives had been contaminated by a third-person point of view?"

"More times than I can count."

"Among the ordinary, Jasper was a rarefied character. During our final meeting, we spoke at length about expressing gratitude at the individual level, not for a faceless collective. He brought me up to his apartment and proudly showed me that very chest. The following morning, while Mrs. Rodin lauded some new infrastructure program, Jasper's name inconspicuously appeared on the ticker together with other dangers to humanity."

"To Jasper Turner," Antony said. "In remembrance of the

time we shared. I thank you for your friendship. And for the wisdom you im—" He choked up, aborting his salutation.

Nathaniel solemnly elevated his glass. "Cheers."

Despite depriving Jasper of the friend label, sorrow seemed to mutate Nathaniel's mien. The ceremonial clink connected the two bar-side citizens. In Nathaniel's display of grief, Antony reconciled his mistrustful intuitions. All of Antony's leeriness from the earlier alias episode abated.

"Jasper and I forged an intimate bond over the course of a decade," Antony said. "Our discussions spanned the gamut of subjects, from superficial banter to divulging our hopes, dreams, and deepest fears. Yet, prior to this afternoon ..."

Nathaniel nodded. "Go on, friend."

"Prior to this afternoon," Antony grudgingly proceeded, "I had never laid eyes on perhaps his most cherished possession."

"I cannot speak with certainty, but I'm quite confident that you have. We both know that Jasper was more the self-effacing than the grandstanding type. Yet he boasted of his retirement gift whenever possible and took delight in showing off the calls he had learned." Nathaniel paused and swallowed hard. "In all likelihood, that treasured exchange was pruned from your accessible recollections. Without consent, those memories were stolen away."

"That's preposterous. But I've been drinking, so who am I to determine what is possible and what is not?"

"Let's revisit your capacity to discern on another day."

Nathaniel smirked before reestablishing a serious tone. "Maybe you can help me shed light on a related matter for now."

"In regards to Jasper?"

"More specifically a maritime disaster he had witnessed. The topic came up when we were together in his apartment. Straight away, he became tentative and sped through a halfhearted story. Burdened by a secret, I surmise, aspects were left unsaid. On a subtler level, I sensed that there was something he wanted to confide, something potentially dangerous. Our chat was cut short by his nurse. Jasper and I said our goodbyes, and we never spoke again."

"I'd venture to guess that he was deliberating whether or not to show you this." Antony pulled the crumpled cargo manifest out from his pocket and placed it on the bar top. "Have a look."

Given the momentous prelude surrounding the object, Nathaniel seemed surprised by the rumpled condition of the document. Stooping forward, he seized the paper mass. He carefully undid its irregular folds, then smoothed out its creases over the edge of the bar. To ensure that nothing of significance would go undetected, he employed his pointer finger as a guide to peruse the entries. When his escorting digit reached the bottom right corner of the page, it returned to container PANU 808637 3. The record containing the disquieting eyeballs warranted a more scrupulous read.

"What does it all mean?" Antony asked impatiently.

"This world we inhabit is full of secrets. But very few mysteries."

At the onset of a yawn, Nathaniel stretched skyward. Discreetly, he surveyed The Emerald. Antony suppressed the contagious impetus to duplicate the act. Dissatisfied by Nathaniel's cryptic explanation, his glare sharpened with each passing silent second. Once eye contact was renewed, Nathaniel tapped the salient entry thrice, then neatly folded the piece of paper and entrusted it back to its owner.

"My self-preservation instincts implore me to end this exchange and walk away." Nathaniel's face tightened ever so slightly. "However, in hindsight, I mishandled Jasper, and my conscience cannot bear another failure. Ordinarily, we wouldn't broach this subject until a future encounter. Ordinarily, that meeting would take place at a secluded location. But time is of the essence."

Antony waved around the cargo manifest. "A little elaboration would go a long way."

"All in due course." Nathaniel's blink rate increased. "There is much that I will tell you tonight, none of which will be easy to digest. From this point forward, your life will be divided into before and into after. In the present moment, our fates are intertwined. This is an honest account, free from hyperbole. Doom awaits us both if you panic in reaction to my revelations. Do you understand?"

"Not really," Antony said, unconvinced of any transformative potential. "I truthfully haven't a clue what it is you're talking about. But I'm here and I'm listening."

"In an age of ubiquitous conformity, an individual need not be an insurgent to be placed in peril. All that is required is the act of being oneself. An independent thought alone is evidence of deviance. When living under a magnifying glass, a single step out of line is the equivalent of a dissident dash.

"Under the vigilant eyes of Pansophical, you flaunted your individuality. Yesterday, the name Antony Sartori populated a watch list along with thousands of other minor lawbreakers. Today, Antony Sartori was labeled a danger to humanity.

"Public Safety will raid Sanctuary Village later tonight. They'll ransack apartment 7F for illicit materials. If you're apprehended, neither fair nor unfair hearing will be held. In the best case, you'll be banished to a quarantine camp. In the worst case, you'll spend the rest of your days being tortured in a detention center."

Antony's lips quivered. "How in the world do you know of such things?"

"It just so happens that Praxis does not lack ingenuity when it comes to the technical realm. The suspicious person reports piled up at the DSGS following your schoolyard brawl. As far as affairs to come, we intercepted an internal communication between Benton and Sergeant Bannister forty-five minutes ago.

"Welcome to your personal hour of peril. Encircled by everlasting darkness, I offer a torch to enlighten, along with a path to physical freedom. All will be revealed, but now is not the time to dawdle. We must move quickly."

As Antony reflected on his dire predicament, sensory memories attached to his confrontation with Pan-Youth produced a series of immersive mental scenes. A medley of sights, sounds, smells, and haptic perceptions demanded that he relive his defiant deed. Visions of Kennard frantically clambering the backstop amid derisive cheers appeared within his imagination. Antony inwardly detected the earthly scents of the infield dirt. He felt the metabolic strain within his muscles as they struggled to subdue Robert Owen. Throughout it all, in the background, echoed the bumptious teen's sinister warning.

Don't trick yourself into believing that this heroic act will go unnoticed, old timer.

"That vicious little punk was right." The fulfillment of the prophecy sapped Antony of his vigor. His respiratory rate slowed, and he crumbled onto the bar. "It's only been a few hours, and it has already come to pass."

Nathaniel placed his hand on Antony's bowed back. "Being ousted from society is a terrifying proposition, I understand. Adopting a defeatist attitude will only ensure our demise, however."

"Why me? Is this my reward for opposing moral repugnance? Is there no leniency for a former Pansophical engineer who helped pave the road to prosperity?"

"Years ago," Nathaniel said soothingly, "I stood in your

shoes. My thoughts from then are revived by you in the present. I assure you, in retrospect you'll be eternally grateful for being awoken."

"My death warrant has been drawn up." Antony rolled his chin across his sprawled-out arm and set his sightline on the purveyor of confidentialities. "It's all over for me. There's no evading the omnipresence of Pansophical."

"On the contrary, life thrives in their blind spots."

"Blind spots? Rewind. Did you say what I think you said?" Overcome by revulsion, Antony gagged. "Are you … a member of … Pra—"

"In fact I am. And if you aspire to be a free man by day's end, you'll consider yourself one of us as well."

"Out of the question," Antony spat back.

"Think this over carefully. Rarely are we granted such control over our fate."

Slivers of optimism reframed Antony's state of mind. "Well it appears that you've made a grave miscalculation, Nathaniel. What's stopping me from tackling you and exposing that inconvenient truth of yours?"

"Before you betray me in the hopes of earning absolution, a few reminders." Nathaniel calmly counted them off on his fingers. "No longer are you some inconsequential curfew violator. That blemish on your record, combined with the rebellious acts of today, signify a pattern of disobedience. Not to mention there's the complications caused by that document within your pocket, which any mid-level bureaucrat would classify as contraband to the highest degree. Reading it alone borders on treason.

"Three strikes. Regardless of the information you possess, the Pansophical Corporation will not be granting you a pardon. Dreams of acquiring one are delusions to be dismissed."

Antony averted his gaze. "This can't be happening,"

"It can and it is," said Nathaniel firmly. "No more procrastinating. Our conversation has attracted the attention of a loyalist busybody. It's time for us to leave."

The reference to an eavesdropper injected a sense of urgency within Antony. He sprung up from his slouched position and impulsively slapped down upon his thigh. Alternating between flexing and extending his fingers, he verified that the cargo manifest was secure by dragging his grimy nails back and forth across the folds of the concealed material. Nathaniel's appeal to logic successfully brought Antony's incipient snitching machinations to a grinding halt.

Only two conceivable courses of action existed: contrived ignorance or radical acceptance. Adopting the former involved designating Nathaniel as nothing more than a disaffected deceiver. It entailed hours of binge drinking until all was forgotten. Adopting the latter involved disavowing dogmas and renouncing his citizenship; it entailed embarking into the unknown. Within his rational mind, no amount of cognitive dissonance could protect the option of tantalizing nescience. Try as he might, he could not explain away the intel Nathaniel divulged.

"Desperation compels me." A sense of shame washed over Antony's physiognomy as he embraced the unthinkable. "I'm not ready to die. And I'm not willing to sacrifice myself to appease the masses. There's something inexplicably illusory with this world. At the very least, I'm determined to live long enough to figure it out."

"All the answers you seek will be revealed in time. Right now, we need to separate to divert suspicion, though."

"And then?" Antony asked.

Nathaniel spoke softly. "In my absence behave normally. Remember that everyone around here is none the wiser. Avoid the urge to overcompensate. Finish your beer and settle your bill. Do nothing out of the ordinary. If anyone asks, you drank too much and are calling it a night. If they happen to question you about our conversation, speak disparagingly. Tell them that I'm an irritating out-of-towner who couldn't keep his mouth shut. When you get outside walk three blocks west to the newsstand on Pontius Avenue. That's where we'll meet."

"Understood," Antony said with nod.

Nathaniel hopped off his stool. He stared down Ivan as he plodded toward the restroom, then spun back to Antony. "Follow my lead while we're on the streets, and keep the dialogue to a minimum. Be ever vigilant, my friend. Godspeed."

On Nathaniel's way out of the establishment, he dangled his arm over the optical turnstile and snatched Ivan's sketchpad from the abutting table.

"Goodbye, Ronald Hasslet."

Nathaniel vanished on the heels of the mechanical farewell.

Antony focused on the road ahead as opposed to Nathaniel's departure. The game plan was categorically simple. Nevertheless, envisioning the upcoming solo leg left him unnerved. Here was a man taking his marks, with his feet planted in the starting blocks, preparing for a life on the run. He suddenly apperceived the breadth of his vulnerability within the present. Not even the familiar comforts of The Emerald could allay the feeling that his perfidy was exposed. To avoid being overwhelmed by the enormity of the situation, he broke down each task into its elementary movements.

Deliberately, Antony wrapped his fingers around the pint glass. The chilly sensations that prominently characterized the object anchored his attention. Every point of contact was consciously identified. He elevated his beer off the bar to a suitable drinking height. Along his personal frontal plane, he slightly angled his wrist, sending the flavorsome ale through his open lips. Teeth and tongue alike felt the frosty wetness as the liquid entered his digestive tract. He repeated this sequence every forty-five seconds or so. Once his glass was empty, he casually told Floyd that he would pay off his tab by the end of the week, then staggered in the direction of the exit.

"Slow down, boss," Ivan shouted while rushing out from

the restroom. "Where'd your buddy go?"

The raspy accosting stalled Antony's teetering progress. Notwithstanding Nathaniel's warning, the question caught him off guard. Standing face-to-face with the surly inquisitor was his first test. Antony's designs of projecting himself in a quotidian fashion could not weather the heat of the moment. In an exaggerated manner, he purposely ramped up the drunken nonsense.

"Sir Ivan," he slurred, "what is it that you require?"

"That buddy of yours." Ivan pointed at the pair of unoccupied barstools. "Where'd he go?"

"Beats me." Antony awkwardly shrugged. "Beats you. Beet salad." He forced out a laugh.

"Everything all right there, boss? What's up with you today?"

"The magical powers of alcohol." Antony twirled around his finger as if it were wand. "I've been transformed."

"Hmmm." Ivan looked Antony up and down. "So, what was the deal with your buddy? Ran out of here, barely touched his beer."

"How would I know?"

"Seemed like you two were becoming pretty chummy."

"Certainly not," Antony contended, suddenly serious. "I only wish I had a muzzle to silence that jerk."

"Is that so? Because from where I was sitting"—Ivan leaned in close with a narrow-eyed stare—"that's not what I saw."

"What you saw was a Seraphs fan. If you've met one, you've met them all. Arrogant asses without exception. How many times was that guy going to remind me about the eleven championship banners hanging in São Pau—"

"Bah. I shoulda known it was nothing more than two blockheads talking about sportsball."

Typically Antony would retort this belittlement. In the here and now, he gladly surrendered his personal honor to avoid the limelight. He gave no response as Ivan strode past. Antony's path to salvation was unobstructed, but only for a split second.

"What in the devil?" Ivan roared. "Where is it?" He dropped down onto all fours and crawled about hysterically.

Antony monitored Ivan's frantic movements. He patiently waited for an opening to slink away without further confrontation. Presumably spurred by boredom, two of the Pierson sisters peeled away from a long-winded Albert anecdote and joined the search party. When they approached Ivan, Antony pounced.

Once outside, he scampered into the abutting alley. He gazed up at the sparse stars that penetrated the light pollution. Angling his frame rearward, he transferred his weight to his heels. As his spine collided with the exterior of The Emerald, he heaved a sigh of relief. He heard an invective stream chock-full of profanities and references to a stolen sketchpad through the walls. Following a half-minute of vulgarities, Ivan's tirade concluded.

For the nonce, acknowledging the omnipresent nature of the axiom of impermanence was inescapable. Over a single evening, the retreat Antony once held dear had been converted into a minefield of misgivings.

Over billions of years, the luminous heavenly bodies overhead would inevitably fade to black. Desperately clinging to a transitory state was a pointless exercise; everything eventually bowed to the forces of change. In spite of the prosperity Pansophical propagated, a revolution lurked on the outskirts of the monolith. Tonight, compelled by the survival imperative and feelings of derealization, Antony embraced reformation.

CHAPTER THIRTEEN

An augmented reality billboard promoting the civic responsibility of communal surveillance gave Antony pause on his flight from authoritarian oversight. The heedful directive from the Department of Safety and Global Security embodied humanity's collective vigilance through an interactive mosaic of eyeballs. The photomontage was composed of visual organs from citizens across the skin complexion spectrum. There were close-set eyes and wide-set eyes, upturned eyes and down-turned eyes, protruding eyes and hooded eyes, with iris pigmentations ranging from the lightest of blues to the darkest of browns.

Antony scanned the assemblage for real-world likenesses. He saw himself. He saw friends and foes. He saw everybody he'd ever known. Provoked by paranoia, he flipped up his collar and buried his chin into his chest.

Each westward stride brought the unaccompanied stretch of his emigration closer to an end. When the cherry-colored finish line on Pontius Avenue entered the margins of his purview, he hastened his pace. One block away, the people forming the newsstand queue asynchronously stepped forward. Nathaniel moved from the on-deck circle into the ordering recess. He reappeared two minutes later carrying the pilfered sketchpad along with the latest edition of *The People's Voice*. Before stepping onto the sidewalk, the shrewd recruiter swiveled his sightline in search of shadowing Samaritans. Once the coast appeared clear, he addressed Antony.

Nathaniel flashed a commendatory grin. "Greetings, my friend. I'm delighted that you didn't get sidetracked on the way over. Appears that we're in store for a rainy evening. If we hurry, we'll be able to elude the downpour. Our wellness retreat is less than twenty minutes away."

"Today has been exhausting," said Antony in a subdued tone. "I look forward to a peaceful night."

Neither spoke another word until they neared the squalid doorstep of their destination. They drifted down a dingy backstreet on the border of the city's industrial district. Dumpsters brimming with decomposing matter lined the passageway. Nathaniel pinched his nostrils. Antony was unprepared for the putrid incursion of his olfactory receptors. A deep inhalation triggered his gag reflex.

"My apologies," Nathaniel said while handing Antony a pack of gum. "I always forget to warn the newcomers. Our retreats tend to not be in the most pleasant parts of town. The aromas inside are far more palatable."

Amid the dilapidated storefronts, the Inky Lyceum was

the lone establishment to still render services. An orderly row of miniature Pansophical flags protruded from the upper facade of the tattoo parlor. Tribalistic persuasions similarly embellished its main window. Center stage among this chauvinistic artistry was a vivid depiction of a mountain range featuring the carved likenesses of Pansophical's Board of Directors. At the base of these granite sculptures, hordes of painted citizens bowed down before their corporate saviors.

Whereas Nathaniel hustled indoors, Antony marveled at the mural. The minty breath freshener alleviated his queasiness, diminishing the unbearableness of the neighborhood. Adrift in recollections of bygone days, a sense of camaraderie percolated within him. He hypnotically placed his palm on the shop window, metaphorically merging with the congregation. His bewitching dreams of deindividuation were quickly terminated by Nathaniel, who knocked on the other side of the glass.

Following a prolonged blink, Antony identified a laudatory citizen near the outskirts of the scene dressed in a brown overcoat. "I'm no longer one of you." He scratched away his acrylic doppelgänger using his fingernail. "Evidently, my days of worshipping with the masses are over. Evidently, we now exist as enemies. Only time will tell whether I've chosen correctly."

Nathaniel extended a beckoning finger through the doorway. "Quit loitering and get in here."

Antony ceased explicating on his adversarial relationship with the idolizers of Pansophical and headed into the shop. On the threshold, however, he paused once more. Half outside, half inside, he inspected the antiquated security turnstile. An out-of-order notice was duct taped to the metallic glass flap of the swinging gate. In lieu of traditional greetings, the defective device spewed a continual stream of robotic gibberish. Stirred by wariness, Antony crouched down for a closer look. Apprehensive about disclosing his whereabouts, he popped open the turnstile's service panel.

A thunderous voice arose from the parlor's foremost cubicle. "Leave it alone. Can't you see it's broken?"

Antony raised his sightline but averted his eyes at once. A shirtless behemoth with a black paisley bandanna wrapped around his Neanderthal-shaped skull assumed receptionist duties. A ginger horseshoe mustache framed his tobacco-stained choppers. Ink strokes of the macabre variety painted his pasty skin. Over the decades his muscular build had been overrun by opportunistic fat cells. Notwithstanding his flaccid biceps and prominent paunch, he exuded an air of intimidation. Tattooed at the base of his throat was a wooden marionette control bar with severed strings. Directly below, his given name blazoned his chest in an Old English typeface: "Maddox."

"The prestigious Inky Lyceum," Nathaniel grandly announced. "Rumor has it that there isn't a finer tattoo shop west of the Mississippi."

"Prestigious?" Maddox scoffed. "Who'd you hear that from?"

"Word travels fast among the aficionados," answered Nathaniel.

"Yeah, yeah, yeah," Maddox said. "None of those type come around these parts."

"My cousin Lucius would beg to differ."

"Is that a fact?"

"It is," Nathaniel said. "Here is where he blossomed as an apprentice. His praise for this place knows no bounds."

"Oh, I remember L. J. all too well." Maddox slammed his fist on the cobweb-strewn display case. "If he ever shows his ugly face around here again, I'll tar and feather the bastard. Unless you're lookin' for the same, time for you to tell me what I can do you two for?"

"Who you tar, and who you feather, is none of our business. As for the matter at hand, the piece that I want will require an artist with exceptional skill. An ant farm with tunnels winding around my bicep, tattooed hyper-realistically and to scale."

Looking on in reticence, Antony attempted to make sense of the befogging exchange. He jumped to his feet under the presumption that Nathaniel was about to be trounced.

"All right smart-ass. We can make that happen." Maddox slogged back into one of the stations while he spoke. "Wait out there. Both of you need to log in. Then whoever is gettin' inked needs to sign some shit."

With the threat of physical violence seemingly extinguished, Antony strolled around the parlor's reception area. Atop a coffin-shaped coffee table, fractured baboon skulls bookended a collection of cruddy leather-bound portfolios. Cockeyed canvases composed by middling artists plastered the walls. A pair of disturbing life-sized portraits of the mummified body of Ötzi the Iceman flanked the entryway. Along the splotchy ledges that partitioned the workstations, coil machines dangled, and needles soaked in chemical baths of disinfectants. An atonal hodgepodge of distorted guitar riffs, primordial growls, and breakneck percussions blared from a floor-standing tower speaker.

In the act of absorbing the seedy ambience, Antony wondered why any sensible person would patronize an establishment of this sort. Moreover, he questioned the logic of stopping for body modifications given his endangered status. Insecurities swirled within his frontal lobe. By no means was this the safe house he was promised. Deprived of confidence, he sunk his teeth into his collar and helplessly gazed at Nathaniel for reassurance. His request for relief went unnoticed.

Maddox emerged with a portable RFID reader and a clipboard in hand. "Pansophical should be sendin' out someone to fix our piece of shit gate sooner or later. We've been usin' this old-ass citizen logger for weeks."

As the mammoth tattooist drew near, Nathaniel spun around and straightened his posture. Maddox flipped on the low-frequency handheld reader. A seal from the Department of Vital Records and Statistics was engraved into its side. He elevated the device to within a few centimeters of Nathaniel's nape, then depressed its trigger. A green light on the reader's backside came on shortly after.

The tension underlying Maddox's bearing receded. He turned to Antony and twirled his index finger aloft. "And now you."

"But ..." Antony's head oscillated between the men in consternation. "But ... but ..."

Nathaniel flashed his palm to slow Maddox's advance. "May we have a minute?"

"You got it," said Maddox as he withdrew to his receptionist post.

"I know what you're thinking," Nathaniel said. He placed his arm around Antony's shoulder. "Years ago, when my role was reversed, I panicked at this exact moment. All the fears are justified, but they're based on a false premise. I give you my word that there's no need to worry."

Without demur, Antony acquiesced. While stretching out his collar to expose his implant, his physique submissively contracted. Awaiting the scan, he monitored Maddox's rearward actions via their reflections on the framed artwork. The mirrored scene was soon cast in the yellowish hue of the reader's indicator light.

Seeking elucidation for the colored designation, Antony whirled around in an ignorant frenzy. Before he could articulate his incomprehension, Maddox slapped him in the stomach with the clipboard.

"Time to sling some ink." Maddox ushered the men down a hallway with an openhanded gesture. "Go back that way and wait while I lock all this shit up."

Puzzled, Antony took the consent forms, but he didn't go anywhere.

Maddox lumbered past him on his way to a wall-mounted security panel. When he armed the system, the music stopped. The turnstile clicked, locking into place. Amorphous metal blinds descended over the windows. He manually double-checked these fortifications, then nudged Antony toward the private stations where Nathaniel was waiting.

From the door at the end of the hall's middle hinge, Maddox removed a faux pin to reveal a tiny red button. Once pressed, a second security layer materialized to safeguard the premises. Crisscrossing lasers beamed from imperceptible holes along the parlor's perimeter.

Antony suspected that a lethal concatenation of events awaited any trespasser who breached the primary line of defense and disturbed the labyrinth of optical tripwires. Within his imagination, he visualized the explosive train leaving the station. Electricity flowed uninterrupted, heating blasting caps throughout the circuit. Precisely placed bundles of dynamite detonated. In devastating fashion, the entire building was razed.

As Maddox opened the door to the private station, the

poignant odor of disinfectants seeped out. Resembling an operating room, the workspace stood in striking opposition to the publicly visible areas of the shop. Two articulating arms were suspended overhead. A plate-sized magnifier was attached to the lower arm. From the other hung a shadowless hexagonal light fixture. A black powder–coated tool chest, capped by a rubberwood slab, stretched across the rear wall. Below its labeled drawers, eight heavy duty casters provided the workbench with mobility. In the heart of the room sat a tattooing chair upon a hydraulic base.

Through Antony's callow eyes it became apparent that the Inky Lyceum's ostensible shadiness was a well-constructed facade. The observations he had gathered over the past ten minutes began to make sense. The cleanliness of the back room served as another data point to substantiate his theory.

Nevertheless, it wasn't until Antony noticed the wave-scattering fractal lattice covering the pearly white walls that he became convinced that this was an incubator for subversion. Years earlier he'd designed the control system for a stealth drone constructed of a similar metamaterial. Within these confines he was sure that all was hidden from Pansophical's pervasive gaze. Standing outside the surveillance state, he winked at Maddox in appreciation of the guile he exhibited.

Once the safe space was sealed off, Maddox seized Nathaniel for a crushing embrace. Akin to a bumbling boa constrictor having a go at affection, Nathaniel's arms were pinned. In this abrupt outpouring of emotion, Nathaniel's sneakers were detached from the jasmine-colored floor.

Nathaniel squeezed out an irritated appeal. "That's … quite … enough … you big oaf."

"My bad," Maddox said, releasing his grasp. "Gettin' back in the swing of things since Charlotte went down has been tough."

"A terrible tragedy," Nathaniel said. He caught his breath while adjusting his disheveled blazer. "Many great men perished in that massacre."

"Many were my friends," Maddox bemoaned. "I was lucky that day. Lucky as hell that I made it out of there alive."

"One of the fortunate few."

"I'll never forget the sound of those alarm bells. Everythin' else is a blur."

"Forgive my callousness," Nathaniel said. "Pansophical may have won that battle, but the war is underway."

"They'll pay for everythin' they did," Maddox said, his voice hollow. "They'll pay for everythin' they're doing."

"All in due time. Until then, we plot and regroup. Speaking of the latter, over there is my wide-eyed recruit Antony. As for myself, the name is Paine. Nathaniel Paine. But my friends call me Nate."

"Carryin' out these identity checks always screwed with my nerves, Nate. Now whenever a new face walks through the door, I nearly lose my shit. Takin' life one day at a time.

Good to meet you both."

"I'm Maddox." He offered his hand to Antony. "Welcome to the team."

"Relieved to be on board." A limp handshake matched Antony's softly spoken words.

"Speak freely," Nathaniel insisted. "There's no need to exercise restraint any longer. You're among friends."

Antony shuffled his feet. "Charlotte was a ... a terrible tragedy." He parroted Nathaniel out of a sense of compulsion rather than conviction.

Weeks earlier, the fateful incident in Charlotte had commandeered televisions across the planet. Prefaced by counterterrorism reports, the pillaging of the Praxis base was declared a global imperative. Antony had watched the carnage while unwinding at The Emerald. He spent that evening absorbed in footage of the tactical raid. With Camille Rodin on the play-by-play, the onslaught was presented as a rousing success. If this subject was broached mere hours ago, Antony above all would have lamented the fallen Public Safety officers who sacrificed themselves for the welfare of the citizenry.

There and then the narrative fissured; one story became two. He suddenly viewed the broadcast's supposed candor as spurious. Through an inverted lens, the protagonist morphed into the antagonist.

"All of this," Antony said, "it's ever so difficult for me to wrap my ..."

"Acceptance won't be instantaneous," Nathaniel said.

"Nor will it occur solely by your own efforts. For years you've been held hostage, bound and blindfolded. From time to time you've glimpsed the truth through frays in the fabric. But your captors sewed patches in haste. Only by lifting the delusive veil will you see rightly once again. Help is what you require Antony, not empty encouragement. Take a seat. Let's start the procedure, Maddox."

"The truth is a bitch like no other," Maddox said. "Could take months, even years, for you to get a handle on this crazy shit. I for one am still figurin' it all out."

Antony's angst over misplaced allegiances was allayed. He plopped down on the tattooing chair. At the same time, Nathaniel made his way over to the tool chest, where Maddox gathered supplies. From a refrigerated side compartment, Nathaniel grabbed a bottle of water.

"I propose a trade," Nathaniel said, taking the clipboard and the boatswain's call off Antony's hands. "Clearly you could use a dose of hydration."

"Suppose it would be wise to drink something nonalcoholic." Antony gulped down a mouthful. "Thanks."

"Hold on, rook," Maddox said. He glanced up from the chair's remote control. "Lowerin' your ass down."

Antony took one last sip before settling into a recumbent position. "So, this life-changing procedure, what exa—"

"Undeniably life-changing," Nathaniel said. "But more accurately it's a restoration of the natural conditions of mankind."

"All the same from my ignorant viewpoint," Antony said. "For the sake of my sanity, care to enlighten me about the details?"

"Really nothin' to it," said Maddox. "That implant of yours needs to be tweaked."

The unpredictability gnawed at Antony. "That's all well and good, but wh—"

"Goddamn," Maddox said, shivering. "Feel that draft? Freezin' my balls off here. That reminds me, you'll want this. Heads up." He tossed a microfiber quilt onto Antony's lap, then slipped on a long sleeve tangelo-colored crewneck.

"Great," Antony said, enwrapping the lower half of his anatomy. "All snug. Now can one of you please tell me what exactly this procedure involves?"

"That piece of shit in your neck"—Maddox pointed emphatically—"needs to be drained and reprogrammed. Easy as ABC. Soon you'll be a free man."

"A free man." Smatterings of pessimism colored Antony's tone. "Yet a man exiled from society."

"Who the hell told you that freedom was free?" Maddox asked angrily.

"Isolation is a temporary cost," Nathaniel calmly clarified, "and hardly our preference. Combating Pansophical's menticide from within the system was never feasible."

"Life inside is all I know." Antony rubbed his nose. "Liberty has always been a given. Before today, calling it into question was unthinkable."

"Accepting servitude is effortless," said Nathaniel, "demanding freedom requires courage. If presented with the option, Antony, would you return to the illusory universe of yesterday? Could you in good conscious sacrifice yourself to serve as fodder for those who engineer consent?"

"No. Never."

"Slowly but surely, you'll remember what existence was once like." Nathaniel smiled. "By and by, you'll realize what it could be like again."

"I do wonder." Antony paused. "If everything I believe is a lie, how can I be confident that you won't lead me astray?"

"Evidence is forthcoming. For the time being you'll have to take my word that the so-called protectors of the people destabilized our memories to ensure control. In that despotic other world, those who are united as one have been cognitively castrated. They've been rendered docile by chemical straitjackets. The citizenry governed by the Pansophical Corporation live a life without liberty. Arguably ... it's not a life at all."

Fueled by the inconceivable, Antony exploded into an upright seated position. As he construed the significance of the bombshell, his hand gravitated toward his cervical vertebrae. He intentionally outlined the boundaries of the delivery system with his extended middle finger. Bit by bit he integrated the disturbing psychological episodes from the day into this shifting paradigm.

A willingness to believe that one's reality may not be

what it seemed was merely the first step. By identifying the underlying mechanisms of the corporate sovereign's manipulation, Antony arrived at stage two. The veil of benevolence that Pansophical used to carry out its ghastly machinations suddenly became transpicuous. In the vacuum created by his explosive epiphany, his frame crumbled, returning to a supine position.

"How? How could they do this to us?"

With a clenched fist, Maddox pounded his palm. "On many nights I've asked myself that question. In between tossin' and turnin', I dream of torturin' those sons of bitches for answers."

"If confronted with your wrath, the board would give rationalizations aplenty," Nathaniel said. "But not a single one would be satisfactory. Since the dawn of civilization, the justifications for enslavement have been repeated ad nauseam. Throughout history, the delusional visions of the anointed have commonalities. In the here and now, we revolt against its latest manifestation."

"The memory lapses," Antony said with a forceful blink, "the feelings of dissociation — nothing more than the handiwork of Pansophical." He voiced his insights with incredulity. "All of this time it's been them, nudging me closer and closer to insanity. Can it really be that my days have been spent navigating a perverted reality of Pansophical's making?"

"I'm afraid so," Nathaniel said. He placed his hand on Antony's kneecap. "They're culpable across the board. By expunging the past, Pansophical has hijacked the present and staked a claim on our inalienable right to command the future tense."

Chronological ambiguity loomed. The mystery blanched Antony's countenance. He feared that nothing could prepare him for the unvarnished truth. His thoracic cage was replaced by the parallel jaws of a vise. Each rapid breath turned the handle, tightening the bony enclosure's grip on his organs. Contracting his diaphragm, he filled his lungs to capacity. On the exhalation, he blurted out the inescapable question. "When did this all start?"

"Historical accounts haven't been easy to come by," Nathaniel replied. "Few resources survived the Purge of Falsities. We've pieced together the events from the materials we've salvaged. There's gaps in our knowledge, but we do know th—"

"Wait," Antony interrupted in a panic. "Just wait. It's way too much to bear."

"Difficult to digest would be an understatement," Nathaniel said. "Let's dive into the particulars of their nefarious operation tomorrow, after some sleep."

"Okay." Antony emotionally disengaged. He flipped onto his stomach as the numbness flooded his essence.

Maddox prepared the operating theater. He swapped the tattooing chair's headrest for a face-cradle, then clamped a flexible gooseneck arm onto its frame. A makeshift table was created by attaching a stainless steel tray. On his first supply run, he dropped off a syringe-styled discharging gadget, a serial cable, a handheld electron microscope, and a set of magnetic picks and probes. Returning to the tool chest, he next retrieved a tub of antimicrobial wipes along with a pair of gloves.

"Before we get this show on the road, you need to strip, rook. Jacket off, and anythin' underneath. The anti-tamperin' dye destroys everythin' it touches."

Antony obeyed without saying a word. He compacted his body, tucking his bundled legs. With his hindquarters flush against his Achilles tendons, he erected his spine. After unfastening the buttons of his overcoat, he flung the garment into the corner. His green-and-yellow polo went along the same flight path seconds later. Bare-chested, he pivoted from kneeling and planted his face into the cushioned horseshoe.

Maddox laughed. "Blanket wasn't for your legs, rook. No worries. I got you."

He tugged the quilt free and shook it out. Near one of its edges was a reinforced cutout encircled by discolored blotches. With cutout and implant aligned, he draped the quilt over Antony's exposed torso.

"Good to go," Maddox said. He angled the surgical light overhead, then pulled the magnifying lens over the operating site. "Ask if you got questions."

Antony grunted approval.

In the absence of procedural inquiries, Maddox commenced with safety measures. As he slipped on his exam gloves, he unleashed an earworm onto the soundscape. Humming all the while, he cleaned Antony's implant. Using an antimicrobial towelette, he performed a series of clockwise spirals starting at the center of the electrochemical system. He reproduced this purifying action in a counterclockwise manner in the interest of being thorough. Last but not least, he wiped down the probes designed to magnetically snare the contrivances of coercion.

Right before he inserted a sickle-shaped tool into Antony's refill port, he replaced his hummed harmonies with a howling chorus.

> "Peo-ple for-get.
>
> Fuckin' forced to for-get.
>
> Peo-ple for-get.
>
> Maddox here is gonna remind you,
>
> Maddox here is gonna remind you!"

Carrying the punk rock tune, Maddox probed the depths of the implant. In search of non-deployed nanobots, he slowly explored the titanium confines of each micro-reservoir. After every other one, he examined the sickle under an electron microscope. No nano-stragglers were to be found in the first eight reservoirs. Chamber number nine remained hermetically sealed.

The pointed probe punctured the airtight enclosure, disrupting the cohesive force binding the membrane. Florescent orange dye erupted from the refill port. Maddox withdrew his tool to inspect the objects of mental manipulation. At the nanoscale, drug delivery vessels peppered the sickle's smooth surface.

"Goddamn robots," Maddox said with a snarl. "Pieces of shit have messed you up enough." With a flick of his wrist, he casted them into the garbage. "To hell you go."

Following a second sweep to corral survivors of the initial purge, Maddox switched tasks. Stabbing downward, he penetrated the implant with a translucent discharger. Its multi-pole needle interconnect split lengthwise upon entry. A closed circuit was formed when its conductive tips contacted the battery terminals inside the refill port. Electrons flowed from anode to cathode, draining the implant's chemical energy. In the process, the gadget in Maddox's hand adopted a bluish glow. The color intensified to represent the depth of discharge. Forty-five second later, its barrel started to blink.

"Done." He extracted the needle and placed the discharger back upon the tray. "And now time to reprogram that bitch."

The TTL serial cable required for the final step was contorted by a caboodle of crimps. Maddox straightened the cable, rolling the insulated sheath back and forth between his sausage fingers. Little by little, he worked his way from its four single-pin housings to the female USB receptacle on the other end.

Seeking to corroborate the diagram inside his mind, Maddox inverted his sleeve cuff to uncover a tattooed electric chair schematic. A seemingly innocuous inked multiplexer concealed the key to Pansophical's technological shackles. Under his breath, he conveyed the pin header connections hidden within.

"Ground to pin seven. Ground to pin seven." He muttered each instruction before he connected the wire, then reiterated it as a form of verification. "Receive to pin four. Receive to pin four. Transmit to pin five. Transmit to pin five. Power to pin one. Power to pin one."

Once the interfacing link was in place, Maddox removed an encrypted flash drive from his pocket. In the act of plugging the peripheral into the cable's open end, his fingerprint initialized an override of the microchip's bootloader code. Seditious zeros and ones flowed over the wires. The unique identifier assigned to Antony Sartori by the Pansophical Corporation was overwritten by a spoofing program. Emancipated, Antony would henceforth traverse the public sphere shrouded in algorithmic anonymity.

"Bada bing." Maddox plucked the pins off one by one. "Bada boom!" He yanked off the quilt and slapped the newest Praxis enlistee on the back.

The good-natured whack left behind a handprint, yet Antony languidly rolled over with a blank expression, without comment.

Antony stared up at Nathaniel.

"Welcome to a reality uncolored by deception," Nathaniel said enthusiastically. "Tell me, my friend, how does it feel to once again dwell within a pure state of nature? How does it feel to regain your humanity?"

Antony rose from his reposed position. "Wish I knew."

No longer were the neural substrates of Antony's memory at the mercy of insidious chemical antagonists. His fundamental right to privacy had been reclaimed. Nevertheless, palpable change was absent. Overlooking his liberation from thralldom, he perceived the procedure to be anticlimactic.

"The fog will recede," Nathaniel promised. "The self-accusations will cease. Eventually, uncorrupted free thought will chip away at the years of systematic indoctrination."

"One can only hope," Antony replied with his pupils downcast.

"When forced into a world of unending pretense, we forget what we are capable of; we forget who we truly are. The memories, Antony—they will return."

As Antony listlessly dressed, Maddox vigorously tugged the workbench away from the rear wall. His might was exerted in brief bursts. Underneath there were galvanized cables fastened to the floor. Inch by inch, he peeled back the tiles to uncover a trapdoor. "Let's go, you bastards." He grinned, then squeezed inside the hatchway.

Shepherded by the tattooed gatekeeper, the men descended the dimly lit staircase. Nathaniel closely trailed

Maddox, and Antony lagged considerably behind. On the first landing, the trio passed under an aluminum archway that emitted ultraviolet light. On the next, they were blasted by frosty streams of air that smelled of ozone. Eleventh-hour safeguards against pestiferousness Antony presumed.

Apathetic to threats of Tembakoo, he continued quietly ahead. His eyes adapted to the darkness. After several flights of stairs, the Praxis lair below began to take shape. Leavened by smidgens of curiosity, his attentional spotlight panned the abandoned light-rail station.

Outside this clandestine stronghold, habitual distrust divided the meek. Inside, camaraderie was forged within the fires of inescapable truths. Exhausted emotionally, Antony felt nothing. Be that as it may, optimism percolated beneath the surface. In the company of these men, he trusted that the Pansophical Corporation would fall. United in defiance, he was confident that Praxis would rewrite the fables of prosperity echoed by the masses.

CHAPTER FOURTEEN

ircadian sirens aroused Antony. Thrusted into the waking world, he tossed aside his comforter cocoon to reveal a set of foreign flannel pajamas. Unfamiliar surroundings materialized before his groggy eyes. Apart from the Victorian-style hospital bed, he pinpointed an oil painting and an espresso-colored desk with a matching chair as the room's only furnishings. Rustic whitewashed bricks enclosed the diminutive subterranean space. A corroded iron door barred the single point of entry.

Pushing through sleep inertia, Antony bestirred his drowsy frame. He performed his morning stretches on autopilot. For each exercise, he counted to thirty aloud. His cerebral blood flow was replenished over the course of his routine. Recollections of yesterday cropped up amid this cognitive revival. Consequently came the realization: Praxis and himself were now one and the same. Anxious energy accelerated his internal timer. He released the spindled headboard that served as his balancing aid partway through stretching his quadriceps. The prospect of clarity and a caffeine fix called for his attention from atop the writing desk.

An emerald banker's lamp illuminated a continental breakfast spread of fruits and pastries. In the center of the desk, Antony's clothes awaited, washed and neatly folded. A stack of burgundy scrapbooks with gilded dates along their spines towered above the wooden surface. Adjacent to this chronically arranged corpus of Pansophical prehistory sat the former property of Ivan Myshkin, which Nathaniel had snatched from The Emerald. A handwritten note was taped to the sketchpad's cover. Penned in cursive, Nathaniel offered guidance.

Survival was once solely dependent upon our ability to accurately perceive the real world. The rise of civilizations, however, birthed deception at scale, ushering in an era of propaganda. The purveyors of falsehoods have fine-tuned their perception-molding schemes over the centuries. Enhanced by technology, the reality-flouting tactics employed by our modern-day tyrants are unmatched. The very neural pathways that define humanity have been short-circuited. An obscurant layer has been constructed between our conscious experience and objective reality.

But you, Antony, need to see it for yourself. Nullius in Verba. Free your mind of preconceptions. As you put together the pieces, assert truth no matter the consequences.

Before delving into the suppressed annals, Antony poured himself a cup of coffee from the thermal carafe and grabbed a banana. While he peeled the potassium-laden produce, his field of vision climbed the brickwork. The visceral masterpiece that hung above the workspace was paradoxically a complementary mismatch among the austere ambience. Awash in brightness, the chilling composition depicted an execution unfolding. Through the lens of realism, an infantry unit unleashed their muskets' fury on a doomed trio. Standing aside from the firing squad, a disinterested sergeant prepared to deliver the coup de grâce. Impressionistic brush strokes portrayed an apathetic audience perched upon the rear wall. The inspired creator's signature honored the bottom corner of the canvas, "Manet."

Save for the traditional attire and primitive firearms, Antony regarded the painting to be contemporary in nature. His eyes hopped around the historical cast. He wondered what part he would play in a modern reenactment. Was his fate personified by the condemned or an executioner? A faceless eyewitness or the impassioned chronicler? Eventually the passage of time answered all; in the present, only the naked truth could shed light on his path and where it would lead.

Anxious to jettison his tendentious blindfold, Antony cleared the desk of nonessentials, then spread all the books out for inspection. Electing to ease into the unknown, his exploration began with Ivan's sketchpad.

Meticulous accounts of The Emerald's happenings filled the pages of the pilfered property. A nightly register logged the comings and goings of customers. There were personality profiles of regulars and conversation snippets from suspicious strangers. The final entry included a lifelike portrait of Nathaniel drawn as "Ronald Hasslet."

Skimming Ivan's surveillance efforts allowed Antony to finally fathom the dour barfly. Ivan's devotion to Pansophical elicited a blend of loathing and pity. Enriched by an understanding of micro-level motivations, Antony prepared himself to face the macro-revelations to come. Following a deep breath, he dropped the sketchpad to the floor and immersed himself into the archives. Newspaper clippings from the previous half-century were housed within pages upon pages of protective plastic sleeves. Taken as a whole, these articles told the story of a diabolical conquest.

USA TODAY

PANSOPHICAL AIMS TO STRENGTHEN DEMOCRACY
5/23/2034

(San Francisco) In the wake of worldwide concerns over electoral integrity, the Pansophical Corporation announced on Tuesday that it will be teaming up with nonprofit organization the National Institute for Equity (NIE) and nonpartisan think tank the International Institute for Inclusion (Triple I). According to NIE President Janice Walker, the partnership will employ "Pansophical's expertise in blockchain technology to combat discrimination and improve election transparency." The NIE was founded in 2024 using a US federal grant designed to promote social justice. Triple I actively collaborates with liberal democracies to curb hate speech on social media platforms. For over twenty years it has published quarterly reports on inclusivity trends and measures of marginality.

PEOPLE'S DAILY

CENTRAL COMMITTEE PRAISES PANSOPHICAL FOR SAFE CITY DEVELOPMENT
1/11/2037

(Guangzhou) The number of Safe Cities in the Guangdong Province has increased threefold under the Communist Party of China's seventeenth Five-Year Plan (2035–2040). During last week's plenum, Chinese Premier Liu Qingtong stressed the importance of coordinating social provisions inside each Safe City. Qingtong singled out the Pansophical Corporation for pioneering these synergistic efforts and credited their "peaceful technologies" with "boosting social stability." The Internet of Things (IoT) giant has worked closely with the Ministry of Public Security since opening a robotics center on the Sun Yat-sen University campus two years ago.

THE NEW YORK TIMES

NATIONAL INDUSTRIAL REFORM ACT: REDEFINING AMERICAN BUSINESS ETHICS

2/26/2038

(Washington, DC) Senator John Hamilton's (D-Calif.) initiative to save capitalism is underway. Last September, Hamilton's National Industrial Reform Act (NIRA) was signed into law with overwhelming bipartisan support. Under NIRA, mega-corporations that neglect the welfare of the general public will be prohibited from operating within the United States. Corporations are scrambling to get into compliance with only six weeks remaining in the grace period. The Office for Responsible Capitalism will issue its first federal charter on Friday to the Pansophical Corporation. Andrew D. Fields, Pansophical founder, cheered the shift toward a culture of interdependent accountability and rebuked the "immoral, greedy practices" of his competitors.

SÜDDEUTSCHE ZEITUNG

PANSOPHICAL CEO OUTLINES ASPIRATIONAL AGENDA, PROMOTES CORPORATE SOCIAL RESPONSIBILITY

10/28/2038

(Munich) Keynote addresses at the annual European Symposium on Nanobiotechnology rarely disappoint. Andrew D. Fields, founder and CEO of the Pansophical Corporation, has raised the bar. Over a captivating hour, Fields showcased innovations capable of bridging the Internet of Nano Things (IoNT) and the Internet of Robotic Things (IoRT). The exhibition in hindsight was purely an appetizer. The main course began midway through a standing ovation, when Fields silenced the conference room of engineers and scientists to passionately advocate for progressive capitalism.

"A corporation's right to exist is granted by society. The inhumane corporate governance models that once lined the pockets of greedy shareholders are a thing of the past. It's time for us to recalibrate our moral compasses. It's time for companies to act in the interest of all stakeholders. It's time to reboot the system. The Pansophical Corporation will from now on benevolently serve all humankind."

After touching upon a host of humanitarian causes, Fields set his sights on disease eradication. "Today, we [Pansophical] blaze a trail with a pledge. In the hopes of strengthening public health surveillance systems, in the dreams of discovering new miracle drugs, we will be donating 25 percent of all future profits. Here and now, we show the world what it means to be socially responsible."

EL TIEMPO

CURRENCY SUBSTITUTION: ECONOMIC CRISIS SOLVED?
1/3/2041

(Bogotá) Hyperinflation has ravaged the Colombian economy for months. Emergency efforts to halt the peso's debasement by the Banco de la República de Colombia

(BRC) have failed. Demands for radical change by the Colombian people have grown louder by the day. At long last they have been heard. In what has been called a "reckless act of desperation" by the International Monetary Fund, the BRC has announced that it will launch a hybrid-fiat currency in partnership with the Pansophical Corporation.

Bancor (Ƀ) "shares" will be physically distributed by the BRC and will now serve as the country's official legal tender. BRC President Milagros Gómez expects the bancor to "solve Colombia's money problems by improving payment efficiency and by stabilizing purchasing power." Each environment-friendly bancor smart note includes a tamper-proof blockchain-enabled microprocessor to allow use with or without an internet connection. A permissioned transparent ledger will guarantee the authenticity of all transactions. To prevent money laundering, banks will be verifying identities and performing source of wealth checks for all peso/bancor swaps.

DAINIK BHASKAR
TERRIFYING VIRUS SPREADS THROUGH TAMIL NADU
12/12/2052

(Chennai) Nearly a quarter million cases of a mysterious disease have been detected in the state of Tamil Nadu via the Integrated Disease Surveillance Programme. Signs of the outbreak first showed up in fishing villages along the Bay of Bengal. Epidemiologists theorize that the epidemic's epicenter is Kamarajar Port, where a hazardous shipping container was lost overboard in an accident weeks earlier. Known as "Tembakoo" among the locals, the virus appears to disrupt the body's acid-base balance. Autopsies of the infected frequently report corrosion of the cardiovascular system as the primary cause of death.

Tamil Nadu Health Secretary, Dr. Anil Gokhale, refused to speculate on transmission vectors or contagiousness but did assure the Indian people that "the situation is under control." Rapid response teams are currently repurposing antiviral drugs to treat the infected. Trials to confirm the effectiveness of these medications are underway. While hospital overcrowding could prove problematic, Dr. Gokhale is "optimistic that a cure is on the horizon."

Anyone experiencing an onset of extreme skin sensitivity or a graying of complexion is strongly encouraged to seek medical attention.

LE FIGARO

MIRACLE VACCINE GRANTED EXCLUSIVITY IN PERPETUITY
5/8/2064

(Paris)   Over the span of twelve years, the Tembakoo pandemic has killed billions, tragically reducing the global population by nearly 70 percent. On Thursday, the European Medicines Agency awarded the Pansophical Corporation a lifetime exclusive license for their Tembakoo vaccine as a token of appreciation. Newly appointed CEO, Lenny

Fields, played down the license. Fields instead focused on the future and highlighted the legacy of the company's recently deceased founder, Andrew D. Fields. "My father's altruism and foresight deserves to be celebrated until the end of time. But today is a new day. As the Pansophical Corporation moves on, we vow to expand upon our humanitarian mission. We vow to pave the way for an age of boundless prosperity."

THE PUNCH
REFLECTIONS ON THE BLACKOUT
6/13/2068

(Lagos) For three long weeks, Nigeria's mobile networks were crippled by outages. Democracy Day celebrations nationwide had to be canceled. Millions of panicked Nigerians were left unable to connect to voice, text or data services. After twenty-four hours of no reported interruptions, life is returning to normal.

Nigerian Communications Commission (NCC) official Ladi Ojukwu blamed "a SIM-less botnet" for carrying out a "DDoS [distributed denial-of-service] attack on major telecom providers." The NCC had no luck mitigating these attacks. The botnet was seemingly shut down voluntarily yesterday morning. Investigations are ongoing, but Ojukwu fears "that this could have just been a trial run."

MICHAEL S. MILANO

THE PEOPLE'S VOICE
AN ASSAULT ON THE PILLARS OF THE DIGITAL AGE
9/30/2073

(London) A nightmare scenario descends upon us. Our global information infrastructure has been compromised. Four months ago, the destruction of several underwater fiber optic cables fractured the internet along continental boundaries. Last month, entire territories were cut off from the internet when a high-powered microwave weapon fried a satellite constellation. An international investigation, spearheaded by the Pansophical Corporation's security team, has identified Praxis as responsible.

The savage organization broadened their despicable attacks on Friday. An arsenal of cyber-weapons, bearing an intrusion signature attributed to a Praxis hacker, was deployed on root servers throughout Europe. Root server clusters are the backbone for the Domain Name System (DNS). Without the DNS, the internet will be rendered unusable.

Humanity remains in a state of psychophysical shock. We continue to mourn our losses. We fear Tembakoo mutations. We long to restore the former vitality of our institutions. As editor in chief of *The People's Voice*, I, Camille Rodin, appeal to Praxis in earnest. Please end this madness. Please stop targeting our communication systems. Hasn't mankind been through enough?

Antony indistinguishably reproduced his activities within the subterranean sanctuary for four consecutive days. Each morning he woke to breakfast and a freshly curated archival collection. He spent afternoons assimilating factualness into a backdrop flush with false flags and poisoned by propaganda. At nightfall, Nathaniel swung by for supper and earnest discourse. The two forged a special bond as Nathaniel tugged on deceitful threads to hasten the unraveling of Antony's misbeliefs.

Now that Antony was unencumbered from the fear that unified the herd, the blurriness receded. The big picture came into focus, and he began to comprehend society's hallucinatory underpinnings. Days earlier at the Inky Lyceum, an avalanche of questions overloaded his brain. Privy to the unfiltered past, his answers to those very questions now converged upon veridicality. His insights unveiled a political economy abducted by corporatism, a civilization transmogrified by the grandiose delusions of tyrants.

As Antony advanced through the third stage of his awakening, he couldn't help but marvel at the fortitude required of Praxis members. Feelings of inadequacy prevented him from exploring the lair. Aside from short strolls to the restroom, he confined himself in order to ruminate over his faults.

On the dawn of the fifth day, a portable file box was left in place of the scrapbooks. The Pansophical Corporation's dossier on Antony Sartori sat inside. Within the plastic organizer's hanging folders were academic progress reports, college recommendation letters, security clearance interviews, and employee performance reviews.

Whereas these biographical records evoked little reaction, the character evaluation compiled by Praxis struck a chord. Printouts of scrapings from obsolete social media platforms filled the rear of the file box. Mirroring terminal lucidity, the years flashed before his occipital lobe.

First of the photographs featured a blithesome five-year-old Antony. Donning reindeer pajamas and a Santa hat, Antony unwrapped a programmable robot on Christmas morning. Fast-forwarding several years, there was a blog post detailing a birthday party at a Harlem Globetrotter's game. In the center of the page was a caricature of Antony roaring with laughter, picking his father's nose with a giant foam finger. A snapshot of a corsage from a decade later marked his introduction to heartbreak and the end of adolescence.

Dormant memory traces were rekindled throughout his connectome. Episodic recollections germinated from the residuum of the nanobots' deleterious handiwork. Incidents spanning the emotional gamut sprouted from his fertile mindscape. Within his wetware, vivid daydreams materialized, treasured conversations replayed, and turning points were relived.

Behind the social media cache, a manila envelope with

surveillance camera still shots awaited. Last of these photos captured Antony and Dominique at the black tie grand opening of Tidal. Champagne glasses in hand, with arms intertwined, he toasted his gorgeous wife.

Antony had endured her absence for over twenty months. All the while he had remained enamored even when unable to truly recall their time together.

The emotional wounds of yesteryear ruptured along their duplicitous sutures. Amid this turbulent fissure, his grieving process was upended. Anger transposed acceptance. The crimson roses adorning Dominique's gravestone had withered away long ago. Humankind had all but forgotten the departed. To immortalize the memory of his one and only, he placed hand over heart, then swore to shed the blood of the vile executives of the Pansophical Corporation.

"No matter how long it takes." Antony's clenched teeth shredded his vocalizations. "No matter the cost. Vengeance will be mine."

Hammurabi reciprocity would not suffice. Fantasies of inflicting inhuman torments on the miscreants at Pansophical's helm filled him with pleasure.

Later that evening, Nathaniel stopped by for a visit. When he entered, Antony was hunched over his paper-strewn desk, surrounded by darkness. Nathaniel brought comfort food in the form of lasagna along with a twelve-pack of beer.

He flipped on the lights. "Everything okay there, my friend?"

Antony looked up. "What do you think? My own well-being is no longer of consequence. Revenge is all I desire, nothing more, nothing less."

"Despite how it appears," Nathaniel said as his eyebrows flattened, "all is not lost. There's more to this fleeting existence. How would Dominique and Jasper have wanted you to live out your days?"

"Wouldn't they be here to answer that question if not for Pansophical? Instead our civilization has been ravaged, and all that I hold dear has been stolen away."

"Each of us have had our share of retaliatory impulses." Empathy seeped out from Nathaniel's words. "It's natural. I've harbored them myself for years with little signs of waning."

"Then you understand better than I."

"I do." Nathaniel walked over and set Antony's dinner down upon the desk. "But I choose to pay homage to the deceased by liberating the enslaved and by ensuring the survival of the autonomous mind."

"Those things don't concern me."

"Do you not pity the billions under Pansophical's control?"

"No," Antony said bitterly. "They mean nothing. But they'll be free when all is said and done."

"Singularly seeking revenge is a dangerous game, my friend. Under the guise of justice, the urge to avenge has destroyed many men. With my own eyes I've seen it jeopardize everything we fight for."

Nathaniel paused. He stooped down and placed his hand

on Antony's forearm. "The onus is on you to avoid being overwhelmed by these emotions. And that begins with forgiving yourself."

The blood-soaked visions within Antony's mind dimmed ever so slightly. "How can I do that?" His gaze dipped. "I'm culpable ... undeniably so. In good conscience, how can I ignore the role I've played in those heinous deeds?"

"Self-reproach will get you nowhere, Antony."

"I should have seen what Pansophical was becoming." Antony buried his face into his palms. "I could have resisted."

"Conquest and deception go hand in glove. Outside these walls, Pansophical is seen as the benevolent savior of mankind. Everyone who has joined our crusade has expressed contrition for being complicit at one time or another." Nathaniel took a step back. "Being blameworthy requires knowledge before the fact. Post hoc moralizing is unreasonable, pure and simple."

Preceded by a deep breath, Antony reemerged from his shameful shell. "That's one way to frame it."

"Think back to your days as a Pansophical employee. Did you ever once believe that your creations were evil upon conception?"

"Of course not."

"Then why allege that in hindsight? While technologies are inherently neutral, their implementations are not."

"There's truth to what you say. But it's little more than a trivial comfort." Antony pressed his lips together. "How long did it take for you?"

"For me to ...?"

Abashed, Antony glanced over. "To forgive yourself."

"It happened the moment I let go of that which was beyond my control."

"And what about the homicidal daydreams? When will they fade away?"

A sense of gravity drained the compassion from Nathaniel's countenance. Following another backward stride, he responded while standing in the doorway. "Pacifism is never an option when facing an enemy that lacks a conscience. We rouse to action in the pursuit of justice, knowing that we take up arms for the sake of humanity. Our plans for reprisal are in motion. Speaking of, there are other matters that I must attend to before sleep. Goodnight, my friend."

In solitude, Antony's self-discovery continued. He flipped through the photos of his former life over and over again. With Nathaniel's wise words reverberating in the background, he tamed his rage. Slowly but surely, the layers of his guilt shed away.

Twelve hours later, as the arrival of daybreak stirred surface dwellers overhead, the allure of sleep summoned him to bed. Restlessness stymied his slumber, however. Hours of ceaseless fidgeting ensued. A tap at the door eventually offered refuge.

"One minute." He dragged himself out of bed and threw on his clothes.

"Good morning! Good morning!"

The rapturous reception was delivered prior to the establishment of visual contact. The door sprung open. Antony's sightline descended onto a doe-eyed little girl wearing a lavender-colored shirt under a pair of denim overalls. Yellow bows adorned her afro-puffed pigtails. Between her milk-chocolate cheeks beamed a bucktooth smile.

"Rise and shine," she said as she skipped inside. "Just as the sun dispensed of the darkness, within you ... within you—"

"Morning," Antony said lethargically.

"One second." Foreshadowed by a wink, the adorable visitor turned away. "I'll get it, I promise." She slyly peeked at the index card that sat inside the central pouch of her overalls. Spinning back around, she started anew. "Just as the sun dispensed of the darkness, within you, Mr. Sartori, rationality will vanquish the emotional storm."

"Such youth," said Antony, "yet you speak as a sage."

"Wasn't that the best wake-up message ever? Mr. Paine told me you'd love it." She clapped once with delight. "We wrote that together ten minutes ago."

"Kudos are in order. But before all else a question: who might you be?"

"The name is Lomax, Destinee Lomax. But my friends call me Dez."

"Pleased to meet you, Dez." Antony grinned. "Where is that collaborator of yours at the moment?"

"Ot-nay ere-hay."

Antony picked at the crusty corners of his confused eye sockets. "Huh?"

"Ot-nay ere-hay. O-day ou-yay understand-way?" She giggled. "That's one of our secret languages. Shhhh."

"Consider your secret safe."

"Uperduper-say!" She bunny-hopped over to the desk. Bursting with inquisitiveness, she shuffled through the photographs scattered about.

"Pay heed to the brilliance of that, Mr. Paine, and you'll be just fine kid." Antony purposely cleared his throat to recapture her attention. "Mind telling me where he is? In English preferably?"

"The Human Action Council meets twice a week." Destinee looked up from a teenage photo of Antony, then tapped her rainbow-banded wristwatch. "At eleven o'clock sharp."

"Is that where we're going?"

"I wish. I've tried to sneak in so many times. But my disguises never work. Whoever catches me says the same thing." She deepened her high-pitched voice and wagged her finger in mimicry. "Dez, you know you aren't old enough to be in here."

Feigning shock, he dropped his jaw. "Age minimums for the council?"

"Worst part," she said, stomping in a huff, "is I don't know when I'll be able to join. On April 21, I'll be eight years old. Thank you very much. April 21. I can't wait. Maybe, just maybe, they're waiting for me to turn eight."

"We can only hope," Antony said with a chuckle. "To be honest, my memories of that age are a work in progress."

"Really? I remember each and every day of my whole life. Pick a day, any day, I'll tell you what I did."

"Is that so?" He skeptically accepted her challenge. "How about two months ago from yesterday?"

"Well, I finished reading *Little House on the Prairie* yesterday." She nodded with pride. "And two months before … I checkmated Mr. Paine while playing as black, and we celebrated with ice cream sundaes."

"Very impressive. Two months ago I lived in a world of make-believe. And I spent all of yesterday wading through hazy episodes of my personal history."

"Oh, boo bear. It must've been hard living up there, being brainwashed and all."

"An indescribable ordeal, for conceptions of an external reality do not exist when you reside within a bubble."

"If you say so," Destinee said with a shrug. "Do you know my friend Spencer who used to stay in this room?"

Antony proceeded to loosen up, hinging at his hips. "I do not."

"Him and his papa are learning the lay of the land too. Spencer is different, though. He doesn't laugh. I've never even seen him smile. He misses his fancy toys."

"The citizens in that world"—Antony pointed upward in between stretches—"have embraced their technological trappings with open arms."

"Maybe that's why Spencer can't make sense of anything. I've been teaching him our real history. Mr. Paine always says that doom awaits the foolish who don't respect the past."

"Young or old, acceptance and acclimation take time. Easy to lose track of it down here. Incredibly, only a week has passed since my own blissful unawareness was punct—"

The realization that Destinee inhabited an alien milieu stopped him mid-response. He straightened his posture. In front of him was an innocent creature, unsullied by historical negation, spared of revisionist readjustments. Here stood an effervescent child reared within a culture medium of truth, bred to live not as a subservient sheep to be sheered and slaughtered but as an autonomous human being.

"There's something unmistakably special about you, little lady. Have you always called this place home?"

"This place?" Destinee's eyes darted from wall to wall. "No. No. No. I've never stayed in any of these deprogramming rooms."

"Figured as much. But what I meant was, how long have you lived in this particular hideout?"

"All my life," she said. "I was actually the first child born down here. Can you believe that?"

"For me," he said with a half-smile, "the suspension of disbelief has become the norm."

"Out of our whole community, I was first. First. It's true, I swear."

"That's all the evidence I require." Antony paused. "Out of curiosity, how many others are there in this community of ours?"

Keeping a tally on her fingers, Destinee rattled off residents. When she reached the sixteenth name, she gave up. "Better idea." She threw up her hands in excitement. "Let me introduce you to everyone! That's kind of my job today. You know, to show you around."

"Hmmm. Intriguing proposi—"

"Come on." She bounced on the balls of her feet. "Let's go!"

A sense of comfort quelled Antony's internal monologue. In the little girl's company, he set the past aside. The time had come for him to quit brooding over his personal shortcomings. He was ready to acquaint himself with his fellow apostates.

As Destinee escorted Antony through the dank tunnels, she relayed the inner workings of their parallel society. Along the way she pointed out escape routes. Over the unceasing hum of the air filtration system, she spoke of evacuation procedures.

First stop, the communal sleeping quarters. The extravagant comforts that fueled an entertainment-fiending culture of escapism were nowhere to be found. Life bordered on privation inside the lair. Clean clothing was provided, the whereabouts of toiletries were imparted, and Antony was assigned a bed.

From there the teensy tour guide led the newcomer

through an empty dining hall on the way to the subterranean farm. Under geothermal-powered glow lights, a submersible pump sent water runoff through the channels of a hydroponic vertical garden of fruits and vegetables. An electric fence split the space, protecting the plants from the livestock. Chickens, goats, and pigs rounded out the community's diet.

Past the mechanical rooms, beyond the medical facilities and the gym, stood the armory. A weapons specialist greeted Destinee and Antony at the door. He showed off the base's panoply of arms with zeal. After a cautionary word, he gave them earmuffs and goggles, then ushered them through the deadening discharges of the shooting range.

At the two-hour mark, the tour arrived at its final destination, the library. A reservoir of prehistory rested at the fingertips of inquisitive minds. There were tubs of artifacts, bookcases brimming with classics, and archives of newspapers and magazines. Huddled around a table, a group of teenagers categorized a trove of materials recovered from a quarantine camp. Forsaken lands, bestrewn with rotting corpses, served as asylums for forbidden knowledge.

From start to finish, Destinee introduced Antony to the other Praxis members. A name, a face, a story. In one way or another, each referenced a former existence. Some vowed vengeance, others fierily expressed a moral obligation to fight for freedom. A jumbled mass of encounters formed within Antony's temporal lobe.

"All done. It was lovely meeting you, Mr. S." Destinee

pranced off. "Lunch time!"

"Wait up," Antony called out, trotting behind. "I could use some sustenance myself."

"Lunch waits for no man," she shouted as she pirouetted. "Mr. Paine wants to check up on you." She stopped and pointed back at the conference room. "Wait there, okay? He'll be out soon, I promise. Toodle-oo."

At Destinee's behest, Antony lowered his buttocks onto the benumbing concrete to abide the conclusion of the council meeting. Every few minutes a hubbub arose from behind the closed door. The cabal filed out a half-hour later. One after another, they stepped over him without acknowledging the obstacle.

A leggy woman in her thirties, dressed in pinstriped trousers and a black turtleneck, shuffled out at the tail end of the procession. Snake-styled rings coiled around her fingers. In contrast with her playful pink pixie spikes, her facial features had been marred by stress. Anxiety drained the dewiness from her lips. Puffiness underlined her icy blue eyes.

Bringing up the rear with head inclined, Nathaniel tramped forward. He absorbed the woman's instructions with rapt attention. Following an uneasy hug, the two traded well-wishes and she scurried off.

Nathaniel glanced down at Antony and extended his hand.

"There he is," said Antony, pulling himself up to his feet.

"How goes it, Nate?"

"Well enough." Nathaniel's pupils drifted back to his pink-haired confidant. "What about you? Everything go smoothly on your tour?"

"My new living arrangement is far from ideal. But I'll survive."

"Yes," said Nathaniel, barely paying attention. "You will survive."

"Truthfully," Antony said with a chuckle, "I was under the impression that the room service would continue until the end of my days."

A smirk cracked Nathaniel's visage. "Pampering aside," he said, reestablishing eye contact. "Any questions about how things operate down here?"

"Nothing comes to mind."

"Any concerns about emergency procedures? Destinee reviewed them, I presume?"

"The only subject she touched on more were the lessons she picked up from a certain someone. Destinee thinks the world of Mr. Paine."

Nathaniel smiled broadly. "Now that warms my heart. Whenever my hope starts to dwindle, I envision a future pioneered by that remarkable little girl."

"Remarkable," Antony agreed, "and as cute as can be. Kudos, you've taught her well."

"Over the years we've grown close. In all but name, I've taken her on as my protégé. She reminds me of my daughter in many wa—"

"Daughter?"

"Scarlett would've turned thirteen next month." Nathaniel's eyelids drooped. His speech slowed. "She was Destinee's age when diagnosed with Tembakoo."

"I'm so sorry."

"We're all burdened by the dead, my friend. We're all haunted by unspeakable truths. It's the losses we've suffered and our dreams of liberating humanity that bind Praxis together."

"The bond you speak of, it's tangible. I sensed it myself this morning."

"The men and women who fly the flag of resistance form our family. Accept them, and they'll embrace you like no other. Don't hesitate to ask anyone around here if questions come up as you find your bearings. For now I must leave you."

"Wait. What do you mean, leave?"

"Don't you worry,"—Nathaniel thumped Antony on the shoulder—"it's only temporary. The Recruitment Council has been monitoring a genetics engineer who was red-flagged by Benton. I'm heading up to Calgary to make our pitch."

"When you planning to return?"

"Hopefully the end of the month. But there's no predicting how these missions will play out. Surreptitious intelligence provides the preface. On-the-ground fact-finding tells the real story. I'll orchestrate a chance encounter in the next day or two to see whether he's prepared to be awakened."

"Whoever he is, he's about to have his reality turned upside down. Anything at all I can do to help?"

"Wish there was, but this is a solo operation. Once you're settled in, we'll find a suitable assignment for a man of your talents."

"Whatever it takes. I'm ready."

"As luck would have it, we're dunking you into the maelstrom tonight. At 18:45, find Emilie. She'll be awaiting your arrival in the situation room." Nathaniel pointed at a maroon door fifty yards down the tunnel. "You'll be serving as an extra pair of eyes for our brethren in the field."

"That I can do. Although"—Antony scratched his head—"you will need to remind me—who's Emilie?"

"The commander of this very base," Nathaniel said. "If you saw the woman I was speaking with moments ago, that would be Emilie. She would've introduced herself, but her mind is elsewhere. Our meeting just now grew contentious over an intelligence report. She authorized this evening's offensive after a heated debate. Our pieces are being positioned. Tonight, we cast our mating net."

"Yet you're leaving?"

"I would prefer it to be otherwise. But we cannot risk losing an asset such as Mr. Shannon, nor can we postpone this multipronged operation. Opportunities are rare in this life that we live, Antony. Godspeed."

"Thank you, Nate. For everything." Antony spread his arms outward. "Best of luck out there."

Nathaniel responded in kind, stepping forward to embrace. A pair of hearty back pats signaled the termination of their hug, then the men went their separate ways.

With the bulk of the afternoon to spare, Antony popped into the dining hall to satiate his hunger before retreating to the communal quarters. The previous night of connecting the mnemonic dots left his sleep reserves depleted. Anxious to part with his conscious mind, he flopped down face-first and drifted away.

Hours later, gung-ho for his first Praxis mission, Antony bounced out of bed. The extended siesta nearly repaid his sleep debt, and adrenaline offset the balance. He jogged through the tunnels in search of the situation room. From a few strides away, he detected traces of sanguinity spilling out of its open door. He slowed his pace to catch his breath. Standing aside the entrance, he craned his neck to investigate.

Akin to a pregame locker room, exuberance was amplified recursively through emotional contagion. Low-fives, high-fives, and hyped-up hurrahs accompanied the radicals' preparations. The lone exception was the appreciably apprehensive Emilie. Incapable of suppressing her jitters, she compulsively buzzed around, rechecking anything and everything. Upon meeting Antony's gaze, she beelined for the door.

"Finally," she said, hurrying him inside.

"Delighted to make your acquain—"

"No time. Follow me." She scooted toward a cluster of white laminate desks with neon green partitions. Along the way, she briefed Antony. "You'll be manning the crow's nest for our green operation. We have a crew of five disguised as the janitors of a pharmaceutical warehouse. Once inside, they'll be swapping drug vials for saline solution. The window of opportunity is short. When the clock strikes midnight, the loaders arrive to ship off the whole batch for vaccination day."

As the Praxis commander approached the green team's mission control, she grew quiet. A brawny twentysomething in an orange camo hoodie sat at the head station. A syncopated bass line with interweaving kicks and snares emanated from the speakers of his virtual reality headset. Outlined by a pencil-thin beard, his egg-shaped dome bobbed rhythmically.

Emilie peeked over the man's shoulder, then straightened up to face Antony. Her gaze narrowed. "The warehouse is a half block from the Inky Lyceum. It's an industrial neighborhood. The streets should be deserted. You're on lookout duty. You'll be monitoring the live feed from our drones. Be on red alert. If you see anything out of the ordinary, and I mean anything, warn Ryker here immediately."

Upon hearing his name, Ryker swiveled his headphones to free his cauliflower ears. The lens of his goggles became transparent when he made eye contact. "What up, yo?"

"How we looking over here?" Emilie asked. "Communication systems online?"

"We all good, Em."

"Eyes and ears on the warehouse?"

"No doubt."

"Public Works approve our cleaning request?"

"No double doubt."

"And what's Rosalyn's status?"

"Roz and the dummy vials are on the move. Meeting up with the boys in T minus ten. What I tell you, Em?" He smirked. "We all good."

"If anything changes," she said as she whirled around, "let me know immediately." She zipped over to the blue team for an update.

Color-coded desk clusters with built-in holographic platforms occupied the four corners of the situation room. A sped-up simulation of each team's respective operation played out overhead. Probabilities associated with contingencies scrolled along the top of these projections. A timeline highlighting objectives for the multipronged offensive appeared below.

A simulated uprising unfolded before Antony's eyes.

Three holographic Praxis rebels in hazmat suits hovered over the blue team. The trio boarded a ferry full of the infected. Their destination, Vancouver Island. After disembarking, they headed for an abandoned car dealership to digitally hot-wire some wheels. En route to the Greater Victoria Public Library, they sped down the coast, setting hydroelectric plants ablaze.

For the blue operation, artifact retrieval was secondary.

In the grand scheme of Praxis's plans, disrupting the electrical grid paved the way for the treacherous deeds to come. As power was diverted, a rolling blackout would give the violet operation a tactical advantage. In Portland, where a violent clash was inescapable, pouncing on the element of surprise was key.

On the hologram floating above the violet team, a weaponized outfit of twenty-five infiltrated a fortified waterfront compound. The Portland platoon split up once inside. Some raced for the Public Safety barracks to ambush reinforcements. Others plundered away. The operation's primary objective was entrusted to the combat engineers. Demolishing a quantum data center belonging to the Department of Vital Records and Statistics was their responsibility. The platoon was scheduled to rendezvous on the Columbia River just before denotation.

In terms of logistics, the green operation and the yellow operation were analogous. The former was set to take place in a pharmaceutical warehouse, the latter at the North American headquarters for the Department of Information. Both operations were slated to kick off the moment the servers in Portland went down. Both were preceded by a forged cleaning order. The phony janitorial staff in Seattle would swap Tembakoo vaccines for harmless injectants. Their counterparts to the south would substitute vile propaganda for staggering truths.

The rebels in San Jose were tasked with scouring the

IT offices inside the Department of Information. Success or failure for the yellow operation hinged on them finding files related to the network's topology. Once the network was mapped, they'd load a remote access Trojan onto the department's master server. A backdoor to *The People's Voice* would be opened. Subliminal seditions would soon sprinkle the organ of the Pansophical Corporation.

Antony grinned. He visualized this cunning offensive inciting a chain of events; he imagined a swelling resistance that refused to be quelled; he thought to himself, Pansophical will rue this day.

Full of optimism, he went around the horn greeting his teammates.

"Name's Felicia." A flaxen-haired girl wearing wired monaural earbuds flashed over a peace sign. Her black earbud was plugged into a Citizen's Radio. Her white earbud was connected to a laptop that appeared to control the microphones planted outside the warehouse. Presumably, Felicia complemented Antony's lookout duties by focusing on the auditory realm.

Across the cluster, a steely-eyed gentleman with a sloping forehead kneeled upon his chair. He saluted Antony. Through his round tortoiseshell glasses, he revised his Bayesian simulations with real-time inputs.

On top of supervising duties, Ryker fulfilled the role of liaison between green mission control and those in the field. Via his immersive headset, he vicariously experienced the frontlines. Simultaneously, he grooved away. Without missing a beat, he acknowledged Antony with an upward nod, then exaggerated the movement in reverse, urging the newcomer to sit down.

Configured as a cockpit, nine monitors formed the crow's nest. Live feeds from hovering drones spanned the displays. As a whole they produced a 360-degree bird's-eye view of the industrial district. The system's knuckleduster-shaped controller charged wirelessly atop the desk. Its navigational commands were written along the station's walls.

Antony read over the instructions before settling into his seat. He slid his fingers through the controller's rubbery ringlets. Individual cameras within the surveillance triptych were selected by way of a point. Pinching and stretching gestures zoomed in and out. A finger snap activated night vision. If a second followed in close succession, a thermal filter was applied. After a little experimentation, he restored the system's default settings with a shooing motion.

"Attention everyone," Emilie said. She stood inside an elevated semicircular desk at the front of the room. "As we all know, I'm not one for giving speeches. None of us need to be reminded of the stakes."

She paused. As she referenced each operation, she locked eyes with its mission control head.

"Vancouver Island has boots on the ground. Blue operation is fifteen minutes out from the starter pistol. Violet operation,"—the tension in her face ratcheted up—"move out on that second explosion. Yellow and green, hold your positions. As soon as the DVRS goes up in flames, it'll be your time to shine. Let's do this."

The gravity of the moment muted the ensuing cheers. From that point forward, it remained quiet. Barring an occasional encoded message, the only sounds to be heard belonged to Emilie's chunky heels. Periodically, the commander performed figure eights around the clusters. The cadence of her clacking served as her anxiety barometer.

Praxis had expected casualties, but the evening was drawing to a close with nothing more than minor injuries. The rebels from the blue operation had returned to home base with backpacks of literary contraband. The platoon in Portland floated downstream with the data center's flames far off in the distance. Under the moonlight in San Jose, the seeds of awakening had been sowed.

Meanwhile, the janitorial impostors in Seattle were disposing of signs of tampering while conducting a final walkthrough. Nearby underground, an amorphous aberration on the fringes of the crow's nest caught Antony's attention.

A mechanical mosquito complicated his investigation.

In size and shape, the insect ornithopter was virtually indistinguishable from its organic counterpart. All similarities ended there. The ornithopter's photovoltaic wings harvested energy from artificial light. A micro-needle served as its proboscis. Electroactive polymers replaced muscle function, and a signal processing unit constituted its brain.

Whizzing around, it buzzed Antony's eardrums. Whenever he selected a camera, it landed on his outstretched finger. When he directed the magnification spotlight, it darted through his contracting gesture. Time after time, he swatted at the pest and missed.

Several minutes passed before the mechanical mosquito left Antony alone. Shifting to reconnaissance mode, it retreated to a perched position upon his collar.

Antony scanned the surveillance triptych. Down the block from the warehouse, a pair of stray dogs barked at a visual distortion. He kneaded his orbital sockets with the heels of his hands. He'd been starring at these screens for so long that he was starting to see things.

Efforts to rub away the mystery were to no avail. Viewed through his freshly lubricated eyes, the shimmering mirage remained. Superficially resembling heat haze, it was erratic in motion, shapeshifting in form. Paralyzed by perplexity, the visual filters at his literal fingertips had slipped his mind.

Felicia shortly detected that something was awry. "Strange," she whispered, "why's there static?"

Antony looked over. While she considered whys and wherefores, her winsome appearance turned ashen. A moment of clarity pulled Antony back to the crow's nest. He pressed his middle finger and thumb together.

Snap ... nothing to see.

Snap-snap ... the heat signature of a Public Safety squadron illuminated the monitors. The officers advanced on the warehouse. A gargantuan figure with a predacious gait quarterbacked the assault.

"Bannister," Antony said, his lips trembling. "It's Bannister." The Sergeant's scarring scowl was conjured up on the wax tablet of his mind. "It's Bannisterrrr!"

Building upon the reverberations of Antony's cries, Felicia sent the place into a panic with a bloodcurdling shriek. Amid the hysteria, Emilie and the other teams scrambled to assist.

Antony rocketed to his feet. As he stepped away from the crow's nest, he felt the mosquito bite him. He slapped the side of his neck but missed the pest once again.

His field of vision strayed from the crisis. A memorial to fallen heroes emblazoned the rear wall. Swallowtail Praxis flags bordered the columns of engraved names. Antony could not help but quale at the sight.

In his heart, he knew that the crew inside the warehouse would be joining these heroic souls before night's end.

The lair's evacuation alarm drowned out his solemn thoughts. Upon registering the blaring forewarning, Antony's amygdala triggered his survival instincts. Mid-dash, his consciousness began to wane. One step from the doorway, his vital force shriveled into a state of sedation.

CHAPTER FIFTEEN

An enveloping darkness filled Antony's field of view. Were his eyes wide open or sealed shut? Only the haptic feedback from blinking allowed him to distinguish between these diametric positions. For the moment, the contact between these protective folds of skin served as his lone existence proof.

An expanse of murky grays gradually replaced the pitch blackness. An iridescent torrent then swept over the colorless limbo. In its luminous wake, Antony's visual acuity was restored. The intimate surroundings of his Sanctuary Village apartment came into view.

How? How on earth did I get here?

He scrounged up memory morsels, seeking to bridge the temporal gap. Nathaniel? Maddox? Destinee?

If not disaffected delusions crafted within the land of Morpheus, Antony could conceive of no plausible explanation. He drew lines of demarcation between what he perceived to be fact and fiction. Rewinding the clock, he latched onto the last day that made sense, then assigned it the label of yesterday. A week's worth of rebellious recollections were dismissed as a preposterous dream.

The ninth of October, a day marked by the bestowal of Jasper's prized possession. Antony recalled the memento prompting an emotional evening. When it came to what else transpired at The Emerald, he constructed vague conjectures. Counting on history repeating itself, he figured that he had drunk himself into a stupor. In all likelihood, Clara had helped him home. A blackout would explain discrepancies and discontinuities.

As he wrapped up his suppositional timeline, his attention shifted to the current moment. With his voice box rendered quiescent, he internally conducted a perfunctory body scan. Head, shoulders, knees, and toes—the childhood tune revealed dormant body parts in turn. All the physical symptoms of sleep paralysis were present. Thus, he was unsurprised when a malevolent aura saturated the environment; he was unruffled by the adumbral creature that skulked about on the outskirts of his viewing window. Familiar with the script, he watched the surreal scene unfold with apathy.

Enrobed within a white cloak, the cadaverous figure fetched its tools of torture. All the while laughing sardonically, it performed its abrading handiwork. Back and forth, it dragged the triangular file through the rusty gullets of the backsaw. With each pass, the file's ridges reshaped the tooth line of its cutting complement.

The ominous cacophony elicited no fear. Antony was uncharacteristically lucid for a hypnopompic hallucination. Employing Dr. Winfield's advice, he directed his attention to the act of wiggling a single finger. The path to unencumbered wakefulness was by way of minuscule movements. Steadfast focus was required to pierce the vivid visualization.

Ninety seconds of tormenting preparations passed before the creature released the file from its bony grasp. The coffee table below brought the tool's free fall to an end. The clang reverberated through the soundscape as the shadowy specter advanced on its frozen target. Rancorous intentions propelled its gangly limbs. Dramatic swings of the handsaw offset its elongated strides.

Tingling sensations kindled Antony's extremities just as the faceless figure arrived bedside. From head to heels, Antony's reanimated muscles twitched. He once again presided over his own motor cortex.

Yet his movements remained inexplicably hindered. Imperceptible restraints rendered his arms and legs nugatory. Floundering about, he no longer felt constrained by internal forces but by external mysteries. In an act of desperation, he snapped his jaw shut, sinking his teeth into his lower lip. The firing of his pain receptors failed to vanquish the nightmare.

"I've been waiting for you," said the specter.

The gruff presage stopped Antony dead in his tracks.

"Repulsive are the minority who cast doubt on our

budding utopia. Wretched are the few who forsake salvation in earnest. We gave you everything that you could want. Now we'll take away everything that you have."

The specter's declaration punctuated the theatrical phase of its macabre production. In act two, sinister intent would translate into an asset forfeiture of gruesome proportions. After refashioning a pant leg into a tourniquet, confiscation commenced with a crosswise incision.

The serrated blade breached Antony's epidermal shield several inches north of the kneecap. On the warpath, the razor-sharp regiment marched over the subcutaneous tissue, through the underlying fascia. Facing negligible resistance, the jagged invaders pushed ahead. They traversed the crimson rivers. They waded through the rapids. At the creature's command, they transformed the landscape into a meaty wasteland.

When his hamstring was sliced, he howled in delirium. When his tendons were carved, a searing sensation redefined what he believed to be bearable. While the slashing of his femoral artery moments later was painless by comparison, the bisected vessel would be responsible for inducing physiological shock.

In between labored breaths, Antony's attentional spotlight dimmed. His cold, clammy anatomy reached its breaking point three minutes into its sadistic dismembering. Just as his nerves were severed, everything faded to black.

Silence occupied Antony's sonic awareness upon coming around. The confines of his apartment had been replaced by the unsettling white walls of a padded cell. In lieu of a sofa, there was an inclined psychiatric bed. Other familiar furnishings had been swapped for a medical trolley, full of equipment. A quantum computer sat up top. Save for a blinking cursor, its screen was blank. Dangling from the hook of a telescopic IV pole, a mustard-colored solution bag hung above the electronics.

Fluid flowed through the infusion tubing. On the opposite end, a central line catheter poked out of Antony's bare chest. Navy sweatpants concealed his bandaged stump. Padded leather cuffs shackled his other extremities to the steel rails of the bed.

A semi-transparent mirrored ceiling provided a befogging look beyond the rubber room. The footwear and pant legs of passersby was all that Antony could discern. What was his ceiling, was their floor. The citizens bustled along for the most part. A slow-footed woman in loafers was an exception. Bending over, she placed her hand on the ground. As her eyes fell upon him, her lips curled.

Antony shied away from her expression of repugnance. A reflection of himself in the ceiling's corner became his object of focus. Adopting a third-person perspective, he bore witness to a tragic existence.

Secured by a chin strap, Antony's cranium was encased within a multi-modal neurophysiology cap. Underneath the black spandex, he could feel the conductive gel on his shaven skull. Electrodes and optrodes blanketed the cap's surface. Each one sprouted a wire, linking man and machine. The bandpass filters of an amplifier were on the receiving end. One shelf up on the medical trolley, an oscilloscope displayed his brainwaves by frequency.

Drawn to the bobbing pixelated bands, Antony withdrew from the reflected image. His pupils bounced from a flattened delta wave to an active alpha. He traced its crests and troughs. As his grogginess receded, the cerebral wave's beta brethren came alive. Under a firestorm of action potentials, Antony processed the circumstances that constituted the present.

A reality check came in the form of a minimalist eyeball sticker on the side of the machine. The thought of Pansophical sent a jolt through his nervous system. He sprang up, but the bicep bonds bridled his burst.

A fresh vantage point emerged with his neck extended past his elevated shoulders. Only now did the glassy hemispheres on the white rubber floor become visible. If not for refraction, the recessed projector lenses would have went unseen. Dotting the floor, they in essence turned the padded cell into a holographic studio.

Antony stared at his discovery in utter disbelief. Piercing through the corporate despot's trickery, he pieced it all together. In the here and now, his perceptions mapped onto the physical world in high fidelity. The backdrop of his amputation was apparently part of an augmented nightmare. Once the drugs were factored in, any absurd scenario could be imbued with verisimilitude.

The prospect of a perpetual existence within this manufactured reality plunged Antony into a self-pitying spiral. On the way down, questions cropped up from the Broca area of his wetware.

What have I done to deserve this fate? Why? Why me?

The latent features of his neuronal activity were extracted and deciphered. His subconscious thoughts were shortly reproduced upon the monitor.

"Why?" He read the tail end aloud. "Why me?"

The dehumanizing infringements overloaded his emotional capacity. He screamed while lashing out spasmodically against the fetters. Around and around he writhed in futility. Eventually, the exhaustion of his oxygen reserves would put an end to his hysteria.

Mind and body alike were enslaved within this dualistic panopticon. Asleep or awake, vocal or silent, there was no refuge. The last shreds of Antony's self-sovereignty had been stripped away.

At his moment of capitulation, an inconspicuous door on the far wall cracked open. Through squinted crosshairs, he locked onto the most powerful person on the planet. Antony did not recognize the chairman at first. In place of the illustrious attire of a Pansophical board member, the man wore a matte white tracksuit and matching slip-on sneakers.

Without the benefit of a camera forcing perspective, Fields was noticeably shorter than any citizen believed.

Fields's mustache stretched above a derisive smirk. "Do my eyes deceive me? A senior level defector, a modern-day unicorn, here in the flesh? Cannot remember the last time that we captured one of you mythical beasts alive. I traveled many miles to take a gander." The chairman sauntered around, checking out his prisoner from all angles. "Now, where are my manners? My name's Leonard."

The lights throughout the room dimmed. Antony's sightline drifted overhead. Before the ceiling lost its transparency, he saw the outline of a crowd starting to gather. He compressed his lips, wishing to disappear.

"Apparently my reputation precedes me. No reason to hold your tongue, Mr. Sartori. As I'm sure you've deduced, whether you elect to jabber away or keep mum, there's no secrets here."

Fields motioned to the monitor, but no verbal response from Antony was forthcoming. The waiting game was abandoned before long. Feigning friendliness, Fields spread his arms out wide.

"How about we start over?" He softened his tone. "As a sign of good faith, I'll kick off our chat with a confession. All my life I've viewed the arts as pointless. A waste of time and resources without exception. Watching Benton and our surgeons breathe life into that nightmare of yours, however, was an absolute thrill. Tell me, did you enjoy the performance?"

"You." Shallow breaths rushed in and out of Antony's flared nostrils. "Are ... evil."

Fields scoffed. "Spare me your moral judgments."

"Evil," Antony repeated, his words dripping with acrimony. "Unequivocally evil."

"Good or evil? Black or white? Polar opposites at their core, but if you zoom out, you'll see them to be inseparable. Dualities underlie all aspects of the universe. Life cannot flourish without balance."

Antony's frame quavered with rage as Fields waxed philosophically. "Consider the natural world. Acres of forests sit outside these walls. Tree after tree, ravaged by beetles, who have attracted woodpeckers, who fill the stomachs of the bobcats. In the end, each is consumed by the earth. Prey and predators alike, destined to decompose into a thick black humus. It's from the putridness, from the foul decay, from the humus, that life in all its glory germinates." Fields approached the bed. "Only the shortsighted scorn the virtues of destruction. A visionary arrives at a dying forest and courageously sparks a match."

"Are you serious?" Antony shouted. "Did you release Tembakoo on purpose? The circle of life is no justification for wanton slaughter!"

"The dead are nothing more than ripples on the pond. Understand, our species is still in its infancy. Three hundred thousand years lie in humanity's past, but billions of prosperous years are to come. Eons and eons, all hinging upon existential risks. Stamp them out, and we unlock our cosmic potential. The models speak for themselves. Thanks to Pansophical, our civilizational trajectory is once again on the rise."

"We're talking about human beings." Antony balled his fists. "Not a coldblooded calculation, you goddamn psychopath!"

Full of fury, he leapt at Fields, forgetting all about the restraints.

"So close," Fields said, stepping back, "yet so far. The problem is that you act as if a tragedy transpired. Look long-term. You'll find it's to the contrary. Pansophical is paving the way for the vast number of generations to come. It will be the unborn who grow up post-scarcity, on a healthy planet, and colonize the stars."

"Forget the unborn! The victims of Tembakoo fill mass graves in the present. This isn't a hiccup on the way to ful-filling your demented fantasies. But a tragedy that will be felt for centuries. So much pain and suffering. So many people, wiped out of existence, each unique, with hopes and dreams. Entire lifetimes have been spent lamenting loss."

Antony's eyelids drooped. "Losses like my beloved Dominique." He choked on the syllables of her name. "For me, a queen to be worshipped. For you, a pawn t—"

"To be sacrificed," Fields said condescendingly. "A small price to pay for paradise."

"This world that you've created is no paradise. Only

a madman would believe otherwise. Blinded by mega-lomania, you're unable to see the hellscape before your eyes." Straining against the shackles, he lifted his arm and pointed at Fields. "One day"—he thrusted his finger—"the downtrodden will rise up. When they flood the streets, Pansophical flags will burn. And before that day ends, the masses will find you, Lenny. And they'll tear you limb from limb for their amusement."

Rosy patches mottled Fields's cheeks. "It's been a long time since anyone has called me by that name."

Antony had apparently struck a nerve. The color soon spread, imbuing Fields's ears with the redness of raspber-ries. Antony grinned at the sight of these ruddy chinks in Fields's armor. With the clock winding down, there were no trivial wins.

"Lenny, Lenny, Lenny, when all is said and done, they'll string up your tiny corpse for all to see. The people will dance in the streets when they learn of your death."

The swipe deflated Fields's self-assured posture. His chin dipped, and he clasped his hands behind his neck.

"Did you honestly think that statues would be built in your honor? Did you honestly believe that the history books would sing the praises of little Lenny?"

Fields accepted the gibes in silence. He stepped away and directed his gaze overhead. Meeting the eyes of his own reflection, he forcefully dragged his palms down the length of his face. Lingering resentment twisted his abashed countenance anew.

"Is everything okay?" asked Antony.

Below a furrowed brow, the chairman bared his teeth. He spun the dial on the IV's flow regulator, then nudged his way onto the bed using his hip.

"Lenny, what do you think you're doing?"

"Say it again, you betraying ingrate." Fields reached inside Antony's empty pant leg. "And I'll introduce you to an existence of unfathomable torments." He dug his stubby fingers into the stump's suture line.

Masking the pain, Antony smiled. A final provocation seeped out from the confines of his mind and popped onto the screen. "Go to hell, Lenny."

"No reason to go anywhere, Mr. Sartori. For you, hell is here." Fields gave the residual limb another squeeze before hopping off the mattress. "Appears that someone could use a reminder. On my cue, Benton, launch Tartarus."

The drugs caused Antony's heart to palpitate. A sense of dread crept up on him as he started to grow woozy.

Fields let Antony be for a moment. He pulled a white stocking mask out from his pocket and resumed pacing. He slapped it against his thigh while walking back and forth. When he put it on, the holographic projectors came alive.

As the mind-melting phantasmagoria began, Antony lost his grasp on reality.

Beyond the crumbling ceiling, a star-strewn sky emerged. Where once there were walls, shrubs sprouted.

Muddy water bubbled up through the fissured floor. An island of peat moss surfaced to complete the room's transformation into a bog.

Meanwhile, Fields entered a state of metamorphic flux. Each facet of his being was synthesized independently at random. Transitory transmutations of body parts amorphized his anatomy. Over the course of time, the biological mass solidified.

"Jasper," Antony said, blinking hard, "is that you?"

The familiar face beamed with delight. Around his neck, partially hidden by his bushy beard, hung the boatswain's call. Jasper straightened up. He cleared his throat, then piped away.

Partway through an elaborate mess call, blow flies arrived on the scene. A plump maggot peeked out from the whistle's buoy. Others wriggled around the collar of Jasper's buttoned flannel. The faster he played the notes, the quicker he decomposed.

Lost in the illusion, Antony's sweaty hands twitched. Through dilated pupils, he watched on in horror.

Tinges of purple discolored Jasper's complexion. Rigor mortis set in, yet he piped on undeterred. Blisters formed, blisters ruptured, segments of his skin sloughed away. As his body swelled, fluids were expelled. The carrion fauna population boomed amid the active decay.

Jasper's swan song was cut short by the liquefaction of his innards. The boatswain's call splashed down, disappearing under the water. Its rotting performer followed closely behind.

Splattered by immaterial droplets, Antony suddenly became aware of his own awareness.

"Enough already," he cried out. "None of this is real!" The padded walls dulled his screams for sanity.

"None of this real." The sentence would serve as Antony's anchor. His exhalations steadied to restore a modicum of calm. "None of this is real." He repeated himself again and again in the quiet of the virtual wetlands.

In time, the biological life cycle was simulated in reverse underwater. Fresh muscle tissue revived the cadaver. Upon a planted knee, the recomposing skeleton rose up into a kneeling position. Arteries and veins connected its regenerating organs. Networks of nerves branched out from its developing brain. Throughout its cells, elderly Y chromosomes were erased and replaced by their youthful counterpart.

During the final phases of rebirth, Antony backslid into unawareness. With his anchor aweigh, the passage of time slowed. In astonishment, he looked on as soft supple skin spread over the lithe female frame. Blonde locks flowed over her shoulders, onto her perky breasts. The intimate traits of his true love materialized. At twenty-five years of age, Dominique stood in the nude as a goddess.

"Oh, Antony," she said, flipping back her hair. "I need you now, more than ever."

The last time he'd heard her mellifluous voice felt like a

lifetime ago. Tears welled in his eyes as she closed the distance between them. Her swaying hips stalled just outside his reach.

Foreshadowed by a seductive smirk, she snapped her fingers. Everything flashed; the world was made anew.

The Sartoris were transported to the empty Grand Appointment Hall of the Eastlake Immunization Center. Nearly three decades had reshaped Dominique's features. Sorrow pulled at the corners of her lips. In a leather jacket and jeans, she was dressed as she had been during their final frozen moment.

"If only there was a way for us to rewrite the past," she said with a sigh. "How I wish we could grow old together and do all the things we had left undone. But there are no second chances, my darling. We always end up right back here." Her glassy gaze sunk to the floor. "Nothing ever changes. Soon we'll part. And I'll be all alone, haunted by one lingering question. How could the man I adore live with himself knowing that he failed to save me?"

Between the surreality of the external and the mind chatter of the internal, the present became too much for Antony to bear. Mirroring his first encounter with grief, he retreated into the realm of numbers. Via the assiduous trivialities of an arithmetic series, he muted existence.

"1,000." He squeezed his eyes shut. "999 … 997 … 994 … 990 … 985."

"Well, well, well," Fields yelled over him, "deep down

you're just like all the rest. Citizen and dissident, one and the same, both eager to squander their days away with distractions. And to think, only minutes ago you wanted me to believe that humanity was underlain by uniqueness. Fact of the matter is that all men crave to escape reality."

"945 … 934 … 922."

"Tell me, what led you to believe that you were any different?"

"895 … 880 … 864."

"Because in actuality," Fields jeered, "there's nothing special about you. Or your Praxis pals."

"829 … 810 … 790."

As mental fatigue slowed Antony's pace, Fields groaned in annoyance. "How much longer do you plan on wasting my time with this nonsense?"

"769 … 747."

"Skip to zero and be done."

"724."

"Zero. And. Be. Done." Fields punctuated each word with a clap. "Unless you prefer I send in the surgeons for round two."

Antony brought his chin to his chest. He muttered a number under his breath, then slammed his head into the pillows. At his wit's end, he snapped at Fields. "What do you want from me?"

"What every man wants: an opportunity to be heard."

Antony cautiously surveyed the cell through his eyelashes.

"No reason to hide." Fields peeled back his mask, then tucked it away. "The mind games are over as long as you promise to be a good boy."

"Fine." Antony allowed his eyes to open. "Have your say if you must."

"Some dance for the carrot, some sing in fear of the stick. All it takes is the right motivation to unlock a man's potential."

A smug smile spread across Fields's face as he closed off the flow of Antony's intravenous drip. He strolled away with his hands clasped behind his back. After planting himself in the center of the room, he resumed his didactic discourse.

"At heart, you and I agree: human beings are remarkable creatures. But contrary to what you believe, the roots of human exceptionalism are not grounded in self-awareness, reasoning capabilities, or the powers of communication. It is plasticity that sets the species as a whole apart. For you see, man is the rawest of raw materials. Each a blank slate when exiting the womb, each pliable even as an adult. With a little foresight, a man can be molded to achieve any end. Through education, through social engineering, perfection becomes a possibility."

"Yet you chose to indoctrinate us all, to create a flock of sheep instead. Educate the people. And free thought would upend this world."

"Substance over semantics, Mr. Sartori. Forget your Praxis programming. For a few minutes, cast aside their romantic fantasies of an individualistic utopia.

"Since the dawn of humanity, survival has required cooperation. When Homo sapiens branched off the tree of life, they did so as a social animal. The individual, then as now, is a vapid concept, an abstraction unable to be conceived of in isolation. There is no man without mankind. And there is no mankind without a cumulative culture to bind together generations.

"A desire for autonomy is maladaptive by nature, for all citizens exist for the sake of society. On behalf of the ethical whole, they each must relinquish their rights and accept the privileges they are given. Herein lies the social contract that unites our civilization. It is a shared obligation to the greater good that drives the collective will."

Antony humphed, then shook his head. "Ideologies obscure the most heinous of acts."

"Correction, Mr. Sartori. Denying the laws of history would be the heinous act. Experiments with liberty have failed time and again. The days of democratic regimes based on individualism have come and gone. One by one they devolved into mob rule. And in their decivilizing wake, progress slowed, well-being suffered, and the culture's moral fabric disintegrated. To top it all off, the age of individualism placed our planet in peril.

"The Pansophical Corporation had a moral duty to take action. The time had come for self-sacrifice, not self-interest; planning and organization, not fabled notions of spontaneous order. Understand, our institutions had to be reoriented for the long term. Our society's moral circle needed an expansion. Rich fulfilling lives await our posterity. Thanks to Pansophical, mankind moves closer to its apotheosis."

"No matter how you dress up the road to serfdom, all of its travelers end up under the thumb of a tyrant." Antony pulled a stream of cool air through his nostrils. "Sadly, you're unable to imagine what life could be like if actions were voluntary and we abolished the leviathan in all its forms."

"Chaos is what you advocate," Fields said, folding his arms. "And you call me a madman?"

Antony slowly surveyed his shackles. From the get-go, it was clear that no counterargument would suffice. No words could tear down the dogmatic walls built by Fields's will to power. There was but one way for Antony to expedite his escape from this abject existence; there was but one way to freedom.

"Well." Antony's hope-sapped sightline drifted back to Fields. "Maybe I'm not one to say. Maybe I'm just a fool who's been chasing a pipe dream. Maybe mankind would be lost if not for Pansophical."

"Is that right?"

"Yes, Mr. Chairman." Antony bowed his head. "Long live Pansophical."

"Even the most irrational of beings sometimes stumble into the light." Fields chuckled. "Now say it again, but this time like you believe it."

Antony surrendered to the shame. "Long live Pansophical!"

"And now as loud as humanly possible because nothing else matters."

Antony knew that, in truth, his conviction, or lack thereof, was of no importance to Fields. The satisfaction the chairman derived stemmed purely from breaking his adversary. As Antony screamed in compliance, Fields smirked and walked away.

A pair of psychiatric assistants entered the cell with a wheelchair. They removed Antony's cap, then unbuckled his restraints and pulled him out of bed. They wheeled him down a hallway into a bathroom. After a shower, they gave him a black jumpsuit along with a script to memorize.

In a windowless room, inside a cage, they set him down upon a metal chair and handcuffed him to a wooden table. Before a camera and an irascible team from the Department of Information, he repeated his lines to exhaustion. Fumbles in his recitation prompted reshoots. Perceived insincerities in his delivery elicited threats.

In a worldwide address that evening, Fields declared another victory over Praxis.

One week later, Antony was paraded before the masses as breaking news.

"My name is Antony Sartori. For the past five years, I have undermined the common good as an agent of Praxis.

I've committed unforgivable acts. I've disgraced myself. And everyone that I once loved. But worst of all, I betrayed Pansophical. ..."

Scattered among the citizenry, an awakened minority endured. Amid the uproarious rejoice of the mindless, the remnant celebrated this latest triumph with a slow clap.

9 798991 458108